nuni

nuni

JOHN HOWARD GRIFFIN

PUBLISHED BY HOUGHTON MIFFLIN COMPANY,
BOSTON, IN ASSOCIATION WITH SMITH'S, INC.,
DALLAS, TEXAS · THE RIVERSIDE PRESS, CAMBRIDGE

c. 1

by

John Howard Griffin:
The Devil Rides Outside
Nuni

HR

to

Elizabeth Ann
Susan Michelle
and John, Jr.

book one

nuni

book two

vanua

book one nuni

Professor Harper made his way
to the South Pacific Island
of Nuni when his plane crashed
at sea. Soon he found himself
carrying on a strange conflict
against native superstition
and sorcery for the life of a
child.

t he glass is cold to my nose as I cup my hands to the sides of my face and stare through the plane's window to the emptiness of tropical twilight.

Sparks from the exhaust become visible in the fading sky. They strike reflections, which I see as blurred flashes almost against my eye, from the wide gold wedding band on my left hand.

Nudging the heavy curtains farther aside, I look for some sign of life out there in the beginning night; perhaps the lights from another plane or the glow of native cooking fires somewhere in the distance. But the ocean stretches to desolate infinity and I have the impression that we are suspended in vast latitudes of star-chipped greyness, unmoving.

It is an evocative moment, hushing emotions in harmless

melancholy, and I withdraw into it as a hinted pleasure, in the knowledge that it will end when I want it to, when I stir, cough, yawn and flick on the overhead light.

The mood of dusk is contagious and there is silence around me above the muffled roar of the plane's motors, and then the other passengers begin moving about and coughing and making restless noises. Somehow I knew they would.

My pants are twisted as I turn back into my seat, and I reach under the book in my lap and grab cloth to straighten them, vaguely aware of the indignity of my act, seeing in my mind the uncertain puckering of a frown that would be on Susie's face if I were to do such a thing at one of the faculty meetings, and wondering if it has been noticed by the bundle of freckles and wrinkles and corn-powder fragrance that is the emaciated old lady sitting beside me.

A faint clink as I twist in my seat reminds me that the pint of whiskey my brother slipped into my pocket as I boarded the plane in Manila is still waiting to be opened, and I decide to recapture the feelings of pleasure that have inundated me all day at the idea of returning home by going into the men's room and having a drink before supper.

Reading lights have been turned on over all of the seats except mine and pencil-thin rays of luminous white angle down like miniature spotlights in front of me, some of them catching billows of smoke from cigarettes.

I rest for a moment in my seat, feeling the weight of the book against my paunch, and in the half-shadows there is no regret that my paunch sometimes feels so old these days. I am filled with the animality of a comfortable belly and with the temporary luxury of my surroundings, absorbing the chrome and mohair and leatherette elegance as one does

that of a nightclub. Absently I contrast it to the plainness
of our home, to the chalkdust and ink and sweat of my
classrooms, to the school gymnasium with its smells of pine-
oil and leather and adolescence.

A movement from the seat in front attracts my attention
and I look up to see an immense brown-suited man struggle
dignifiedly from his place and lumber out into the aisle. His
full cheeks sag with a firm setting of his jaw as he glowers
toward the rear of the plane. From the general aura of
sleekness and darkness that emanates from his immaculate
appearance, I imagine that he is a person of great importance
and intelligence. Speckled gold highlights glint from his
glasses as he draws himself up to his full height, and the
whole combines into a picture of belligerent determination,
announcing to all present the voiceless shout that he is going,
by God, to the restroom. Watching him, I ask myself why
people in trains and planes can never seem to go about these
things naturally and simply as they do at home, but must
almost always affect either the serene head-lowered humility of martyrs shuffling to their destiny or the enraged,
head-raised defiance of patriots about to hurl themselves at
the enemy.

As he stalks past, floor lights catch a fleeting crisscross
sheen on his pantlegs, and I am seized by an almost irresistible urge to ask: "Sir, where are you going?"

Settling back to wait for his return when I may go for my
drink of whiskey, I debate idly between reading Geismar's
Writers in Crisis or the little paper-bound volume of *Great
Essays* that I carry in my coat pocket with the bottle.
Remembering the demands of my new course in American
literature, I decide to continue reading the Geismar and

flip open the book in my lap to the cardboard page marker.
The reading lamp above my head is flicked on, flooding the
somber pages with a concentrated brightness that repels my
eyes for a moment.

Always when I approach such works I am dismayed by
my deficient kinship with these literary historians, for I can
never write such things. The difference is not so much one
of perception as one of expression, for theirs are natural and
mine are stuffy, even my most casual reviews and articles;
and when they are not stuffy I am betrayed in my hopeless
sentimentality. Adjusting my glasses down to the open
page, I read:

> In the flowing, vivid passages which inaugurate this
> section of 'The Web and The Rock,' Wolfe illuminates
> the meaning of the metropolis, the whole complex
> fabric it has woven around itself in . . .

"Professor Harper?" a voice smelling of perfume inter-
rupts.

"Yes?" I say, inserting my forefinger between the pages
to mark my place and looking up into the stewardess's bent-
over face.

"Dinner will be served shortly, sir. What would you
like to have with it?"

I think I would like very much to have her, but say:
"What choice is there?"

"Coffee, tea or milk. Or — I could get you some fruit
juice," she says in an innocently conniving way as though
the fruit juice were a very special concession for very special passengers.

"I believe I'll just take coffee, thank you," I say with inflated dignity, nodding appreciation.

"Black?"

"Please."

She flashes me a smile of almost mystical respect and disappears into the roar, and I think she must have a fine family background to show such appropriate reverence for professors.

"Ain't she a pretty little one though?" my aged seat companion whispers in a timid cockney accent behind the wall of her emaciated hand.

"She certainly is," I agree, inhaling a faint odor of dentures and cloves and somewhat jarred that the old woman considers me her contemporary whereas I feel much more contemporaneous to the girl. But no, I sink back into the conversation of elderly people discussing the finer beauty of another generation.

She smiles through lips deeply drawn with wrinkles and wriggles her scant white eyebrows high in a gesture of secretly understood approval of the girl, and drops her hand back into her lap where long red and green knitting needles are half buried in skeins of brilliant yarn.

As she takes them up, our attentions are attracted by the stewardess who returns for the order of a pallid young man sitting directly across the aisle.

I am slightly taken aback to see her flash him the same smile of mystical respect that I had supposed was reserved for me and she immediately becomes less attractive in my eyes.

"Reverend Mackay?"

"Uh-huh," he says, closing the black leatherbound book

he has been reading and placing it reverently on the seat beside him.

My aged companion instantly bends toward me, her face prune-wrinkled with enthusiasm, and whispers a moist sibilation against my ear, from which I gather that she has heard he is a mis-s-sh-s-ionary.

He is looking up at the stewardess with a petulance that gives him an expression of consuming sincerity, and I feel certain he will take either the fruit juice or the milk. She flicks something off his tie and leans against the seat, facing him as though she had no intention of leaving him as quickly as she did me.

My companion begins working her needles, tiny veins slithering under the freckled backs of her hands, but her head is completely averted toward the young people and I judge from the rounded bulge in her cheek that she is grinning at them.

Talking with the stewardess, Reverend Mackay absently picks at his chin with his thumb and little finger, holding the rest of his fingers upward as though he were cupping an apple. It is an adolescent gesture of which he appears completely unaware and it arouses some sense of paternal affection in me that softens my distaste without diminishing it.

What can a girl like her see in him that keeps her there glowing and chattering beyond the call of duty? Perhaps she merely pities him as I begin to do. He looks so young, so meanly virtuous and so blondly unkempt with his hair in long strands brushed loosely to one side and angling down toward his ear: the sort of vapidly earnest youth we refer to in the barbershop back home as "watery-assed."

He glances around to notice that he is being observed and

quickly drops his hand from the blebby spot on his chin. As his eyes pass mine I recognize them, for I have seen them in many faces before. They are the feverish, burning eyes that instantly sap all attention away from the rest of the face. They are the luminous eyes of very cruel people and of bankrupt whores and of the desperately sick and of fanatics. They produce the electrically charged expression that Rasputin must have had — a thing never encountered in the eyes of saints or animals.

". . . chew betel nut," he is saying in a pulpit-trained bass voice. "Men, women and even the little children. It's an awful habit."

The stewardess squints her eyes and rolls them up under her eyelids in distress, making little groaning sounds, and from the corner of my eye I see the old woman's needles accelerate in suspenseful interest.

Lighting a cigarette, I rest my elbow on the seat arm and bow my head to the left in an attempt to hear more of their conversation above the grind of the motors.

"I've heard of it," the stewardess says with revulsion. "Doesn't it turn their teeth black or something?"

"Oh yes, and it makes them quite drunk, too. It's hard to break them of the nasty stuff, though."

"I imagine! Oof! Have you ever tasted any?"

"Oh no . . ."

I cut my glance across at him through a haze of cigarette smoke in fascination at the encyclopedia of emotions he has managed to put into those two words: first indignation, then disgust, then pain and finally forgiveness.

My gaze finds the stewardess's lovely face to see if it will not reveal some slight grimace of perception, to see if she is not momentarily affronted by this type of acid goodness; for there is no trace in him of the tranquil honesty of the Mormons or the dignity of the Anglicans or the preoccupied love of the Catholics who serve as missionaries in this part of the world. But her face is marked only with interest and admiration.

Poor devil. Perhaps I am wrong. Why can't I have the good beaming heart of my seat companion whose cheek still bulges with her smile? Why can't I see in him only a courageous young man returning from months, perhaps years, converting savages from their culture all the way down to our civilization. I feel a stirring of true regret that I can't, but when I look at him I see a thousand other viciously righteous faces superposed over the terrible anguish I once read in a drunk's glazed eyes when he stared hopelessly up at me and said: "Show me the man who is virtuous without being either a jackass or a sonofabitch about it — if you could ever find one — and I'll show you the man I might respect," and I know that without the purityranny of such virtuous jackasses and sons-of-bitches to fill men's minds with the guilt of their bodies, many saints would not end up searching for the Grail in the derelict's junkheap.

I turn away, needing the drink more than ever, but the fascination of this youngster — of some seeming good disguising what is inherently evil — picks at my mind, and I remember hearing talk about these new breeds of missionaries who are pouring out from the States with the 100 SIMPLIFIED GOSPEL HYMNS FOR ALL OCCASIONS and their bottles of Sal Hepatica in the presumptuous notion that God has chosen them to "conquer the mission fields for Jesus," and who go about it by replacing betel nut with bubble gum, by replacing ritual dances with our square dances, by replacing nakedness with frocks for the women and jockey shorts, guaranteed not to gap, for the men, and finally by replacing ignorance with our knowledge of the catalogue of sins and other such filth.

Poor Foucauld, I think affectionately, and poor Schweitzer and Dupeyrat — how you must mourn this trashy influx.

I wonder what is keeping the brown-suited patriot back there so long. If he doesn't return soon, I won't have time for a drink before supper.

The plane's vibrations produce two tingling areas in my hips that shimmer upward into my brain and downward into my legs, cloaking me in a sensuous drowsiness that becomes intimately pleasurable. I nudge my glasses and rub stings into my eyes with my knuckles, vacillating between the desire to abandon myself to the moment of animality and the strictures of conscience that urge me to occupy my time more usefully by reading on in preparation for my new course in school. Hell, I can forget school at least until I get home. Hell.

The tingling sensations envelop my body completely and I am swayed with a progressive expansion of happiness that comes when all senses and desires combine into momentary harmony with the universe. I allow myself to drift with it for a time in that self-indulgence of middle age that often accompanies me when I am alone and away from the conscience of familiar surroundings. A detached intelligence seems to float out from somewhere within me, touching parts of my body as though from another volition. vibrating first on the backs of my hands, then on my belt buckle, then on my thighs and then on down the full length of my body, pointing out the existence of all organs in quiescence and the marvelousness of them, without selectivity or modesty, concentrating on each with a delicate vibrancy and relishing the touchings in an offhand way.

In such a mood of quiet exultation I picture again every planned detail of my homecoming, knowing that although we will never speak of it, similar planning is probably going on in Susie's mind: the connoisseur plannings of middle age that seek to focus not so much on the physical activities of reunion as on the emotional coloration of all its aspects into a gratifying whole, satisfying after long experience in ways we never dreamed of in the years beginning our marriage, when the primary need was assuaging the senses in a manner that implied nourishment for the heart rather than, as now, having a primary need for nourishing the heart in a manner that implies enriching the senses.

I am walking up the sidewalk in the halted nostalgia of familiar lawns and porches and parked cars along the street, always slightly changed and always seen as new after separation. Sunlight glints silver from the water tower that rises above shrubs in the back, and I hear a rooster crowing from the neighbors'; plaintive sound in the afternoon that I had almost forgotten. My shoe strikes the first wooden step leading up to the porch when the screen door flies back on its hinges and I gather into my arms a whirlwind of children who sweep me through the door into the living room where there is order and the odor of freshly waxed furniture. Speaking above the babble in all directions, I find Susie's hand and a vague sweeping gladness from the touch.

Georgie and Timmy have bumped my suitcases up the

stairs and are crowding around with Cindy, tugging at my coat and chattering, wanting to see their presents. But Susie tells them to go down and set the table and put on the coffee, assuring them that as soon as I get my clothes changed we will be down with the presents and have supper. The festivity is not destroyed and they dash out the door in the high spirits of their important tasks.

The drumming of their footsteps on the stairs is hushed as Susie eases the door shut and turns with her back to it. We hold to one another for a moment full of murmurings and smilings as tensions drain from my chest and my brackish incompleteness finds its anodyne in that other part of me which fills my arms again.

After a moment there is a mutually understood loosening of the embrace, for that is part of the planning that requires the contained jubilation of casualness and restraint in tested certainty. There is the stepping away and my detached remark that if there is time I think I'll take a bath before supper. Susie thinks it would relax me after the long trip and says that she will draw the bathwater while I am undressing All is consonance in this inner stippling of delight that requires no act of proof to confirm our totality of union, a totality so understood that the lack of stereotyped acts is its greatest proof, and the source of its most intense felicity.

I lower myself heavily to the bed and begin taking off my clothes as the room focuses itself into clarity on a blaze of late-afternoon sunlight that pours through red-checked gingham curtains across the dark wood of the floor and the circular hand-crocheted rug, illuminating the corners with a brightness that makes the room seem as neat and friendly as the kitchen of a Dutch parsonage.

The alarm clock on the table beside our bed clacks frantically above the bubbling roar of bath water.

Naked, I get to my feet to the accompanying groan of bedsprings and wander about the room, gravitating in the direction of the window. Sunlight warms my stomach as I brush curtains aside and look out to the countryside below. Supporting my hands on the window sill, I feel screen wire touching my forehead as I gaze down to the shingled top of our back porch and beyond to the yard neatly punctuated by stone walks. Everything is fresh, everything is full of slanted sunlight that has coolness in it, everything nestles in the comfortable permeation of evening in the suburbs. Beyond the sun-vermilioned struts of the water tower, cattle amble toward their barns for the night; and from the neighbor's yard the chickens enliven the hush as they bustle in white patches after evening feed.

The rumble of water sloshes to silent dripping in the bathroom behind me, and I let the curtains drop and turn back into the room. Susie, trailing the odor of soap and clean clothes about her, arranges my underwear and socks on the candlewick bedspread and then raises her head and closes her eyes to inhale the odor of coffee that begins to filter up to us from the kitchen, looking at me for a moment in that hidden reassurance of understood things.

Standing in the middle of the room and feeling the warmth of waxed floors beneath my bare feet, I breathe in the smell of coffee in answer to her, but my attention is diverted to a movement in the mirror and I catch my reflection absently scratching at the base of its abdomen. The picture, in this oranged light, recalls some portly image from pagan times, and laughter breaks in my chest at the sight of a naked old statue, peering quizzically back at me over the rims of its glasses and nudging its rounded terra cotta belly. In the background, filtered through a mottled fault in the mirror, I see Susie standing with her hand on the bedpost and watching me with a softly indrawn expression of amusement and tenderness.

Cindy's voice, calling for us to hurry and get ready for dinner, is answered by Susie who tells her that we will be there in a few moments and to go bring in the evening paper. A high, squeaking quality is left in Cindy's voice from the terrible fevers of last year, especially noticeable when she tries to speak loud. It gives her speech the poignancy and sweetness of an English schoolboy.

And suddenly all of these things, intimate and subtle — the children, Susie, the smells of evening and coffee, the steamed warmth from the bathroom, the protection within these walls from all the loneliness and emptiness of the world outside — all of these things combine in this moment and in this room to lift me high on the framework of elation, and gratitude swells in my chest for these bodies with their fine shoulders and full buttocks and bustling brains who live with me under this roof, who share unquestioning in this heavy furniture and flowered wallpaper, who share in the table that nourishes us in our mortal hungers and in the affections that nourish us in our mortal loves. The joy of all these things crushes out the distant nostalgia of growing oldness and makes me laugh at the littleness of my occasional regrets.

Susie suggests I had better get my bath before the water cools and follows me into the bathroom. She switches on a light that replaces obscurity with a flood of brightness reflecting from the tiled floor.

I crawl in and splash down on my back with my knees bent and resting against the sides of the tub so that I am looking at the chrome faucets through a topless triangle. Lying still, I feel the line of liquid tepidness ripple to growing calm against my ribs and up under my thighs. Susie hands me a washcloth and sits at the head of the tub. She bends down to unhook my glasses from my ears and lifts them away from my face, talking quietly of the children.

Swishing water over the crease in my stomach, I watch the glistening streak it makes as it dribbles to the sides. Warmness sends its soothing pulse into my nerves and I close my eyes and listen to Susie's voice echoing down into the tub hollowness from above me. My mind drifts into fogged contentment, catching less and less of her words as they mingle into preoccupation with the panorama of designs floating slowly across my eyelids.

An outburst of laughter ricochets through a long tunnel jolting me from my dream, and I open my eyes and stare sleepily at the low-keyed greys of the plane's luxurious interior. The laughter rises again, taunting and empty to my drowsing senses. Two men are laughing a few seats in front of me. I move my fingers and the dead cigarette falls from them into my lap, powdering the blue worsted with ashes before it drops to the floor. I look wearily about and realize that I am surrounded by the shoulders and buttocks and brains of strangers, and there is coldness after warmth and a foul taste in my mouth.

A cough explodes in my throat, filling my mouth, and I spit phlegm into the glowing white square of my handkerchief.

My aged seat companion smiles vacantly at me as I tuck
a fresh cigarette between my lips and strike a match to it.
The flame in my cupped hands appears pink and gaseous in
this light. I inhale deeply and taste the smoke in the hollowness of my intestines, as though it were going down deep
into the pit of my stomach, creating a slight nausea.

All emotions and actions are in the same slow dream of a
moment ago, so similar in rhythm that I glance down to
assure myself that I am not still naked. No, there are clothes
and the hinted odors of cleaning and pressing all about me.
Modesty returns as an encumbrance on the return of wakefulness, a modesty that is so firmly rooted as to be involuntary. This strikes me in deep irritation, and with it the
force of my own total immodesty and its total rightness and
innocence in the jubilant context of home and family.

I glance across at the stern-faced young missionary and
see his unwrinkled youngness against the parched profile
of my aged seat companion, and I cannot help wondering
what occupies his thoughts at this moment as he stares into
the fantasies of his private world, his fervent eyes opened
wide to nothing.

Is he thinking with pride of the shoulders and buttocks
and brains of children? Is he lying naked in a tub listening
to the voice of someone he loves? Is he caressing breasts
that have nourished his children, as his body seeks again the
truths of her body in the renewing knowledge that so much
can be known and yet such truths still not be exhausted?

And if he could see into my thoughts, what would he
feel? Perhaps repugnance or perhaps the challenge to con-
vert, for I know in some hopeless certainty that his mind
would see as lewd those things that are beautiful to my heart.

The vaporous figure of the brown-suited patriot passes

between us as he returns to his seat, cutting off my view and the thread of my thoughts, and reminding me of the drink.

I hoist myself up, stooping to keep from hitting the metal baggage rack with my head, and deposit the Geismar book on the seat. My thighs, touching the window frame, feel as though they are made of cork.

Squeezing past my companion as she angles her bony legs to one side to let me out, I smile down at her in that peculiarly chaste way of such things: the serene martyr's smile of humility. And then to counterbalance it, I stand full height in the aisle and attempt to assume the fierce expression of the patriot.

A sudden buffeting of the plane, like those caused by air currents, throws me off dignity and I support myself by grasping the backs of seats as I stagger toward the rear.

Observing the passengers from this passing vantage, some of them with their heads lolled back in open-mouthed slumber, some of them reading, curled up in the corner of their seats, I am rebuffed by their blank expressions and I hurry toward the comparative friendliness of the washroom.

A hustling disturbance causes me to look up in time to see a gaunt figure in a loud sport shirt dashing to the door where I want to go, holding his hand to his head. I hesitate, not knowing whether to return to my seat and go through this complication of getting up again or to remain here, obviously holding in my bladder and trying to appear casual about it. Glances find me, knowing glances, and one woman even leans out into the aisle to observe me in open curiosity, and I am tempted to announce in a loud voice that I was heading for the washroom only to wash my hands in preparation for a more hygienic evening meal and not for the purposes they obviously imagine.

Perhaps he will only be a moment. I will simply walk forward more slowly and take my —

My head jerks back on my neck and tendons freeze in my clutching hands as detonations blast a sledge of thunder into my brain and the floor drops from beneath my feet. There is no time for surprise. A wall of flame sweeps over me in coolness.

All is diminished to cringings. I want it to wait a moment, to give me time to realize what this whirling is. A whispered "God of mercy" starts in my belly and never gets beyond. I am mixed up in lights and curtains, and my face touches another's flesh, sliding away. I am vaguely surprised not to hear screams as my body becomes glued to hardness with a force that blasts wind from my lungs. A hopeless feeling planes above and beyond, a feeling that things are happening too quickly and that I am terribly alone.

But suddenly there is a flooding that expands the cringings to grandeur. There is no struggling or pain, but distances and shafts of light that are pouring into me to burst my heart with stupefaction as my soul is flung into the spaces of all time. There is youngness in the soaring, and innocence and a spaciousness that ravishes me to the core of my being. There is love that sears to cinder all that was and transfigures it into incandescence of delight. There is a swimming blackness more radiant than its source, and a whiteness and a dazzle floating ever upward into the coolness and the harmoniousness of distilled exaltation. And beyond, there is a faint impact and seeping wetness, far away, in a dream, fading . . .

2

All is changed and sweetness of space becomes bitterness in my mouth and nose, and pressured vomitings against my throat. There are slow twistings through foam-filled undersurfaces (and an amazement that is static, petrified). There is no gravity as my hair floats upward from my head (and amazement settles into understanding, tinged with disappointment). There is a mighty back-swallowing of my lungs (and amazement drifts like dust to sift away the stupor of accepted death).

And then I feel the night against my face.

A cool breeze, flecked with wetness, touches my forehead, and sight, dumb sight, dead sight glimpses a milky haze overhead scored with lacings of radiance like candlelight seen through tears.

Other sight glimpses me from abstraction, glimpses the vision of a bewildered old man dressed in his Sunday best out swimming, not wanting to swim, making a spectacle of himself suspended upright in the water and kicking feebly, trying to stay afloat and holding in the retchings.

My glasses cut into the side of my nose. In silence I strip them away with my right hand and, struggling against the immediate sinking, fumble to place them in my coat pocket.

Sight glimpses again and then focuses slowly until one star gleams through the blear. Treading water, I stare at it in utter disbelief. After a time of death, one star diffused in silence and blackness gently leads me back into life.

But there is no sound. My ears sting with the needling pressure of quietness.

The star fascinates me in that timeless way of great urgency. I blink the membrane haze away and it glistens clean, bobbing violently in the night. It seems that I must stare at it forever before I can bring myself to believe that I still belong to a body, to shoes, to a necktie.

But there is the taste of salt on my tongue and the wet pain of ocean spume in my nose to destroy any remaining doubt. My eyes close in the dementia of sudden exhaustion, and my body is abandoned to the shiftings of the surf while I seem to become nothing but a casual participant. Only the pervading heaviness and wetness are immediate, pressuring me from all sides and filling me with a melancholy that seeks to match the vastness of the water-tossed night.

When I open my eyes I am being lifted high atop a break-ing wave and the ghostly white of breakers cascades about me, shooting sparkles of phosphorescent tinsel into my eyes from all angles. I jerk my head back from the onslaught and, looking up, I have the fleeting impression that my star has been joined by a glittering heavenful, riding serene and detached in the unchangeable blackness. And then I am hurled downward in a somersaulting glide.

Solidity jolts up into my hips as my feet are driven against unyielding ground, but before I can gain my balance my legs are swept under me in a sucking reverse current, and the caul of deafness is torn from my ears as a washing roar surges to the foreground of my consciousness.

My legs flounder, and as I twist to brace myself, my body is swept upward and flung into the soaking darkness. I slither forward in a hallucination of foam that thunders against my eardrums until jagged coral scrapes the full length of my belly and I am deposited on land. Pebbles rush liquidly past and then turn and smash me in the face as the water is drawn back. The ocean leaves me there, draining away and sucking at my clothes with infinite thirst. I crawl forward away from its grasp.

Rocks cut into my water-softened hands until the coral gives way to hard-packed sand that retains the day's warmth against my palms. Strength deserts my arms and I sprawl forward on my face.

I am safe, a speck of livingness surrounded by unknown spaces. I am aware of that as something apart from the things of my body, the immediate ingaspings of my chest and the vertigo of my temples and the bloating suffocation of my heart.

Marshaling strength, I inch forward enough to rest my forehead on the pillow of my gritty hand and stare down, breathing in my own breath from the sand close beneath my mouth. I don't move. I don't ever want to move again.

I wait in a suspended time for my breathing to return to normal and for the trembling to release my shoulders from its pinched grasp. The night is black and full of the ocean's bellowing, but a paleness pervades all sounds, all emotions, all wonderment. Somewhere there is a Professor John W. Harper and classes in English literature at 10 A.M.

A grotesque sinking seems to pull my belly down into the earth and surprised air is forced from my mouth, bubbling into a saliva'd belch that pops against my upper lip. Somehow it makes me want to cry. Nothing else makes me feel the slightest emotion, but the unexpected pop against my lip makes me want to put my hands against my cheeks and weep for a long, long time. It is very hard, terribly hard because that bubble makes me want to cry, but I tell myself I must not. That would be foolish. The sinking draws me further down into the earth, a frightening sinking like lying on a bed dead drunk, sinking, by God, sinking out of sight into the middle of the earth, sinking into a turmoil of feathery silence.

3

My leg. Beyond all the groaning layers of sleep something hurts my leg. Opening my eyes I see unbearable tiredness swimming in mysterious rebuff, but I focus and the world regains its upright balance. The watery glint of a crescent moon is suspended placidly in the sky above me, surrounded by a faint aura of its own glow. I stir and roll completely over on my back and another bubble of saliva breaks against my lips.

Through the canvaslike texture of damp worsted I finger the outlines of the thin metal object that was biting into my leg. I guess it is the key, or perhaps the locket with the children's pictures in it. The children. I choke the thought off, blot it out, bombarding my closed eyelids with kaleidoscopic spangles of nothing, knowing I must escape realizations of things. Reaching into my pocket I grasp a handful of metal and damp lint and drop them on the ground beside me.

Sleep skitters at the edge of my brain but will not return to my body. Where am I? Am I alone? What has happened to make me lie here staring up at the heavens with my jaws trembling? Questions formulate themselves idly through some inner twilight, but there are no immediate answers.

Am I the only one washed ashore?

The weight of my stomach pulls at me when I roll over and get to my feet, and I stagger from side to side and wonder what causes this dizziness. Now, to call out: "Hello . . ." My attentions are divided between my feeble cry and the water that squishes in my shoe.

I shout in all directions until my throat chokes back on the effort, but my voice is buffeted away without echo in the hollow sweep of night and only dampness returns to salt my lips.

Standing in animal stupidity, I listen. My arms are folded across my chest and my hands are tucked under their opposite armpits seeking warmth.

A hinted odor causes me to draw in my breath sharply. It is a familiar odor, an odor of docks and garages, purified almost beyond recognition — the odor of oil. And I remember that search planes sometimes locate missing craft by oil slicks.

No answer. I stand wrapped in mists, tottering against the wind. I stand stripped of all the brilliant garb of safety's assurance, as though I had just had my clothes torn from my body, more naked than embarrassment can measure. My soul, my flesh, my fatness, the strength of my pulse and digestions — all domesticated — loom suddenly ineffectual in this black strangeness.

From some spectre of consciousness I feel that I am being watched by an obscene and merciless curiosity that leers at me from some detached part of myself, taking measurements and noting how man acts when he is stripped of all the complex paraphernalia of his world and tossed on the junkpile of aloneness. This humiliation of being watched sears me with the same desire to cry as before, but somehow I know I am lost if I shed a single tear. There is a cynical smile in the night that seems to judge me and ridicule me in my exposed helplessness before the elements.

So I act, going through my paces in the most private immodesty, but seeking to retain what human dignity is left when there is no more humanity. I act in automaton, with a sort of crafty calculation that comes from no intelligent source, the way a drunk man walks. My mind concentrates on the single thought that I must not let the trembling begin again. For the time I must tread on thoughts as though they were eggshells.

One certainty haunts me. There is no possibility of begging from the skies and the sea and the rock any mark of tenderness that will allow my heart to dilate back to normal.

No answer. I am alone then, or else another, washed ashore as I, cannot hear my feeble shouts above the rumbling surf.

My legs buckle as I fold them to sit back down, and the thought jars into my brain that I am passing through an attitude of prayer on my way to comfort. Habits of the past draw forth an Our Father but the words slither away before

they can be retained and other preoccupations drift in to
replace them, leaving only the vague impression that at such
times man is supposed to pray. But who knows about such
times? Such times are not supposed to be. The sand draws
my brain to the pain of my behind and I shift to find
greater comfort.

I lie on my side with my legs drawn up and think fleet-
ingly that I am in an embryo position. The soured weave of
my coat breathes back at me and I am filled with a thousand
pinpricks of irritation.

Think of safe things. Think and wonder what happened
to the books. The little volume of *Great Essays* is safe here
in my pocket with the whiskey. I can feel their lumped
weight and my hand obeys listlessly, removing them and
placing them on the sand beside me. But what about the
other book, the Geismar book? Who was in it? Lardner
and Wolfe were already dead, but what about the others?
— Hemingway, Dos Passos, Faulkner and Steinbeck — out
there in the ocean somewhere . . .

The reef hovers ghostlike above me. I raise my eyes
without moving my head and see that moonlight has illuminated a faintly glinting wall, a greyish-blue wall that
cuts up into the star-filled heavens. I am at the base of a
cliff, then. Perhaps that is why it seems so noisy here; perhaps the precipice cups the eternal crashings of the tide.
I think of moving my head and following the angle of the
cliff top, but the effort repels me. It is not interesting how
far the cliff extends in either direction along the beach.

Cautiously, in the intimate nest of myself, withdrawn
from the vastness of the night, I attempt to project Susie's
face behind my closed eyelids. Concentrating, I can feel

the sweat spot on my ribs where her breasts have rubbed against me through all the summer nights, but designs swim in the outline of her face and it has no features. I think without much emotion that I shall probably remember Susie's face tomorrow.

Vague fantasies of half-formed prayers mingle with lonely cross-shafts in a floating dream of beginning sleep, gently disengaging themselves from the bulk of wakefulness, drifting away at tangents.

4

Morning brightness is acid in my eyes. Muscles react first as my feet convulse, kicking off the giant sand crab that touches my leg. It lands a few feet away and scurries behind its spidery shadow to the base of the cliff. I watch it scramble out of sight in a jumble of coral.

It seems to me that there should be the odor of coffee, strong coffee, and I catch myself waiting in a somnolent attitude, distantly disturbed by the rumbling emptiness in my belly. Waiting for the aroma of black coffee I breathe in only the flat smell of the sea.

Coughs explode upward in my chest. My hands, when I rub them across my eyes, feel as though they were made of sackcloth and I recoil in pain. When will I smell this morning's coffee? I cross my arms and bend far over to get the kinks out of my back, noting the imprint in the sand where I have slept.

Slowly there comes the clear realization that there will be no odor of coffee this morning, no brushing of teeth, no changing of clothes for the day.

Rejection touches my heart, and sensitivity is replaced by a callousness that knows neither tenderness nor wrath. My head pulses at the right temple. When I think of those at home, it seems to pulse more violently. I think of them sitting by the radio and worrying about me, and I feel I should apologize to them for their grief, as though it were some fault of mine over which I should have exercised better control. To hell with it. Without thinking, I am shocked at this reaction. I would never have believed it of myself, never have believed that because the needs of a man's heart cannot be met, his heart itself will change rather than suffer death. Is that what is happening to mine? How else to explain this sudden coldness in me?

I turn from it, turn to activity that will let me think of other things. Shading my eyes from the glare of sun on water, I gaze about me at the elephantine gaiety of incoming breakers. They exist in another world and are friendless and concerned with nothing of life or death. I face toward the cliff which extends in a broken line far down the beach to the right. To my left, a few yards away, a giant boulder dwarfs me, blocking off the view of the beach in that direction. Water swishes around its base with each incoming wave, leaving a brilliant mirror in its wake that quickly blots into the sand.

My shadow stretches grotesquely before me, lying at a flat angle on the ground and then rising squat and shapeless on the pocked wall of the cliff. I look casually upward, without emotion, as though I were a tourist, my eyes indrawn against the glaring brightness of the precipice face. Its jagged top separates cleanly from the sky, like a lump of white salt glued to a background of infinite blue, making the depth of the heavens appear no more distant than the cliff top.

My eyes water from the crystalline reflections and I turn away and cover them with my fists. In the greenish mottle I think that back home they sit huddled around radios in the comfortable half-light of the living room and wait for news. And how does it sound to them? — the lifeless phrases of a commentator's impersonal voice announcing tragedy seasoned with static:

". . . are notified that only one of the plane's occupants was from this area. John W. Harper, age fifty-seven, of 2308 Roanoke Avenue. Mr. Harper was assistant professor of English at St. Thomas Academy. He was returning to America after a short visit with his brother, Colonel Frank Harper, who is stationed in the Philippines. The two brothers were reunited for the first time since before the war. The missing plane, presumably far off course, has not been heard . . ."

I wonder if they will mention Susie's name, and the children's? Probably not. They never do that on the radio, only in the newspapers. My mind settles into its own ferment of surprise. Something is wrong with me. I have no feeling about these things. I can call forth nothing of the emotions I know I should be feeling. I don't really care about them this morning, neither the emotions nor the family. But it isn't right. Yesterday I lived for them. I took the boys on fishing trips and scraped to buy the piano for Cindy. Every evening I rushed home to be with them. They were my life, always, but now it is changed and all of that is wiped out, wiped clean from my affections. I feel nothing, nothing at all. I finger at my belt buckle, resting my head in one hand, and taste salt on my lips and there is nothing left in the world beyond this moment. I cannot understand it. Perhaps it is connected in some way with the fact that I am not able to remember Susie's face. It's not my fault the plane crashed.

I must find some way out of this stupor, something that will make me move about and act and use my mind instead of standing here like a beaten animal. Any action will do for a start. I open my eyes laboriously and see the glint of objects in the sand. Stooping over, I retrieve the key and the locket and the smeared little volume of great essays, wondering if I should touch the whiskey or leave it here to boil under the sunlight. Some instinct warns me against it, tells me to break the bottle and have done with it now — prattles at me like some pasty-faced prohibition lady, but with a shadow of deeper vision. I slip the key and the locket and the booklet into my pocket and stare at the bottle lying dust-streaked in the sand. A vision of the coolness of water replaces the steaming insides of that bottle, the gurgling, choking, tear-gasping quality of hot whiskey. "Boy, if medicine tasted like this, it sure would be awful, wouldn't it?" my old man used to say when we drank straight from a bottle under the car seat in the summer days of prohibition.

I decide to leave it where it is, to take no chances that might mean the difference between wandering about aimlessly drunk and wandering about aimlessly in search of water that will save my life.

My mind idles into curiosity about the place. Where am I? What do I know about life in the tropics? Before starting out to explore the reef I must think intelligently. I force myself to sit down. What must I do first? Crossing my knees, I lean with my back against a boulder that bites through the thin weave of my coat. Books read in the past, pamphlets in preparation for my trip to the tropics, many ideas return through the casual fog of memory, giving me the impression that if I tried to remember I would know a great deal about life on a sun-baked island. But the reality of this hidden knowledge evades me, and I am lost as to where I must begin.

Was anyone else saved?

Is there water here?

What do I possess that might serve as a —

Behind the starkness of these questions a faint shudder of fascination intrudes on waves of unconscious anger. I think of my training in piety and of the solid foundations of faith that have always given my troubles the health of bread, and I know that the first thing I should do is pray and put myself in God's hands, but something restrains me, something makes such an idea absolutely impossible, for I have neither the peace of falling into habitual prayer nor the desperation of a last pleading. But behind these thoughts, as I am thinking them, on another dimension, there is perhaps simultaneous prayer in my rejection of its forms.

I look for some sign of the plane, a wingtip sticking out of the waves perhaps or some debris, some hope of salvage. The surf eddies in surges, slow and impersonal. No debris floats. At the water line a thick slime of ochre-tinted oil catches rainbows from the sun's glitter; the only indication that a great airliner has sunk to the bottom of these unknown waters. My anger calms into long stretches of desolation when I think of the others in the plane, particularly the missionary who seems now so touchingly young and so clean and so much better through the clarity of death than he seemed when I knew nothing of such clarity only yesterday. I stare out at the ocean's blankness and at the sky's white emptiness and feel wind ruffling my matted hair.

"Rest eternal grant them, O Lord," murmurs upward from my heart. Against the dazzling background of waters and heavens, I see an ill-shaven priest kneeling at midnight beside the deathbed of my father; and when the room becomes silenced of life's rattle, he folds his hands and softly chants: *"De profundis clamavi ad te, Domine: Domine exaudi vocem meam . . ."* And there is something of that in this, only here the room is the world and there it was bound by four walls; and here the chant is accompanied by the sigh of wind and waves and there it was accompanied by the sputter of a tiny gas heater.

I try to shake such thoughts from my head, but all I see reminds me of death's immense calm. I think I must make an act of contrition, but no — not just yet. Coral crags jut on foamy roots from the sea, like great blanched bones crystallized by the sun and salt spray into serene detachment. I feel infinitely small and lonely because I am alive in the midst of this inevitable tranquillity of lifeless activity, so devoid of heartbeat and so crushingly eternal. A tremor shakes my heart and I know I must think quickly of little things, of human things before I am engulfed in the terrifying grandeur that surrounds me, this grandeur that has been here forever and that will go on being here forever and forever rebuffing man in his physical aloneness.

What does man do, then, in such an instance? I ask myself
this coldly. He seeks to protect his mind and heart from
the discomforts of too much space and too many realizations.
He encloses himself away from the boundless infinity of
times and tides and ceilingless heavens by creating a smaller
world of his own dimensions that will not reject him, one
that will not burst the limits of his comprehension, one that
will embrace him with a hint of warmth and protection —
a cave, perhaps, or this cove where the sand has already
known the weight of my body and the intimacy of my
respirations.

But first, he must wander about in search of food and
water. Curdled muscles ache as I hoist myself to my feet.
My hand absently fumbles at my shirt pocket for a cigarette
that is not there.

I begin trudging along the beach, my right shoe squeaking
with each step in the coarse sand. The sunlight obsesses
me, even this early in the morning. It has an unrefracted
quality of the stars about it, a bluish-whiteness, an emptiness
of all density as though it were ablaze in a vacuum only a
few feet above my head. I think of the sun at home as
having the mellow tint of gold; here it has the clamorous
tint of platinum, piercing and bludgeoning to the senses.

My imagination takes refuge in the grove of trees I will
find, with its deep shade and its pool of water, so cold and
clean that plants growing motionlessly in the bottom stand
out in sharpest detail.

My squeaking shoe moves me slowly forward. The sun
strikes flames from the ocean and they reflect like luminous
snakes wriggling on the cliff surface to my left.

Some distance down the water line the precipice breaks

and a gorge leads upward between steep walls, as though the rains of centuries had chosen this route to flow from the upper levels down into the sea. I scramble upward on my hands and toes, over boulders that block the narrow passageway. At the top, I get to my feet, gasping and rubbing rawness from the palms of my hands. The terrain about me looks like solidified salt waves of a sea, tossed and torn and chopped into utter desolation, barren of all growth except a few gnarled bushes with leaves whitened by dust and shriveled by the sun.

Stepping cautiously on top of a coral ledge that crumbles beneath my shoes, I shade my eyes and peer in all directions, looking for the ribbon of water that will direct my search. Dancing through moiling waves of heat, distances take slow shape to my eyes. Beaches of white coral jag out to sea, paling to shades of lime green and dropping cleanly to depthless blues where the coral shallows fall away. To my left the shallows stretch narrowly as far out as I can see, like a path leading nowhere. At its apex, against the ocean's horizon, a formless shadow pulsates for a moment and then disappears like some giant fish turning over — a mirage under the sun-soaked heavens.

The only hope is in action, but when the sky is scarred by a great splotch of platinum sun, I can only react by standing stunned beneath it and waiting in a half-dream for something to happen. Stirring myself I deliberately face west again, to get my bearings and to notice those things that pass unnoticed: that the reef rises in lava-like undulations toward a high point in the south and dwindles downward to the north. Much of it is hidden from view by the earth's roughness. From east to west it is narrow, narrow enough to see across from this vantage. And although I am not far above the lower levels, the ocean appears to shimmer distantly below me on both sides of the reef.

My mind dozes into quiescence again and I must shake my head to clarify thoughts. I will walk westward down the spiny cliff ledge in the hope that the walls of the precipice will be high enough to protect me from the sun as I begin my exploration around the island. That way, I tell myself, pleased that I am using my intellect, I can search to the west in the mornings and to the east in the afternoons, working gradually northward and southward until I have covered the entire territory. In the dazzling stillness, I walk in search of a spring.

5

The tide is low and the beach stretches wide, with coral cavities retaining pools of ocean water. I amble along, close to the cliff that rises to my left. Wearily I support myself against a boulder and step over a jumble of smaller stones that block my turning to the east.

It is not until I emerge on smooth ground again that I raise my eyes to see that I am back in the cove where I slept last night; and it strikes me that I was foolish to return here. What design in man's heart, what homing instinct has made me return to this empty spot on the beach? There is no cooking fire here, no odor of foods, no family to draw me back. But there is the hinted comfort of familiarity, of bleak familiarity that makes this spot less forbidding than another might be.

Sunset, the sky is swollen red and peeling above the cliff

edge and sounds grow in cupped magnification. If I partially close my eyes I have the impression that flames shoot up into the heavens from the shadowed precipice and turning I see that the flanges of inpouring breakers are tinted a thousand blues and pinks before entering the shadow line and becoming monochrome white. Vaguely I am aware that in a photograph this would be breathtakingly beautiful.

Sunset, time for dinner, but no odors of cooking, no family waiting for me to walk up the sidewalk, a folded newspaper under my arm.

Far in the distance the horizon is drawn with a scarlet line separating ocean from sky. I smell my own beginning reek intermixing with the odor of mushroom dampness that heightens loneliness until my insides begin again their tremblings.

To escape all of this I lower myself to the ground and sit with my knees drawn up before me. Pulling out the locket Susie gave me before I left, the locket with the children's pictures in it, I fumble to untie the knots in the silver chain she has worn about her neck. Absently I smell it for some lingering odor of her face powder, but there is only the odor of the sea; and the grit of salt has already begun to choke the chain's eyelets. When I flip the lip open, the children stare at me, false and pale, unbearably cold in their frozen expressions, as though they were looking out on a stranger. I clean my glasses as well as I can on the gummy tail of my shirt and put them on, but the features of my children dissolve into a blear through the scum on the lenses, and I drop the locket and my glasses back into my pocket.

Lonely greys of dusk. Back home they will be around radios. The sand is like stone and it makes me think of my favorite armchair, overstuffed, with red felt worn smooth at the neck rest. Grey fades into the beginning night and the surge of the breakers sounds louder, closer. I move my left hand to get the kinks out of my arm, and my wedding ring clinks against the bottle of whiskey in the sand. The reminder of the whiskey turns my throat dry as though a sudden gust of heat had passed across my vocal cords. That, at least, is something to do, something human, something connected with human activity; not the drinking of the whiskey, but the mere activity of tearing the foil from the top of the bottle and unscrewing the cap. It is an occupation, something to pass the time, something to take my mind from the sounds and smells of this night.

The cap rasps with indefinable overtones of cheap metal as I remove it and smell into the mouth of the bottle. Heat presses dryness against my throat and without further thought I turn the bottle up and feel the tepid liquid bite into my mouth. I drink noisily, holding my throat muscles loose so there will be no choking back.

Fumes explode upward into my nose and I close my eyes tightly against the sting and lower my head. Suffocation panics me for a moment as I inhale gulps of fresh air and exhale moaned belchings. For some other volition I have replaced the cap on the bottle and dropped it into the sand and grasped my forehead in a single uninterrupted motion. The revolt stirs to a climax in my empty belly and my ears are swept by fire. I hold myself rigid until gradually the heavings subside and I can stretch back on the sand.

My face feels feverish to the touch of my hand as all tensions are relaxed into growing contentment. A damp breeze brushes across me and I am sinking into a hole full of stars. Space surrounds me, only space, black space that has the sounds of water and the silence of skies.

6

It is very cold. I straighten my clothes and complain to Susie that she made this pair of pajamas too small in the seat. But these are not pajamas and there is no Susie. I roll over and feel the sand rub into the back of my head. The sky has changed positions and the stars have moved overhead, like a shifted stare.

A sharp feeling of guilt focuses my senses into clarity, like a shout heard somewhere in the night.

"Sir, will you tell me one thing?" something asks from within me in full voice.

"If I can."

"Well, it's about my wife, Susie; my own children even. I can't understand it but somehow I don't feel anything for them. Since the crash it's almost as if they didn't exist. Damn it, it's not right. You know it's not right, don't you?

No, I'm not drunk. Sometimes it takes something like a drink to tear down all this junk inside of you and make you really sober. It takes that to let you think of things you couldn't stomach thinking about otherwise. You'd think I didn't love them. I know I love them but I can't feel it any more."

"Thank God you feel it too."

A cramp doubles me and I struggle against the sudden descent of the heavens that seem to be diving into my face. I close my eyes tightly and wait for the sprinkling of stars to fall over me.

"What's wrong? Do you suppose that when I left them for death back in that plane — because I was happy, you know, and didn't fight against it at all — do you suppose when I seemed to die back there I killed love in life? It worries the hell out of — "

"You're putting on a show now. You're acting smart, trying to be intelligent."

"I'm trying to keep my head and talk sensibly. But damn it, it's not right. You live with a woman seventeen years. You loved her until yesterday — isn't that something? — a time limit. Another thing. You know, I can remember her hands; they were little, but strong, you know, as if she never doubted what she was supposed to do with them. And I can remember how she did her hair, braided and pinned up on the sides around her head to make her face seem a little wider she used to say. I can remember a lot of things about her, just about everything, but for the life of me I can't remember her face at all."

"It's good you can think about something else. In the back of my mind, all I can think about is myself. I'm obsessed by myself. It seems as if my body is a stranger to me."

My voice becomes my consciousness, fading into loudness in my ears. I catch myself with my mouth half open and close it. In the silence the surf pounds its accented roll somewhere out there in the night.

Cautiously I open my eyes. Mists have cleared away from the moon and I stare at the moonlight caught in coral cavities on all sides of me.

"You're realizing how ridiculous you are, aren't you?" I hear my voice again, dulled of all emotion. "You are life set down on a land where nothing else lives. But that's not entirely it. It is more the fact that this could be happening to a man like you. What have you ever done? Gone fishing a couple of times with your boys and had a couple of good drunks. You're not the type for this sort of thing. You wear suits always bought at end-of-season sales and argue with your family about which movie you'll go to after confession on Saturday nights. You aren't made for changing like this."

"I know it. That's one of the things that's been bothering me, but I couldn't put my finger on it. It's embarrassing."

"Yes, such things are supposed to happen to resilient young men who can devise ingenious fishing equipment out of fasteners on their shorts and short-wave radio sets from the filling in their teeth, and who can eat all sorts of strange things with courage and a fearless digestion."

A renegade breaker begins its roll far out and approaches in full swell. I cringe away from the crashing climax as it hurls itself to bits at my feet and recedes into immediate swishing silence leaving its spray to sift down over my body.

"Are you thirsty? Are you thirsty as hell? You know, when a man goes three, four days without water he dries up so much inside there's not even enough liquid left for sweat — or for tears either."

"I know, I know. I've read all the same things you have."

"And about five days is all he can — "

A loud silence settles about me. Tomorrow I will make a home for myself. I will do something human.

7

Without seeming to awaken, I find myself awake and listening. My brain is aware of no definite sound, but rather a dampening of sounds that has brought it from sleep to instant and complete wakefulness. I lie unmoving in a dense suspension of time, straining every faculty to discover consciously what I have sensed unconsciously. My entire being quakes from the impression that someone has been calling me.

There! There it is, heard clearly above the spreading monotony of the surf — the shrill crowing of a rooster. Somewhere out of sight a rooster is crowing.

If there are chickens there is water, and there must be people!

Scrambling heavily to my feet, I stare about me at the

intimate world of dawn which nestles as clean as though I were looking at it through a flawless mirror. The ocean flings its foam-flecked spray jubilantly into the air, and the world that rejected me yesterday turns to me and enfolds me in its affections this morning.

The tide has come in and the pathway leading from this cove is now only a narrow ledge of sand a few inches wide. Once more the crowing, purified as a nightingale's song, drifts to my ears.

Absently, as though it will improve my hearing, I drag my glasses out by one stem and begin putting them on, quelling the vibrations of emotion that cause them to peck at my temples. Though the view is suddenly bleared, the crowings seem magnified and given direction. They seem to come from across the reef, northwest of me.

Before the last crowing dies in echo I am sloshing across the wet sand toward the broken gorge in the cliff shale, holding my glasses in place with one hand. It seems to me that my legs move me forward with exasperating slowness.

My shoulder slams against a petrified outcropping of coral wall, but I am scarcely aware of it, or of the fuzziness behind my forehead, or of the thirst that claws my throat as I shy away and trudge clumsily forward with my left foot on the narrow ledge and my right foot ankle-deep in the shallows. Rounding the corner of the gorge's indentation, I lean against the wall and study the rocky upgrade.

Above my breathing, I can hear the crowing clearly now, floating serene and lively on the chill morning air.

At the crest I pull myself up against a boulder and half stand on one knee for a moment to regain my breath, but my hopes run fast ahead of me. They have forms in my mind, like my own children, rushing forward and then turning to urge me on. I listen again to hear the shrill call that will lead me back into life.

Briefly I regret not having picked up the rest of the whiskey. It would have been a nice gesture to offer them a highball. Probably they haven't had one out here for years. But the ridiculous picture is thrust into my imagination and I lean my head forward in silent laughter: the picture of a disheveled old man, half dead, tottering toward them and trying to be jovial and dignified as he smiles at them through lardy glasses, and with the dust-stained bottle outstretched in offering, manages to croak: "I thought you might enjoy a highball."

Crowing drifts to me again as though it came from the heavens, a different sound this time, much lower in tone. It converges on me from all directions simultaneously, but I cling to my first judgment when it seemed to come from the northwest. Lowering my glasses on my nose, I peer over them until my eyes ache, searching the petrified mass for the most promising way to proceed northward. I decide to follow the reef's central spine in the hope that it will lead downward to a spot wide enough to permit walking on the tide-diminished beach.

The sun bursts out behind me, a pink lamp softening the harsh land and casting a blue shadow at my feet. All is pink — pink shrubs, pink ocean, pink coral — with a pervading pink stillness hovering over all sights and sounds in an imagined fragrance. The soft radiance of this morning counters yesterday's neutral radiance of crab thoughts, fish smells, slug hopes, filling me with an upsweep of exultation that clears the density from my head for a moment of almost intolerable happiness. Its whispering intensity pinpoints my aloneness, for it is a type of joy that cries for sharing, that cannot be contained without expression in the confines of my chest.

The tingling within me urges me forward and I stumble and slide down the ridged ledge to more level ground a few feet below and begin trudging northward, accompanied by the squishing of my shoe.

My mind carries me to another plane that exists simultaneously with my concentration on every detail of the terrain I am struggling across, and my dreams picture the cottage I will find, a cottage with thick walls and a roof of thatch to defeat the sun, a cottage with deep shadows inside and a crock of the coldest clearest water in all the world. There will be children there, and the lively odor of bacon and eggs. There will be a crock of water and a chair, a comfortable chair covered in leather that will insinuate coolness to my seat through the thin weave of my pants.

I gaze at every broken horizon for some sign of the cottage, and glancing back at my miniature volcano I judge that I have come about a mile.

With the garish reflected light from the ocean and the coral, the fine wires of pain become taut in my neck and head, and occasionally I see two of every image — a clear one and a faint one beside it. It makes no difference. Somewhere there is life and water and I am in good enough condition to find it. Nothing matters when there is life to know and water to drink. My face laughs from within and my flesh stretches stiff and burning. It must be very blistered.

The squishing diminishes to a growing squeak as my right shoe dries out.

Another thought touches at my brain with such unbear-able pleasure that I try to dispell it, but the certainty grows that when I have drunk my water and heard the voices of people who at least know what I am, for all their disregard of who I am, and when I have rested a moment in the safety of shade, the faces of Susie and the children will return in living detail to my memory.

The high point of the reef fades into greater distance behind me while I inch my way northward, and my shadow shortens as the morning drags toward noon. I will rest when there is no more shadow. A milky blankness seeps through my brain, obscuring thoughts one by one until there is only the thought of life and the thought of resting for a time . . .

8

I suppose I have dozed or fainted, for the sun has changed positions, and my left hand, which lies open beside me, has begun to swell so that I can hardly close it. I place the burned hand inside of my coat.

Through the layers of stupidity, an image of memory taunts my brain. I attempt to shake it from my being, to look about and think of other things. There, over there is a trackless path, formed by the downward rush of water during centuries of storms perhaps. An image of memory when I was a boy and had a dog. Over there the crazy pattern of nature that allows a chunk of coral to bend over like a naked man with his head touching the ground in prayer. Memory of the dog's death by poisoning. Yes, memory of the living sounds that followed me for weeks afterward when I would hear the dog's panting and the click of his footsteps on the sidewalk behind me, hearing them so vividly that I would turn full of hope and stare at the empty sidewalk. Sounds heard often enough become habit and can be heard even when they no longer exist.

But the rooster's crowing? Yes, I remember, and my footsteps become aimless wandering. At home I was awakened every morning by crowings from the neighbor's barnyard. How often I complained to Susie that I could not sleep for hearing the roosters crow at dawn? For years I complained of that sound.

The world settles into utter stillness about me as I stagger on. I refuse to think of it, but it is there in the sniggering memory of how clearly I once heard a dead dog's panting on the sidewalk behind me.

Salt sores dig into the quick around my waist and between my thighs, and all of the bruises and stiff muscles, forgotten in my joy of discovering life this morning, pulse to the foreground of my consciousness now that the joy is dead, now that I realize the crowing was only a mirage of the hearing.

Heat clamps a breathless fog about me and fills me with a pressure that demands escape, immediate escape. The beginnings of panic tear at my chest and I search wildly for a shaded spot. A segment of green simmers in freshness through a low spot in the plateau. The ocean is escape, calm in its halcyon reaches, and I am drawn to it across sunlit wastes that blister up through my shoes.

My ankle turns dangerously against a sharp projection of coral and my shoe rips open as I regain my balance and flounder down the slope. At the bottom, I fling my glasses into my pocket and pick my way toward the water. The horizon tilts from side to side as though I were viewing it from a rocking plane, and waves flick foam against my face as I wade into the deafening cacophony of the surf. My shoes fill with the water and my ankles are wetted in its promise of benediction to my whole body. Lifting my feet high into the air, I march forward.

Waves, sucking under and furling over in mountainous cascades of white and green, thunder at me with impersonal savagery. They knock me off my feet at first until I learn to ride atop them and float downward in their wake to regain my footing. When they pass, I am left standing in water only knee-deep.

Ripples catch sunlight and slash it into glittering fragments, all of them aimed directly into my eyes. I drift forward with my knees bent double, scarcely supporting myself on tiptoes in the water's heavy buoyancy.

When I get to my feet again, I lean forward and stare down through the unreflected clarity of my shadow. Pocked hollows of coral seem to gaze back at me like eye sockets of coruscating skulls. Traces of spume minnow past, touching my eyelash with their fragile bubbles.

The beach, when I drag myself from the water, is strewn with greyish lumps of crystallizing seaweed. I sink down and bunch some of the damp strands about my head to protect it from the sun, gratified with this hint of inventiveness and encouraged that I am fulfilling in some way the role assigned me.

Lying here on my back, surrounded by the flat odors of wet sand and brine-soured clothes, I think of the picture I must make — an overstuffed Bacchus, his face cherub red from the sun, water streaming from his clothes, his balding

head crowned with a diadem of tangled fibers. Professor
John W. Harper. Classes in Literature at 10 A.M.

The moisture in my clothes evaporates to coolness, calm-
ing me, and I am again struck by the idea that under different
conditions, all of this would be ravishingly beautiful. Yes,
all of this that I see as frightening and hateful is in turn a
miniature paradise depending not on it, but on the conditions of being here. If there were people close by, even on
some neighboring reef, with the assurance of companionship,
this would become a gem of whiteness and cleanness, bathed
in the serenity of soft tropical colors, brushed by a perpetual
breeze. It would be an ideal retreat. Then I could leave my
people and come here and experience the health of removing
my clothes and bathing in the ocean and basking naked on
the beach and thinking and dreaming. But now, because
there is no one else, every act against modesty becomes a
reminder that there is no longer any need for modesty.

Every moment when I close my eyes, then, becomes the
recreation of humanity, of its fragments in static portrait as
they assault my brain through all of my senses simultaneously, without order, images crowding images — the healthful odor of barley soup on a winter's afternoon; the touching sight of a woman, momentarily hideous and ovarian as
she crawls from sleep in the morning; the sound of footsteps
running to answer the telephone upstairs and the sudden
sweet idiocy that comes into my son's voice when he realizes
that his girl is at the other end of the wire; the quick, hesitant touch of midday July rains stippling the backs of hands;
the private night-mellowed taste of another's breath before
dropping off to sleep — fleeting sense images gradually
settling into place to give a more consistent portrait which

takes possession of my consciousness with the tenacity of a trancelike dream.

The breeze stirs a vagrant strand of seaweed about my head and brushes it down to tickle my nose. I flick it away without being able to flick my attention away from the dream, and my vision locks itself to a reality beyond the distant present, to a reality over which I seem to have no control.

It gathers its distangled segments from the mists of lingering tropical sunlight and sound and swims into focus that is static, like the people in an Utrillo painting, posed and unmoving, caught in motion and petrified for the moment, without regard of the preceding moment or the subsequent actions. It shows me a room with another me, a stout and placid fifteen-year-old who needs to shave once a week, a youth who leads two separate lives. He lies bundled up now between the quilts and blankets of his four-poster iron bed with its brass roses carved at the headstead. He does not move, and I must supply in my dream his actions. One life has taken him through the day, through the morning hours in the community school and through the afternoon hours working in his father's country store. Now, after supper and homework at the kitchen table, his second life has called him to his room at the end of a long hall, to the secret hours of solitary night that are the most perfect of his existence. He has already skinned out of his clothes and into his nightshirt in the stoveless room, and has carried his underwear to bed with him so that it will be warm when he puts it on before getting up in the morning. He has opened the door of his marble-top night stand, and fumbled beside the porcelain chamber pot for a match to light his lamp; and

after adjusting its wick, he has moved his clacking jaw close
to the polished glass chimney to gather its feeble warmth.

He lies in bed now, and when the heat of his body has
penetrated the blankets, he rolls over on his back, pulls his
nightshirt up around his chest and arranges his books upright between his legs, using his knees for book ends. And
while winter settles over the countryside, he turns to his
private world of discovery in the peace of knowing that the
stock is bedded down in straw against the cold and that all
is well within the house. Holding his book against his
chest so that his arms will stay covered, he becomes part of
the drama of Stevenson and London, or bastes his ignorance
in the gentle science of Paré's *Journeys to Diverse Places*
and Dr. Chase's *Receipt Book and Household Physician*.

Occasionally he stops on a word he does not know, puckers his lower lip out and seriously copies the word down in
his notebook. Then he looks it up either in Dr. Chase's
Glossary or in the dictionary, memorizes it, and repeats it
again and again to himself with much eye-closed concentration and head shaking for emphasis.

As the rustlings of the house calm to quietness about him,
the overtones of the day die to remoteness and the realities
of the night grow in fascination. Within the intimate protection of these flickering walls covered with latticed designs of giant red poppies, and with the shutters drawn
against the world outside, childhood becomes adolescence
and tentative manhood, manhood filled with the unrestrain-
edly noble passions for knowledge, for faraway times and
places; but most especially filled with the amazements and
fearsome joys of a new strength growing within his body
and soul. This beginning awareness of manhood insinuates

itself into a magical background for all he thinks and reads, groggily suggesting problems as yet neither forbidding nor familiar in the occasional dreams at dawn. He is only vaguely conscious of these things, conscious of a latent force within himself that is distantly connected with health and vigor and nobleness, coloring his little circle of lamplight with a tonality of exultation as the printed words close to his face fade away with the last vestiges of his daily life and he leaves all of this to become part of a better delight. He is the companion and apprentice to Paré, being chosen to accompany the venerable surgeon to sixteenth-century Flanders to treat the ailing Marquis d'Auret. He walks at his master's elbow in the castle gardens and hears him pray to God to bless his medicaments and his hands, to give him the grace to cure the dying marquis. He stands beside Paré in the sweating, stone-walled antechamber of the sickroom and assists him in making a refrigerant for the invalid's heart, eagerly measuring out the oil of water lilies, the ointment of roses, the pinch of saffron, dissolving them in rose vinegar and treacle and spreading them on a red cloth for the surgeon to administer. Or, his path takes him into the more immediate comfort of Dr. Chase's generous friendship, where he listens, filled with wonderment, as the old man explains to him what a womb is; touches him on the shoulder and tells him that the art of baking good yeast bread is the key to a happy home, and that young boys must train themselves with much exercise, hard beds and cold baths into the habits of temperance and continence as preparation for vigorous manhood and virtuous marriage.

When the room has grown colder and the page returns to nothing more than printed paper, blurring this time only

under the pressure of drowsiness, he will push all of the
books to the far side of the bed and blow out the lamp. In
the sudden riotous blackness, he will crawl lower between
the blankets, spraddle his legs out, adjust the pillow about
his head and fold his arms across his bare chest. Closing his
eyes, he will force himself to say his prayers, not because he
wants to, but because he feels incomplete when he does not;
and then, in the same prayerful cadence, he will go over all
of the new words he has learned, drifting to sleep on the
whispered litany of "metatarsus, consecrate, nutritious,
scrotum, ephemeral, aromatic . . ."

I can taste true affection for the child in the bed, but he is
different when I close my eyes again. He sits, dressed in a
college student's clothes, bending over a writing table in a
tiny room in Poitiers. He is becoming convinced that he
must make some sudden bold choice between the animal and
the spiritual. His soul desires to enfold another in the ancient
dream nurtured in him by Dr. Chase — the dream of health
and homemade yeast bread, but his body drags the dream
down into a swampy vision of a whore's belly, seen again
and again in devastating reality of touch and sight. He
smells the reek of humanity, seeing it only as frailty, and he
hates it with all of his love, his body and soul distilled into
a concentrated essence of loving. He looks out and sees the
cooking fires of supper smoking upward from networks of
chimneys, and each chimney tells him of a family inside,
going about their tasks, secure in their protection of body
and soul in the nest of affections born of themselves.

The rooms downstairs in this silent boardinghouse give
off a different reek, the moulding reek of loneliness, of
people who sleep alone, who putter about their rooms in

half-existences, knowing no one in the shared embrace of familiarity and being known of no one. To him there is the obscenely impeccable neatness of death about such lives, a ceramic odor of unshared propriety, of scrubbed affections, antiseptic hearts and waxed souls. He bends over his journal and his hand moves, scratching a cheap pen against cheap paper:

> . . . to break away, to become bigger than loneliness, for there is such a state. Somehow I know there is. But the dream of a newspaper and a woman's soft crying and a toothbrush and a thousand other things holds me back. It is decency, mediocre decency and not love, decency that binds me and will not let me break away, dividing the hope of heaven from the desire for hell. But decency clings softly to the soul — the body rejects it in its own prowling way. Will I ever know the answer? Will I ever know it without first knowing my own children?

And that hand is scarcely finished before an older hand replaces it, a hand with deeper wrinkles across the backs of the knuckles, a hand stained with the scuffed layers of experience, a hand moving a better pen against better paper:

> The night has turned very cold, with rain blowing in gusts against our windows, but the fire has kept the bedroom warmer than it really needs to be. I have been up several times to fill the vaporizer with tincture of benzoin compound for Cindy, who sleeps with almost no congestion now, and to add logs to the fire. In spite

of my sleepiness, there is some profoundly intimate pleasure in stirring about and doing things to keep Susie and Cindy comfortable while they sleep unaware of the storm. These are the secret things of a man's heart, and sometimes, as tonight, they break through the clutter of my life, shed their dullness of familiarity and overwhelm me as though I were living them in all of the startling clarity of newness, so overwhelm me that I catch my heart pounding with disbelief and gratitude. How many times in how many countries have I walked outside of homes, my heart breaking with the knowl- edge of what went on inside of them — the families, the loves and the quarrels, the bodies and the hearts, all of that shared in livingness behind those curtained win- dows. I remember writing in one of these journals at that time that my body and soul were at war within me, that they were separate and inimical parts of my being, finding opposite answers to the same eternal question, and I wondered if I should ever know the one right answer before I knew my own children. Now, as the house sleeps about me, protecting my chil- dren from the night outside, I realize that the answer is not what I thought it would be — not some vaguely pleasant compromise between the two opposing an- swers that would allow me to be at peace with those separate portions of my being. No, it is quite some- thing else. Through some mysterious chemistry, my children make clear to me what has never been clear before: that man is not his body, but his body and soul combined, with the soul pumping vitality into all of the actions of his humanity, sleeping when the body sleeps, making love when the body makes love, suffering when the body suffers, infused with the body in all things, even to the smallest and most banal; and that to look down on man's animal appetites and functions as contemptible impediments to his soul is no compliment either to the soul, which directs them into unashamed health, or to God's creation of man's humanity. It is on such a night as this, blustery, cold, threatening, that these things bring man the sudden comfort of complete clarity. On such a night, they whom I protect become my own greatest protection, and my stomach urges me to be with them, to build up the fire for them, to sit here smoking a cigarette and listen to Georgie's sleep-clumsied footsteps padding to the bathroom and, after a moment, back to his bed to the accompaniment of the flushing toilet, listening to all of these things in flickeringly renewed wonderment; and then mashing out my cigarette and getting to my feet to make a last check of the household; and finally to crawl into bed myself and listen to the fire inside and the storm outside, and to know with a new certainty that I am on the inside of my own —

The sweet odor of a bedroom fireplace vanishes. The soft dampness of vaporized tincture of benzoin compound is throttled in the raw dampness of vaporized sea water. My hand finds my beard and the crusting dryness of my lips, and all freshness vanishes to a view of the cliff overhang. The sun has disappeared around the corner of the reef, throwing me into the cavelike somberness of deep shadow. Time for dinner, time to bathe and dress for dinner; time to shave and comb my hair and change this filthy shirt.

My tongue feels glutinous and clumsy. I won't be able to eat much. Maybe just a bowl of cold rice and cream.

If I hate the sun, I hate the darkness more. I begin climbing back to the top where it will be lighter, stopping midway to catch my breath and to toss aside my soggy crown of seaweed before moving on. I must have light to locate my twin bushes so I can find my way back to my cove. Strange, even its windswept emptiness is a familiarity to which I cling now, as though this familiarity imparted some faint aura of warmth and recognition.

My pants rub the insides of my legs raw. At the top, I drag myself to my feet and gaze about me for some sign of my bushes. The reef lies bathed in warm cobalt tints of dusk, misted with yellow and rose. The sun is a crimson disk, cleanly outlined without radiance and no longer threatening as it hangs near the horizon. Again I see a shadow far in the distance, flat and formless, rising and falling with my eyes' pulsation, a flickering cataract in front of the sunset. What is it, some twin reef as desolate as this one?

Turning my eyes away from the sun, I look back along the quiet, waterswept beach.

I am quaking from within before I realize fully what I have seen. It takes some time for me to blink back the seizure of trembling, for, from this raised perspective, and in the peculiar shadings of sunset, black pockmarks are clearly outlined walking along the beach, stepping around clumps of seaweed and moving on. I look up and down the beach and nothing about it is familiar. I have not walked along it. I approached it from above for my swim.

Sliding, falling, hurrying and slowing, I somehow get down the incline. In the confused pattern of my own footsteps, cut neatly and deeply into the sand, the washed prints of other feet pattern themselves above the water line to disappear around the great boulder that crouches against the cliff like a sleeping sentinel. I did hear the rooster! There is life here. I am not alone.

I concentrate with amazement on the core of calm that paralyzes me in the midst of this maelstrom of emotions. My legs propel me forward, telling my numbed senses that I must hurry before night erases the path from sight; but the calmness within me refuses to hurry. It is frightening, as though I didn't much care, when every particle of my being cares with agonizing acuteness. The calmness suddenly observes all things coming alive about me. That which was monotonous when I had an eternity of time in which to observe it becomes varied and magical now that I must rush past it. The upper crown of the sentinel boulder is struck ablaze with reflections from the setting sun. I am running too rapidly, calling out with no control over my lungs, like a bleating animal.

Around the curve there will be a cottage with a thick roof of thatch and a magnificent crock of sweet water. There will be fish cooking, and a little bowl of rice. There will be people dressed in fresh-smelling clothes, and they will have clean hands and faces. But I must hurry. Color drains from the heavens and the sky whitens behind a first star. The boulder becomes soft purples as I draw nearer. She will be there in soft purples, under soft lamplight, cooking for me. And I will call her Susie. Her face will not be there, but I will never tell her that. Now, with darkness falling, the cottage will look calm in its cove. Light from the open door will reflect a shaft of pale yellow on the sand. My hand touches the rock, rough diamonds.

Around it, another step, the house, neat, hidden in a cove from sight, protected from the frightful night's ceaseless activities. I clear my eyes with the back of my sleeve, blotting them against the sting of rough cloth. Drawing a deep breath, I swallow the tremblings and step out onto solid ground. I open my mouth to shout the greeting.

My shout dies somewhere in the back of my throat as I stare at a barren sweep of grey sand marred by black lumps of seaweed. A cliff rises from ground mists into a massed silhouette against the star-filling paleness, calm, silent, inscrutable. A breaker crashes its monstrous drumroll loud against my ears, rolling water above my shoetops. Evening mists, unbroken by lamplight, veil the dozing alleyway of beach.

When I come to my senses, I realize that my mouth is still open for the shouted greeting and that my head is moving slowly from side to side. Absently, in the humming silence of my heart, I bend forward and follow the hinted footsteps to a point where they mingle with many others and stop. In the last glow of twilight I see the distorted imprint in the sand, the size of a man's body, and beside it a black whiskey bottle.

Reality filters through shock. I am back where I have slept before. I have followed the footprints I made yesterday evening when I wandered dazedly home. I stand above them and gaze unbelieving. A shadowy sand crab wobbles sideways into its hole and their is no life here but mine as night falls. Time to dress for dinner. That is what aches in my brain. Not the dinner, not the water, but dressing for dinner. I lie down in the bed of last night.

9

"Is this the second night? — the third night? — the fourth night? Will you tell me?" I roll on my side. Granules of sand bite into my wrist and my weight compresses my ribs against my lungs with dull pain.

How many days' growth of beard and with what filth on a body full of sores? Think beyond, think of something else. It is wrong to die in filth. Words of St. Teresa of Avila: "If a man had only five minutes in which to prepare himself for death, he would spend four of them making himself comfortable." No, he would spend four of them washing his body, combing his hair, shaving himself. I feel it, you hear? — I hate to die this way, not hating to die, but hating to die in filth.

How is it that I smell so strongly of the odor of sweating

when I am blistering here without a trace of sweat on my face or body? A knot draws to tightness at the base of my brain and I wonder how a tree looks. All things assault my somnolent brain as though I were seeing them for the first time. I think how miraculous an ice cube is. A toothbrush — when did I last see one? A drain plug in the bathtub? Morning coffee and a cigarette? The marvel of life that is somewhere back there, magical now even to its smallest detail. Did I ever sit in an easy chair? — ever? How did it feel? How do newspapers smell on a veranda in August? And what about classrooms at the end of day? — empty chairs and desks still vibrating life, rooms still carrying moist odors of youngness that is no longer fresh after the long day. Did I ever really know all of that? Miraculous. To lie in bed when sheets are clean and smell of summer sunlight. To enter a library or church and be greeted by some subtle density of atmosphere that demands walking on tiptoe and whispering the moment you open the door. To hear talk from someone else's lips . . .

God how remote, how remote and foreign all of that seems tonight.

10

There is the coral always and always the sun, and I must walk always in search of water.

I try to remember how many days — three? four? five? Five days is the limit. Five days and a man sees the sun through a glowing mist and then his eyes recede and he dies.

Thought no longer exists but there is hope. The closer a man approaches nothingness, the more he refuses to admit it. And there is tenderness, even when there is no longer the image of a face . . . there is tenderness until tenderness fills every crevice of being and a man loves gigantically. And the love is his hope.

There! There! A sand crab far from its hole. I jump into the air and land on it with the heel of my shoe. Its legs rake furiously as I crush it into the sand. Restaurants of the

world. Pressed duck with burgundy. Baked pompano.
Roast pheasant. Crab in agony.

The sun, the ocean, the universe gyrate somewhere in
the background, but I don't pay any attention to them.
I can live. The beach is full of sandcrabs. They swarm in
all directions.

I reach down and pick it up. Its claws are not distorted in
death. It lies perfectly whole in the palm of my hand.
None of its liquids are lost!

Exultantly I place it between my teeth to break its armor.
It cracks and I taste grit between my lips and gums. Surprised, I take it away to look at it. Focusing carefully, I see
it become a grotesque and lifeless chunk of coral. I let the
thing fall to the ground. The others no longer swarm.
They cast shadows, motionless shadows. Five days and
how many have passed? For the life of me I can't remember.

I climb to the highest point on the reef and stare in all
directions. The shadow pulsates on the horizon. For a brief
instant, it is brought close to my eyes, inhabiting the smallest
corner of my vision, like a miniature seen through the wrong
end of a telescope. It is covered with trees. Blanched coral
beaches fade into a wild, moss-colored jungle. The tops of
the tallest trees are made luminous green by the sun and the
lower growth is lost in dank shadows. All of it is motionless,
a mass of static color. My eyes ache with the effort and I
am aware of the white ground and the white bushes around
me as though seen superimposed. I look away and then
quickly back. Now there is nothing but a flat shadow once
more on the ocean's horizon. Some trick of the lenses, like
the crabs . . .

I begin walking again. My pants brush against a dew-drinking bush, and drunkenly I bend down to examine it. And I am bending down in a garden in Holland and there are morning mists and tulips and my pants are comfortable grey flannels that do not eat into the ulcers of my genitals and legs. Clusters of giant purple grapes cling to the stone wall. Globules of morning dew drip downward from one grape to another and plash into the sparkling grasses below. The pockets of yellow tulips are filled with rainwater and the soaked air is gently perfumed with smoke from chimneys nearby.

I examine the leaf for a long time. My hand is incredibly red and wrinkled against it. I stand up straight and begin to walk. A searing breeze from the ocean nudges at my face. I raise my hand to rake sweat from my forehead, but my forehead is dry. Waves crash against the reefs below. Then I see the ground coming up to meet my face.

11

The wind blows through a shuddering forest, deep and far away.

Someday I will get to my feet and walk again.

Is this the fourth day? God! Is this the fifth day?

I do not move. The granules of sand beneath my eyes pulsate and draw closer and then swirl away. They fascinate me. In a while I will walk some more.

The sun sets and stars cluster overhead. They are like the sand. They move. They fascinate. They are so young, so terribly young and I can hardly believe that they will go on like that, glittering every night on a world that knows nothing of my existence.

I sleep some of the time, with dreams of verdure, dreams of healthful green countrysides and clear unreflected lakes.

I lie on my side with my legs drawn up and with my hands between them, not needing to move, not needing to think. Strange. A point is reached where even thought becomes waste spilled out on the hem of eternity.

But there is no waste to memory, and no thrift and no time. Somewhere back there a freshly ironed dress, face powder, the face without features from a lifetime ago when I knew her and loved her.

The fifth day? Is it? God.

The waiting, the moments of waiting when there are no more seconds. The moments between life and death or between two sleeps. Moments suspended in time, not counted in seconds.

I think that I must turn to my wife, and with sudden youthfulness, mingled with age and passion into a fragment of tranquillity, ask: "Do you remember the days? — the days when we first started together? — those wonderful days?" and read in her body the answer and feel strangely full of guilt. We are together, then, for a new time in the nest of our bed, breathing the humid air that accumulates beneath the covers, hidden from the world, from the night, safe, pressing against one another to express some mysterious security of pardon; pardon because always when two people love, they must be forgiven one by the other, constantly, without other reason than that love demands it — the security of perpetually renewed pardon born of the delicate balance forever re-establishing itself between two people become one but remaining two. I roll in my bed. My arms reach out to encircle warmth, to find the complete union after all these years, still seeking to have only one heart with hers, only one body, only one painfulness.

The sky is full of night's sharp clarity and there is no warmth of her body in my arms, but I am profoundly comfortable in the silence, the emptiness. I am filled with the realization that I am a fleck of unknown livingness in a world where nothing else lives, and yet tonight there is joy and comfort in all of it.

But I wonder why eternity keeps me waiting in this timeless hole. It surprises me that something that important could be laggard. You expect it to be punctual, immaculately punctual. I lie here waiting, feeling strangeness.

To my left, light glistens from coral diamonds. It is a fine illusion. Perhaps here is the flame that is supposed to blaze up before my eyes recede into my skull.

Fiery reflections slither and dance. I let my head be raised on its tendons. Far away, through the clean blackness, pinpoints of flame cast a glow upward into the sky. Numbly I listen. There is no sound and I am too wonderfully comfortable to move.

And yet the irritating distraction is there, floating beyond my intimate world of now. And then I recognize it and I turn on my side and put my blistered hands against my blistered face. I need water for one tear or I will suffocate. I remember campfires glittering through timber at night when you return after a long day's hunting, and they were like these, glowing in the distance and made close in the clarity of night. These have probably been there every night, bringing my phantom shadow on the horizon close to me, but I could not see them from my cove below.

I struggle into an upright position thinking to shout; but no, that would be useless; to build a signal fire; but no, there is no flame here. The coral shallows that follow an underwater path to that horizon? But it is too late. Lights roar before my eyes, splintering all vision. I cup my hands into a telescope over one eye. I stare at hundreds of tiny lights until they join in sight to become ten or twelve, dotting the blackness without design and casting a glow upward to the lowest stars.

"Hey!" But the seal on my lips refuses to break. "For the love of God, hey!" They will never hear my mumblings. Faint odors of night mingle with my own reek. I try to separate my lips. They feel like wood bark to my trembling fingers.

I no longer try to call out. I crawl, dragging my distended belly like a packsack beneath me. Stars allow paleness to glint about me. I stop at the edge of the western cliff and peer out into its black hole. Invisible breakers foam up beneath me.

Sitting with my legs dangling over the edge, I telescope my hands again. The fires are still there. How far? A thousand yards? A thousand miles? I can feel my face draw up into a grin, a weeping grin in which there is no moistness. How far? And what choice? What difference is there between dying on this chalk-dry cliff and dying in sea shallows? The one is certain, the other less so. If I don't think about it, don't try to —

Blind impulse pushes me to lean forward and I teeter over the edge knowing only that I will go as far as possible. My feet touch the ground, my legs buckle wildly and I am sitting with my nose tingling numb where it has bashed into my knees. The surf bellows forward in crescendo and water lashes around my seat and ankles. I stretch out and allow it to cover me from the neck down. Its tepid wetness seeps into the fever of my body, massaging me and clearing my head a little.

My brain swims off into sleep and I am jerked back to wakefulness with my head lolling on my neck into the water. Lumbering to my feet, I straggle forward over the pocked shallows, bracing myself against the long walls of phosphorous turnings that fling the tinsel of breakers at me.

My senses withdraw against the onslaught. How far to the lights? As each breaker roars on beyond me, I can see the fires over low waters and the fixed grin returns to hurt my face. With each step forward I place my foot carefully, in the prayerful knowledge that I may be stepping down not on the rough ground of now but into the smooth plane of forever.

Slowly, carefully, I shutter my senses deep within me and move forward automatically, feeling nothing, my body senselessly obeying the obsession of its brain, the obsession of those lights.

Suddenly the last fire disappears, cut off by some object, and I am moving with the waves in total darkness. And then there is a swirling envelopment as I am lifted away from the terrain into warm nothingness. I hear my voice from within, moaning "No . . . no . . ." and turn to whimperings of despair as coolness pervades the air of my somersaulting flight. And there is no more solidness beneath my feet.

12

I see broken pieces of brightly colored glass swimming against a background of whiteness. When I open my eyes it is the same. Chips of red and green and amber and blue whirl in circles and I can neither slow them nor tear my attention from them.

Faintly, from across a vast park, music of the carrousel steams to me, the three-square waltzing of the calliope, wheezing brasses and clinking triangles, distant gaiety like some remembered sadness through the glass-spangled forests.

My throat is torn with gulpings. My brain is jerked from my head, brutally, as though manipulated on the tight little wires of a puppet master. It flies to my lips which are rubbed to the quick against a roughness that spouts liquid into my throat in such plenty that I swallow against suffocation. The broken pieces of glass gyrate before my staring eyes. My brain flies to my neck, bent forward with my head pillowed against a hardness that pulls at my hair. The pieces of glass billow up like leaves in the wind and the clanging of the music surges louder as my brain is dragged into my belly, feeling the scorching, the dry heat, feeling wetness that pours down my chin and drops like crystals of ice against the front of my shirt.

I am weeping, wracked with weeping, doubled-up on my side in bed with my face pressed between her breasts.

Somewhere, above the music, a voice full of the sweet antiseptic smells of arnica and iodine murmurs: "You mustn't cry. It will give you a headache."

I bury my face more deeply into the warmness between her breasts and feel her hands cradling my head. And I must weep and gulp to keep from suffocating.

"You mustn't. You mustn't cry. It will give you a headache," she says from far above me, sympathy and laughter and patience tuning her voice to the fading ocean of music. Her uniform smells of starch and sunlight, but close to my nose is the odor of breasts, others, naked ones.

The colored pieces of glass are swallowed in a milky haze, and a formless shadow hovers somewhere before me. There is no more smell of the doctor's office, but the odor of breasts lingers close to my nose.

Gradually, the shadow assumes details, pale and wavery: the eyes of a cat in the face of a cat; the dead concentration of a stare from enormous eyes in a tiny black face and the sound of labored breathing close to my ear. I drink with a contraction of neck muscles and stare until the cat's face becomes the face of a child. His eyes are fixed on me as though he were looking at an animal or a blind man, unaware of a responding intelligence.

I look through drooping eyelids to his miniature stomach, his dust-filled navel. He is sitting astride my chest. All is stillness and I am not sure whether the carrousel music has gone or whether I can occasionally hear its thumping beat in my head.

I open my eyes with all of my strength. Beyond the scraggly rim of a container held to my mouth and made enormous and fuzzy so close to my eyes, I see his face, a child's face, a beautiful child's face of intense seriousness that looks bland from frequent laughter, a vaguely comical face. His lips pucker in a sucking gesture as he concentrates on forcing me to drink. I peer into the blank wall of his face, incredibly old and wise in its unwrinkled sheen. He does not notice my gaze. The odor of naked breasts is the odor of his naked body bending over me. My brain hovers somewhere beyond recall, refusing to co-operate with me, fascinated by the faint music of an amusement park, and I drift into nothingness.

It seems that I sleep to awake in the same attitude, as the cutting pressure is removed from my lips, pulling whiskers at the corners of my mouth and dragging me from my stupor. When I open my eyes, I see him as though from the bottom of a well, peering up through a long tunnel. His beautiful face, his beautiful face . . .

Water has reached its curing charity into my belly and stopped the smoking. I watch the child. Sunlight plays on his dust-streaked nakedness, highlighting blues. Something hangs about his neck. Squinting, I see that they are teeth — a double necklace of some kind of teeth.

He inches down my body until he is sitting on my stomach and lowers his head to listen to my heartbeat. The salt-stained lapel of my coat partly covers the kinky black crown as he nestles his ear against my chest. Can he hear the gathering carnival in my heart?

The music dies on a caught breath, suspended in mid-air. On the sizzle of silence, my heartbeat thumps in my ears and I seem to be waiting, tense, waiting for the unknown, all faculties tuned to expectancy. Then, with no warning, the face of other times bursts back into memory with all of its traits, livingly detailed, as though she were suddenly a part of me again. A tremor sings through my body, changing the very texture of my flesh in its wake. I can see her face and feel all of the emanations of her being. The air is alive with scattering recollections of her and guilt slides lightly from my heart!

The child's head bobs up and his searching eyes open to roundness. Above my immediate dizziness and pain, I try to recollect myself enough to smile and to thank him, but only a scratching groan comes through my lips. I see a network of brown filaments, like cracked porcelain, surrounding his dilated pupils as panic boils up in his eyes. His breath becomes a rapid series of wheezes. A patch of sunlight glistens on one cheek, highlighting a thousand intricate geometrical designs exquisitely tattooed in blue on his flesh.

He supports himself with his hands planted in my chest, frozen like a hound at point, and for an instant our very souls seem to unite in the devastating meeting of our gazes as his eyes recognize consciousness in mine. My lips stiffen with the smile I try to force on them and I raise my hand to pat his leg, to reassure him, but the touch galvanizes him and lightness immediately replaces his weight on my stomach as he springs away and disappears. I have the impression of black nakedness, of stomach and arms and legs and wild squeakings of breathing, all of that somehow mixed in contortions of motion that speed him away.

When I force my head around on its creaking muscles, the sun-splashed beach is deserted. With my eyes at ground level, the scene rises in strange perspective, like an off-angle photograph. A few feet above me, where the sky should be, a solid wall of underbrush bends in a blackish green curve around the arc of the beach. It moulders dank and forbidding without entrance, without a break, impenetrable. To my left, sunlight hisses down in angular rays through giant palms that lean out over the water at a great height. The very earth seems to move with the points of sunlight that drift to and fro on the sand.

The child is gone, leaving no trace. I wonder if this is not another illusion, but no, a roughly halved coconut shell lies still glistening beside me, and when I reach beneath my head, the pillow that has supported it is the other half of the shell. Green-fibered coconut husks are scattered nearby in magnified perspective.

When I close my eyes, the child's remembered face is etched there, a tiny face, intensely serious, but bearing the mark of centuries of sweetness, of unbelievable sweetness mixed with a certain sardonic casualness. And the tattoo marks, visible only when the sunlight struck his face, not marks, but indentations in the flesh, like some ancient two-dimensional bas-relief containing countless minute designs in florid detail.

The weakness grows on my comfort, like some distant flute song played from the other end of a long corridor. I will get up and move later, but now I listen to the weakness that tells me I may rest for a time.

13

A distant odor, an odor vaguely familiar seeps through
my sleep-numbed senses — the soft odor of wood smoke,
fragile and diluted in space, like cold incense.

I open my eyes to deep shadow. Beyond the eternal
whiteness of breakers, the low-flung skies are solid with
twilight's deepest blues, dark as in storm, but cloudless and
filled with stars. Paling upward, grey dusk lingers overhead,
with its hints of purples and pinks. Thickly interlaced palm
fronds are silhouetted in black sharpness high above me,
their ringed trunks weaving in gentle contortions. I lie
beneath their vaulted ceiling and the sky sifts through like
dusk through stained-glass windows. I think of the subtle
glow of a cathedral nave at twilight, and am bathed in its
twin warmth, a warmth of translucent clarity that suspends

all movements into an instant of utter stillness within the heart.

Chilled air, splanged with dampness and stagnation, flows out from the jungle. Not moving, I inhale the intimate odors of nature — the eternal combinations of decaying vegetation, freshness from the sea, dried fish carcasses and my own stench; all of it laced with the unfailing perfume of wood smoke; all of it rarefying the purity of dusk and making it transparent in its mysterious rustlings toward night. I listen to the drowsy twittering of birds, sharply isolated near and far in the jungle darkness, as they chirp compline before drifting into sleep.

Thought does not go beyond feeling, and feeling is limited to the slow inundation of peace and contentment.

Over this land, which becomes like all other lands in the halted moments between sunset and night, I feel that I should be hearing the hushed, distance-distorted sweetness of an Angelus bell ringing out from some ancient parish church; and I imagine that all who hear it are arrested in their attitudes, stopped in the middle of washing their hands, setting their tables, unharnessing their plows, making love or reading their mail, and that eyes are suddenly closed in individual concentrations that join all minds to the same words: "*Ave, Maria, gratia plena: Dominus tecum.*"

The prayer breathes unexpected radiance throughout my body. It catches me in full surprise, and for the moment all else fades into unimportance. There is gold in my brain, gold on my lips, gold in the spontaneous warmth of some hidden companionship, and I repeat the prayer again and again until, putting my hands between my thighs for comfort, I am reminded of my own excremental filth and the gold blurs into the clays and dusts of earth. I will forget the filth, forget it until tomorrow, but the irritation grows into its own obsession, and I know I must find some way of cleaning my clothes and my body. It is good. The gold is gone, but its overtones linger to nourish me, changing everything, the way a street seems changed when you walk out of a museum after having seen a masterpiece. Now, the demands for physical action stir sluggish contentment and give a goal to my wounded idleness. I must get up and wash myself and my clothes; somehow, I must do that.

First, to unbuckle my belt and inch out of my pants and underpants. Peace floats over the atmosphere, the peace of accomplishing motion, the peace of an action that seems immense and distant through all the layers of lethargy.

When they are off, I roll around to one side to retrieve them and begin the slow business of emptying my pockets. The locket, the key, the pocket handkerchief fill my hands with their rusting grittiness, but my wallet seems to be missing. The child must have taken it. But no, I dismiss the thought as an idiotic hangover from civilized suspicions. I must have lost it in the water when I made my way through the shallows last night. Between each series of movements, I lie back exhausted and listen to my halting breath.

Dried salt and coral granules shower down on my bare legs as I remove my coat and shirt and undershirt. The forest exhales its chill and my flesh responds by stippling. I should have waited until morning when the sun would have dried me quickly. Tonight, I will freeze with washed, wet clothes on me. But now that I can feel the clean air of night against my nakedness, the thought of putting filth-encrusted clothing back on is unbearable.

Out there, somewhere, is a reef that taught me to know death. In some ways I can feel a trace of affection for it now. Someday, when I am strong again, I will wade back through those tugging currents and see the place in safety, and someday I will drink the rest of that bottle of whiskey. In the immediate nothingness, deprived of all contact with the world of my world, the thought of such a reminder of that world sends a thrill of excitement through my body. When shall I drink it? Not too soon. No, perhaps in a year I will make the pilgrimage back and study the bottle in my hand and take one drink before replacing it in the sand. That will be my tie with my world, and my years will be measured by the returns for that solemn and holy rite of nature's juncture with the civilization that has formed my life. And that bottle will symbolize all that is left of my past: it will be my wife, my family, my students, my knowledge, my Sunday suit, my recollection of all past sexual unions — everything to which it and it alone now holds the key.

I am shaken with chill from the jungle's damp breath, and the smoke odor comes more strongly on the coldness.

I attempt to bend forward and pick up my clothes, but dizziness swims on gravity's pull to my head and I quickly straighten up. Bending my knees and squatting with my trunk held rigid, I can do it. Without looking down, I fumble for the festering mass of clothes and get back to my feet, hugging them against my chest with my free hand.

And it occurs to me that I am concentrating deeply on all of these things; that I am lost in them, and that I am almost breathlessly excited to accomplish them. Not since childhood can I remember working with such enthusiasm as I am now working to get these simple tasks done.

The sand's texture beneath my feet changes to damp hardness, cold and smooth as close-grained concrete. The thought of the freezing water repels me, but to my astonishment, it flips over my instep and swirls warmly about my ankles for a moment before receding. The brine is perfectly comfortable. Looking down, I can see where it came to on my feet. From my ankle down, it looks as though I were wearing cellophane socks.

I wash my clothes out slowly, catching them at two corners, dipping them into the water and rubbing. One at a time, I scrub underwear, pants, shirt and coat, putting the clean ones between my legs as I finish with them, floating up and down with the waves, alone in the timeless pleasure of warm liquidness that protects me from the cold of the night.

Rising from the water is like rising into a cloud of frost. I hurry on the strength of my discomfort across the wet sand into the dry warmth of the dunes and hang my clothes securely on the branches of a bush. I am aware of the freedom of cleanliness, a cleanliness of my body that glows exultantly through its dripping chill.

Weakness returns full on a glimmering of sensuality within — the sensuality of delight that I have done all of these things for which I am so ill fitted, the sensuality of vague amusement in the exotic night of my first laundrying, and now, sleeping naked under a blanket of sand. The embarrassment of my first days alone, when I blushed to think of the heroic role assigned me, is almost gone now.

14

Thirst and hunger battle in rage against the emptiness of my stomach, bringing me to life through sheer discomfort. In a paroxysm of coughing, I pull myself up to my hands and knees and begin crawling toward the shadowing wall of underbrush where my clothes hang in white and blue patches against greenery, but my attention is attracted to my shoes nearby. Wedged between them, I see two halves of coconut shells, and my pain and fatigue evaporate in the upsurge of curiosity.

In one, a clear liquid catches sunlight and flashes it without movement into my eyes. The other is filled with a thick purplish substance, like lavender mush. I gaze about me at the sun-splashed world of morning, utterly stupefied. Some-one has brought me these things, has placed them between my shoes so they would not turn over or spill out, and has silently departed.

I brace myself on one side, with my left elbow in the sand, and reach out and carefully bring the liquid-filled shell to my lips, watching the sunlight desert it as it comes toward me. It does not have the soapy taste of yesterday's liquid. It is pure, warm water.

I deposit the shell carefully and bring the other one to my lips. The smell is vile, like rotting Irish potatoes mixed with soap. It is probably some sort of root cooked in coconut milk. I dig three fingers of my right hand into it and scoop some of the tepid mixture out. Its taste is not so bad as its odor. Unsalted mush that has the stinging flavor of soap, full of lumps, makes its way downward from my chewing. I realize that it is probably nourishing and force myself to eat all of it, swallowing rapidly. When it is gone, I wipe my sticky fingers in the sand and then wash the taste away quickly with the remainder of the water.

The food acts as a drug. Before I have finished drinking, I am suffocated by the desire to sleep and my arm trembles beneath me. My eyes close in drowsiness as my stomach growls over its digestive burden.

I must at least get into the shade. The nearest shade is immediately before me, in the underbrush. I inch toward it in great sleepiness, scarcely noting the bare footsteps in the sand around my shoes, tiny footprints of a child and larger footprints of an adult intermingling. The child did tell someone, then . . .

My clothes flutter in my face. Reaching up, I drag them to my chest and fall forward through the foliage. Branches converge on me, but I crawl on into a cave of leaves, dark and filled with the warm humid odors of decay. Spreading my clothes out, I lie on my back, in a cocoon of tightly woven greenery through which no sunlight seeps. The last thing I see is a swarm of gnats suspended in the gloom above my nose. They seem miles away.

15

The noise of laughter and shouting brings me to wakeful paralysis. I blink my eyes open and my ears drink in the almost-forgotten sounds of humanity close by. Not moving, I listen to the strange chattering while I become aware of a thousand bugs crawling over my body, tiny bugs that neither bite nor sting. I can see nothing but leaves and branches against my face.

What must I do? The bugs irritate me almost unbearably. I move my hand up to brush them away from my stomach, but the stir against leaves sounds thunderously loud to me and I halt in mid-movement.

The voices sound argumentive, like high school boys discussing a football game. A child screams in anger not six feet from me, repeating one word that sounds like "Ta-eega, ta-eega, ta-eega!" Strangeness and fearsomeness. It is better to lie here and wait, and if they discover me, to remain motionless.

The child spouts forth a long phrase of sharp-syllabled words, and there is scuffling over which an older boy's voice laughs "*Ebira?*" They are obviously teasing the child. Perhaps he has led them here to see me, and now, not seeing me, they are calling him names. I listen to the sound of human voices with a strange inpouring of contentment, much like the water after my long thirst.

A bug makes its way exquisitely up my side to my armpit and I close my eyes and tremble to stiffen myself so as not to slap it. It turns aside and inches across my chest toward my throat, bisecting every nerve in its path.

The scuffling ceases, very much as I remember it when I have entered classrooms, to a tense silence. The younger men speak differently, with respect and are answered each in turn by the cracked voice of a man. Obviously they are greeting him. I listen carefully and repeat after each of them: "Augua Kulangu. Kmai Kakosekani." To these greetings, the older voice answers with the identical phrases.

It brings an element of threat into the innocent-sounding group. But soon, although the atmosphere of restraint and caution is maintained, subdued outbursts of laughter enliven it.

Hands begin clapping and laughter rises to a howl before the older voice screams out the word the child spoke earlier: "Ta-eega!" and the laughter and handclapping stop immediately. He barks something else and footsteps begin shuffling away.

When I think they have gone far enough, and the cries of

birds have become shrill insults to the parting group, I thrash around so that my head is where my feet were and separate the brush enough to peer out.

Before me, scattered over a wide area, I see my abandoned possessions. They have not taken them. To my left, the cavorting black bodies of naked young men and boys, tagging and chasing one another as they are herded off before the old man. He ambles slowly along with the child by his side. He walks slightly humped in the shoulders, but very tall and skeletal, with withered flesh and kinky white hair. There is an air of unconcern about the way he holds a short club in his left hand, something unhurried in his gait that reminds me of a distinguished British grandfather taking his children and grandchildren out for a Sunday stroll.

The child, whose head comes only a little above the old man's knees, marches forward with his little stomach pushed out and his shoulders rigidly squared.

The group passes on beyond a curve in the beach and my chuckling dies to emptiness within my chest. I watch the spot where they disappeared until my eyes water from the glare.

What can I do but wait now, wait in that sense of expectancy I have so often known in the past, wait for something unknown to happen. Trees sway gently overhead and their shadows reach out into the waves as afternoon wears on. The shaded heat becomes more intense, and I drift into a torpor, not resisting it, chaining my mind to the hypnotic repetition of "Augua Kulangu. Kmai Kakosekani," saying the phrase again and again into my beard, dreading dusk, dreading night.

16

Sunlight scorches into the bottoms of my bare feet and I am drowning in sweat. Something of the calm, platitudinous gaiety of morning riots beyond the orange vista of my closed eyelids. Have I slept so long? I open my eyes to the rebuff of a thousand suns and quickly cover my face with my hands.

A sharp, indrawn squeal jerks my loosened senses into a tight knot, and I turn my head in its world of hand sweat, and look through the tunnel of magnified grooves and lines to see a child clinging in terror to an old man's legs. The old man is backing away, his club raised threateningly. Panic shimmers through me but I remember to lie motionless.

"Augua-Kulangu-Kmai-Kakosekani" comes from my

lips almost before I have gathered my wits enough to know what I am doing.

"Augua Kulangu, Kmai Kakosekani," the old man answers gutturally and I am taken aback that he has answered at all. The child pushes his face forward around the post of the man's knee and spouts a stream of language that makes his teeth necklace dangle. The man casually kicks him aside with enough force to send him rolling over in the sand. When he gets to his feet, I notice no fear in his eyes, no anger or resentment. It is as though this were a perfectly natural occurrence with him. He is still jabbering in his monkeyish soprano.

I rise to lean on one elbow, facing them, and nod that I do not understand. The man is rumbling in his throat, jerking his kinky white head up and down and glaring at me with a concentration that tells me he wants me to repeat what he is saying.

"Augua Kulangu," I begin carefully, "Kmai Kakosekani." The child's gaze flies from me to the old man in some dread that I do not understand.

The man chews on something, apparently working himself up to shout "Au-goo-ah!" on the verge of that feminine screech I remember from yesterday. Red spittle appears at the corner of his mouth.

"Au-goo-ah?" I say, imitating him. His frown relaxes slightly.

"Augua Koo-lann-goo!" he says in a more guttural and natural voice with his vermilion lips drawn back over badly stained tushes.

I mimic as well as I can, noticing that the sun strikes bluish reflections from their bodies rather than the copperish ones seen in most dark-skinned peoples.

The child starts to smile, but his expressions are liquid and the smile changes to open fear once more as the old man screams a repetition of the phrase, again and again, like some hysterical theater director.

We go over every syllable of this weird cant and resentment grows on my own despair as he dominates me in his bellowings. He bends forward until his tortured face is only a few feet above me. Ligaments are tight under loose flesh in his neck and a vein protrudes at the side of his forehead. His eyes devour and dominate; dominate the way diamonds do, making me want to draw away from them, but holding me in fascination. I wonder what lies behind them as my mouth repeats his phrases in some distant consciousness, as though we two were doing nothing but staring into each other while two other men, somewhere in the background, were speaking. What does this brilliance hide? — what sympathies, what passions, what weaknesses? What is there behind them that can be touched by another? I see nothing. They are armor, impenetrable and vaguely terrifying, for somehow there is no defense against such eyes. Was this black skeleton ever afraid of anything? And yet there is a mildness about the set of his mouth, a gentleness implied in his hunched posture, in his dried chest muscles and protruding navel, those reassuring reminders of his humanity. I glance at the child. His eyes are human and expressive. What has happened between childhood and age to glaze those of the old man? I cannot imagine what he would look like in pain. And then I realize that these are the eyes of a man who has never known love. They are animal eyes in the face of a man, and they make him untouchable, unapproachable. The child has not had time to lose the natural startings of love within his childish heart and body, and that is why his eyes still live.

Tombani draws his head back and stands to full height, looming above me in a perspective that makes his head seem small and his hips large, that shows me the underside of his withered chest and railed ribs, in an attitude of immodesty so natural and inoffensive as to make modesty seem an obscene invention. The incandescence fades from his eyes and his lips set in a wrinkled line as he peers down at me in grudging satisfaction, and the transformation from a fiendish threat into a sneering old man is quietly accomplished.

I make a sign of drinking and the child, lying on his stomach in the sand, cheerfully supplies the word "BETI!" in a shrill voice that is half laughter.

The old man turns and sunlight streaks from the polished flesh of his shins. He frowns at me and asks: "Eleoguna beti?" with unexpected gentleness. Humanity, then, is in him in the recognition of mortal needs, and even to some apparent sympathy for them. It is like the father who scolds his son in outrage and then, discovering that the child is hungry, asks in this same tone of intimate gentleness: "Do you want something to eat?" in the uniquely human juxtaposition of grave disapproval and the approval of accepted basic needs. Perhaps my tie with this man will be on the most primitive of all bases, then, the basis of his understanding of the animal functions involved in physical living.

The child, on the old man's command, rises to his feet, dusts sand from his stomach, and ambles away presumably to get me a drink.

The old man cradles his triangular club to his chest and

sinks cross-legged to the ground in front of me, his fierce expression of disapproval only slightly attenuated with his generosity in giving me a drink.

"Eleonguna beti," he begins again, in the tiresome, anger-tinted repetition that taught me the other phrases.

I get to my feet and limp on sore limbs to the brush where I break off a long, thin branch and strip it of leaves. He is watching me, his brow full of wrinkles, his eyes squinted almost closed, in an attitude of cautious alertness. I sit down and smooth the sand out between us with my palm, and, using the branch as a marker, print the letters: "E-L-E-O-N-G-U-N-A — B-E-T-I."

An expression of curiosity flickers across his face and he chews more rapidly on something in his mouth. For an instant his heavy brows are lifted and he wears the dumb, chewing-gum expression of interest I have noted with such irritation in my own students. He is completely absorbed in the patterns of letters I have made, and I sense the ridiculousness of a turnabout in our roles, wherein he ceases to teach and becomes the student. But only for a short time. He catches himself and draws back with the universal expression of ignorance, the sneer, and resumes his role as teacher.

Through this torturous method, I am battered and badgered into learning what I judge to be the greeting, and other expressions such as "I want a drink," "I," "you" and "It is good."

A black movement down the beach attracts my attention beyond the old man's head. The child gravitates toward us, holding the coconut shell before him like a chalice in both hands.

When he hands me the cup, I take it and say: "N'doku

mamati, kulangu," and he replies with the same words, saying "It is good." I do not know whether he is speaking of my language or simply acknowledging my thanks. I drink deeply in their presence but remember to save enough to wash my glasses.

With pointing and ear bludgeoning and startings of fury, I am taught that their names are Tombani, the patriarch, and Veedlie, and they pronounce my name as Jon, very nearly Joan.

Veedlie stands before me with one knee crooked, a tiny child with the same sweet and wise eyes, slightly sardonic, scratching at a patch of dried irritation at the base of his left ribs. I watch as he waddles over to one of the many fallen coconuts and squats to pick it up. It is larger than his head, but he carries it high and marches to a sharp outcropping of coral. He smashes the coconut down on it, using the coral's spine as a knife edge and turning the coconut in his hands with each blow. When the green husk has been mutilated, he kneels and places it between his knees, and, holding it in place with one hand, he strips it upward with the other, tossing the fibrous segments to one side. I notice the old man squinting at him with a benign expression of disinterest, almost as though he were dozing. Veedlie takes the stripped nut, aims carefully and throws it against the stone without actually releasing it from his hands. It breaks open with a sharp pop and falls into almost equal halves in his palms. He sips from one and then the other before breaking them into smaller pieces from which he can pry out the coconut meat. He brings me a chunk of it, bluish white and dripping, and I chew it with them. It is ripe and richly flavored, but so difficult to chew that my jaws soon feel pierced.

Without ceremony, Tombani gets grunting to his feet.

Little Veedlie is immediately at his side. The child picks up the triangular club and hands it to his elder as they begin walking away together. They do not even glance at me.

It is midmorning. I chew on the coconut, staring at the double circle of indentation where Tombani sat in the sand, relieved that they are gone. Solitude is comfortable, more comfortable than the nerve-stringing presence of the old tyrant. I feel as though a disease had visited me, and that its last traces do not disappear until the tall black body trudges listlessly around the curve of the beach and out of sight.

A sense of well-being pervades me from the simple knowledge I have gained from watching Veedlie open the coconut, relief from a tension that was never really defined — the tension of helplessness in hunger and thirst. It is a source of safety, telling me that I can eat and drink forever, if necessary, without their help, for there are giant green-husked coconuts on the ground as far down the beach as I can see and they cling in clusters beneath the daggered crowns of trees high above me. But the well-being is tinctured with regret. It would be better to be alone than under the domination of eyes that are dead to affection, eyes that speak only in degrees of contempt. It is better not to be known at all than to be known in soul-shriveling disapproval.

Rehearsing the words I have been taught, I go and lean against the slanted trunk of a palm tree, sitting away from my sand-tablet dictionary, and learn by writing them again and again from memory in the sand between my outstretched legs. "TAEEGA — NO," I print, and "KULANGU — FRIEND?" and "EL — YES," and "INAU — I."

Loneliness vamps down on me, and I struggle away from it, stooping to print with my long branch: JOHN W. HARPER, as though it were some proof of my existence, and then, like a child:

> SUSAN HARPER
> CINDY HARPER
> GEORGIE HARPER
> TIMMY HARPER

The sand brightens beneath my bare feet as I move from one giant letter to the next, brightens as my weight compresses out water.

The air is suddenly still and I look up to see tension in the gathering overcast of clouds. This is the shout of silence, the most ominous of all. I climb back to the soft dune and sit above my dictionary facing the ocean. Waves rise and pitch forward in walls of greyness. Not a leaf stirs. The birds' chatterings surge loud on the waiting silence and it occurs to me that they save the moment from utter desolation.

The earth looms near and full of restless inevitability, reducing the mysteries of eternity to their cycles of life and death, of birth in springtime and slumber in autumn, of forever new youngness and shriveling age, of the patterns of life repeated on and on forever without reprieve, of new passions and fading ones, new learnings and passing ones. I see the whole of it in such an instance, stark and stripped, full of cruel glory, never changing, as inexorable as the perpetual inpouring of waves on this beach. Individuality is submerged in the flux and flow of all the eons of time. It shatters the mind, more so the heart, for the human whisper counts for nothing against the tides: and the human whisper cringes under the greater designs of eternity, crying in final prayer: "God, let something love me." I struggle against it, feeling that I could be washed from sanity, and that only God can bear the fullness of such a vision without dismay. I need the smaller segment of vision, need to be the participating human rather than the stupefied observer. I shake my head and feel my jaws quivering, trying to bring the world back to human dimensions, to the size of hungers and thirsts, lusts and prayers, to the comfort of nerves and muscles, to the security of affections — the smaller frame wherein place and personality are not swamped in the splash of all things.

From far away, the rumbling approaches through trees while trees above me remain calm. I hear the shuffle of leaves draw closer through the jungle, and I wait, tracing its speed as it bears toward me.

Rain pours immediately out of the west in almost horizontal shafts before a wind that catches palm fronds and twists them violently. Giant drops splatter with the loudness of hail against tree trunks. The wind screeches in gathering force as I flounder out of my clothes and hang them on a branch. A coconut thuds to the earth nearby, and soon another. I hurry out into the open near the water line where I will be safe from them.

Rain pelts me in full mercy, driven by hurricane winds, and I can see the convulsed treetops through a milky veil in the bubbling intimacy of the tempest. Darkness settles so heavy that the rain appears white. A long filament of lightning gashes the charcoal skies from midheaven to the horizon, and a moment later, thunder cracks the atmosphere like a thousand reverberent whips from which I instinctively duck my head. In the half-gloom, the elements unleash their forces against heaven and earth, and there is no human sound, no living sound . . .

I massage my hair, massage my flesh, expose myself to the downpour, rinsing myself as though I were under a full-fauceted shower at the gym.

With final clubbing drops against my feet, the rain stops as suddenly as it began and slithers eastward over the sea. I watch its majestic progress, a slanting shadow of darkness between clouds and ocean.

Looking down, I notice that the names I have printed in the sand are washed almost clean, and the blankness of the beach finds a twin blankness in me, blessing heart and soul as birds resume their singing in the newly silent aftermath of storm.

17

Tombani's naked foot, hard as a crab's claw, nudges grit into my ribs, awakening me to a light so brilliant that all objects seem to swim in mercury. He stands over me, holding two coconut halves which he brings down in a squat to my chest. I blink back the sun-blear and have a momentary view of sparkling palm daggers and a sky of infinite blue above his cottony head.

"N'doku, kulangu," I mumble sleepily, taking the dish of purplish mush and digging into it with my fingers. Its sour stench floats upward into my face and my stomach ridges in caution.

"N'doku mamati," he answers without a trace of interest.

I swallow the warm mush, and wipe it from my whiskers with the back of my hand before taking another bite.

Perhaps alone here with me, he will show me another side of himself. It may be that he was blustering and dominating only because he had an audience before. Bullies in a crowd are capable of becoming friendly and sympathetic when the crowd is not around.

I smile, attempting to break down his reserve, but he sits there, not two feet away from me, chewing something, his lips red with saliva, his eyes half squinting in relaxed alertness. I think of a red-eyed and skeletal bull ruminating his cud, mean and unpredictable. He is truly inhuman, then.

I drink the warm water down in gulps, hearing my swallowings against the background of screeching birds and then clean my fingers in the sand as Tombani rises to his feet. I hope he will go, but he merely moves over into the shade and gestures me to follow him. For an instant I hesitate between going to him immediately or retrieving my clothes from the bush and dressing. His bellowed repetition decides me and I follow him meekly, dressed only in undershorts.

Stopping only to pick up my writing branch, I walk barefoot to the shaded spot he has chosen and sit crosslegged on the damp ground in front of him. He mutters something through his endlessly chewing lips and when I make no move to obey he tosses his head impatiently and screams the command which I still do not understand. His fist thuds into the earth in his volatile rage and he leans far forward so that his nose almost touches the ground before me and smooths the sand with both hands. Then, sitting back, he points imperiously to the cleared space.

I print carefully, in capitals: "TOMBANI." He peers

feverishly at the patterns. Underlining the word, I say: "Tombani — that's Tombani."

He mumbles something about its being "n'doku," which probably means "pretty" in this instance instead of "good."

And suddenly the detached picture we must make is thrown full on my imagination: two elderly men, one fat and bewhiskered with thinning hair and red skin, the other skinny and unwhiskered with kinky white hair and black skin, sitting naked beneath a palm tree making pictures in the sand; all of it serious, all of it natural to the time and place; and I look toward the east, toward my invisible reef somewhere out there and wish I might be away from this black ball of whims and caprices and bellowings and sneers, this spoiled child who inhabits the body of a patriarch.

He holds up his hand and touches each of his fingers with the forefinger of his other hand, repeating "ririkinger" each time, his voice taking on the teasing tone of a chant. I write in the sand: "FINGER — RIRIKINGER." He points to his eyes, and then to his nose and lips, chanting the word again and again until I have spoken it and written it, and then going on to the next one until I have learned all the parts of the body except the intimate parts. To my surprise, he ignores them as though they did not exist. There must be some taboo attached to them, then.

He begins with the functions of the ear, mouth, nose and hands and on down the body, but again ignores the intimate functions entirely.

By noon we have inched back several times to make room for the growing list of words, and my brain is very tired from the constant bludgeoning of Tombani's fanatic repetitions. His voice becomes almost hypnotic, as though

he were in a trance, rising to screams and then lowering to
moans, sharply staccato one moment and mumbled another, with his eyes following the emotion of his voice,
blazing almost yellow in his head and then squinting to
slits of blackness.

His toes wiggle in emotion, making his large, bony
feet as expressive as his hands, and I notice that there is a
wide space between his big toe and the others.

But suddenly I cannot go on, suddenly the back of my
neck seems to stretch taut, but I know of no way to tell
Tombani I am tired, tired almost beyond desperation for
no reason that I can know; so I simply stretch out on the
ground on my side, cradle my cheek against my hand and
pretend to sleep.

"Igoi au kola?" he asks harshly.

Not understanding it, I simulate snoring. He rises and
stands above me, nudging me with his toe, irritating me to
a point where I am almost ready to throw away my hope
for survival by knocking his leg away with all my force.

I hear the soft padding of his footsteps moving away and
some of the tension drains from me. Lying perfectly still,
I wait until he will have a chance to disappear out of sight,
but almost immediately he is back, stepping over my body
and squatting on the ground in front of me.

When I open my eyes slightly, I glimpse an old man
sitting like a statue, beginning to wave a palm frond over
my body to stir the air; and I lie here trembling in stupefaction, pretending to sleep with no hope now that sleep
will come.

book two vanua

18

My heart relaxes a little. For the first time in weeks, Tombani has not arrived to awaken me with a foot in my ribs. Little Veedlie came alone, carrying a rolled coconut jacket in his hand. His hair has been bleached white in strange resemblance to his grandfather's grey head.

He answered my greeting with childish casualness, offering no explanation for Tombani's absence and giving no reason why his hair is dyed. Depositing his coconut husk, he squats nearby with his necklace dangling forward, scooping a hollow in the sand.

I cannot bring myself to ask about Tombani for fear I will learn that he is only delayed, that he will be here later to electrify the air with his thunderbolts of abuse and insults, telling me of my insignificance, telling me of my

worthlessness. Each word he utters takes on more degrading coloring as I understand more perfectly the language.

I sit with my head lowered and resting on my updrawn
knees, looking down at my beard which has grown fully
now, a Brahmsian beard spreading out over my sun-
browned chest with a predominance of grey hairs woven
through the blondish mass, wiry and curling stubbornly in
all directions. The air is still, steamingly hot.

Raising my head, I watch Veedlie with what interest I
can muster. How dead is all emotion within me. Very
white smoke rises from the coconut shell which has partly
unfolded itself. The fibrous inside smoulders like a punk
with pinkness of living ash around the blackened center of
a small hole it has burned. Why has Veedlie dyed his hair?
What is he doing here alone this morning? I watch him
digging the hole with his bare hands.

When is the last time I saw smoke? I look at it dully
as it moves swiftly upward in a straight line and spreads
out to disintegrate a few feet above Veedlie's sweat-
streaked back. Everything is dull and without interest. It
is the vast underspreading of disinterest that tells me of my
death, and only now do I realize the full extent of Tombani's damage to me during these many long weeks. Each
day he arrives with more children who sit around us in a
circle as he behaves with superb cruelty, taunting me and
ridiculing me before their grave and sober eyes. In this
way he has given me much knowledge of the language,
the customs and the taboos, but that knowledge has been
suffocated beneath the more subtle knowledge that no one
here cares in the slightest for my existence, cares in the
slightest whether I live or die. That is what kills. It is not

that they hate me; there would be some refuge, some defense against hatred, but there is none against the weaker, sicker passions of aversion, simple indifference and contempt.

Strange how savages could do this to a supposedly educated man; strange how all the education of the civilized world cannot counter the simple growth of emotions, cannot nullify the feelings of death when respect and affection are denied you. I know these things intellectually, and yet I can do nothing about them. I know that not even a saint can live without some sense of personal value. There has been this unconscious choosing between the body's continued existence and the soul's healthful anger to a point where I have had to sacrifice even the defense of human dignity in order to feed and water my body. Everything has gone but the will to live, reducing all appetites to the basic ones of the flesh, deadening all passions except those two irascible ones of fear and its resultant despair.

But realizing it clearly, as I do this morning in the hinted peace of this cove, I know there must be some way to solve it; to return myself to the world, which is what the natives call this island. The world now is Nuni and there is no other world to them. Where is the withered passion of hope? Is it as dead as I have thought?

No, this morning there is a spark of it in Veedlie's impersonal mildness; hope too that something may have happened to Tombani to prevent his coming back long enough for me to recuperate from his constant bludgeonings. I raise my head to look at the child, who places small branches in the scooped-out hole and covers them with rocks. My heart is frequently torn with tenderness at the involuntary gestures that occasionally slip out from the guileless souls of these children without their ever realizing it, and I know that if any emotion has saved me from complete destruction, it has been this one, which is love, love that is soft and good, love hidden in the growing turgidness of my soul. Veedlie kneels in infant wisdom and holds the punk against the kindling, blowing sparks into the wood until flames begin to catch, and in this moment he is not a savage with a strange heartbeat, but all the children in the world.

Turning his back and holding his head away from the smoke, he wraps an enormous green navundi leaf around a coconut drinking shell and carries it into the underbrush toward the river.

Would he come and talk with me? There is some invisible constraint to silence this morning. He ignores me as though I weren't here, and yet he is obviously doing something for me with that fire. I sit paralyzed to the spot, my eyes lowered to the stomach flesh which hangs loose over my diminishing paunch, trembling at the thought of talking with the child, of hearing words from his lips that might not be abuse, of glimpsing a smile that might be kind, or a flickering warmth in his eyes that might hint some affection.

As I raise my head to call to him, Veedlie turns and waddles down to the ocean's edge, and I close my mouth on the fragile filament of hope, retaining it alive and waiting to see what he will do.

His body is silhouetted round-bellied and featureless against the sun-scattering breakers as he hesitates for a moment and then bends forward over one of the pockets where the tide has left its refuse. He apparently locates what he wants, for he lies full length on the plateau of smooth-washed sand and lowers his arm into the pool until the water amputates it at the armpit.

When he carries the thing back, I see that it is a black sea slug. He drops it into the shell and places the shell over the heated stones. His right arm is sheathed in dripping blackness, much darker than the rest of his body.

Burying my head again, I wait to hear his footsteps pad closer, and I pray, as I have taken to praying recently, in the instinctive knowledge that when man is reduced low enough, nothing else is left but God. But somewhere in those darkened spaces at the edge of consciousness, I feel that such prayer is a confession of defeat, the last grudging recourse to a help beyond me, a proof that it is better not to live than not to love.

Today, in the midst of these dust-syllabled prayers, I see myself in detachment, as I often do. Now, it is an old man with the long hair and beard of a patriarch, his eyes closed, a round ball of humanity, and I am revolted with the sight, revolted to see a man reduced to snifflings for touches of affection.

I stare at the image of myself seen from another dimension. There is shame and there is doubtful cringing. Where is the praise for the design of Infinity? — the soul-bursting praise for the sun and the moon and the stars? — for the winds and the rains? — for the seasons and the creatures and the plants? Because a pain transpierces a belly, is all of this lost? Is man that impoverished, that spent?

Something touches my bare foot and I open my eyes. The view through the restricted frame of my thighs is alive in sun-and-shadow clarity. I see my two feet planted firmly against the sand, see every crisscrossing pore of dusty flesh across the backs of heel tendons, and between them, facing me, the miniature black feet of the child rising upward to kneecaps of dried mud and thighs and genitals and the lower circle of belly. He seems unaware that he is partly standing on a curling snail's shell that pushes up two of his toes.

The overflow of my prayerful anger urges me to raise my head and say: "What do you want, you little beggar," but the sight of his small feet, of that curve where his toes are bent up by the shell, and of his tiny toenails, ragged and white-edged, dissolves the harshness from my mouth and I look into his face without speaking, while the old fatigue returns to spread throughout my body.

How sober he is, standing there rubbing at the corner of his eye.

"Endoa matamo?" I ask, and he answers that yes, his eye does hurt, that all eyes in Vanua hurt, that everyone in Tombani's village has sore eyes.

"Don't scratch it, kulangu," I say and immediately his salt-streaked arm drops to his side. Surprised that he obeys so perfectly, I tell him "Kalao" out of curiosity to see if he will obey my command to smile. Instantly a smile spreads across his face, a smile that is at first only a mask, but that becomes merriment as though this were a game.

"You are handsome when you smile," I say, feeling my own face relax with the contagion of his enjoyment. "You must smile often."

Grinning, he points to his swollen eyelid where I see a pinhead sore that suppurates slightly, and mumbles that it hurts. He says it in such a way that I do not know whether he is offering this as explanation why he seldom smiles, or whether he is merely repeating the information already given.

"You come to Vanua for Maigna's death," he announces with a completely different voice of great solemnity. It is the voice I have heard a thousand grade-school children use in declamation programs, a rehearsed voice, uncertain and filled with poignant overtones of a duty that obviously represents something important beyond my understanding.

"What?"

"You come to Vanua for Maigna's death."

I feel my hands clasping around my knees so tightly that my wedding ring bruises the back of its finger. The unformulated fear that I am being called to witness an execution opens a half-world of new vistas. But nothing is definite, nothing defined because most of such conjecture is too horrible to bring out into the open.

"What is Maigna's death?"

"Maigna's death is he is dead," he answers, dropping his declamatory style and reverting to his normal wheezing soprano.

"Who is Maigna?" I ask as my hands relax.

"Maigna is the dead one, dead this night," he says with childish exasperation, apparently frustrated that I cannot seem to understand this obvious and simple fact.

His voice is begining to imitate that of Tombani, sharpening steadily toward rage.

"Kalao!" I command sharply. Obediently he spaces his lips apart, showing his teeth, and then the forced smile becomes an open laugh.

"That's good."

"Very good," he affirms.

There is some awakening of delight, some unfolding intimacy between the child and myself as we talk freely, as we even laugh and joke over this accidental discovery that he will break into a smile the moment I command it with the word kalao. The shales of tension slip away slightly and I see a new vitality in the beauty of this cove as the heat of morning increases, greasing all the folds of my body with sweats.

"Why is your hair white, kulangu?"

"For the death of Maigna," he says casually, fluttering his sore eyelid and puckering up his face as though it were itching almost unbearably.

"You belong to Maigna?"

He nods his head in affirmation and tells me that he is Maigna's son.

The flesh loosens across my forehead as a movement of sorrow for him flows through me.

"Kalao!" he explodes, pointing his finger straight into my pitying face and laughing. "Kalao, kalao!" he insists, still manipulating the eyelid against its itching.

I pull up the corners of my mouth into a smile, but I am taken aback that he shows so little concern over the death of his own father. Shadows move and sunlight catches tattoos on his cheeks, which are puffed out smooth in childish gaiety. There is no sign of grief, or even sadness. Was I really correct, then, in my guess that Nuni is a world without love?

Veedlie raises his arm and nuzzles his face against his shoulder, brushing his biceps across his eyes before flinging his arm back to his side.

"How is your father dead?"

"Dead how? Dead by his — " He frowns down at his feet and his mouth chews without sound on words he apparently cannot find to express himself. "Dead like this," he says finally, illustrating Maigna's death with utter simplicity by folding his fist as though it were holding a knife, shoving his belly far out, and dragging the imaginary knife across it at the level of his navel.

"But why?"

"He is too old to go to Zinai!" he explains, looking into my eyes with an almost pleading expression, seeming disturbed and impatient that I do not understand these simple things, that I do not understand how anything could be more natural than for a man to open his abdomen when he becomes too old to go to Zinai.

"What is Zinai?"

"Zinai is the bent trees growing together. It is away from Vanua. Maigna can't go to Zinai, so he is old enough to die."

When I try to understand how Tombani's son is old enough to die while Tombani is not, he can make nothing of it and screams that Tombani is not too old because he can still go to Zinai. So long as he can go to Zinai, he has no right to die.

It occurs to me that they do not know what age means, for they do not measure time in any way except night and day. A man is "too old" only when he can no longer go to Zinai. Until then he has no age except those of tattooing and the change into puberty.

"Why do I go to Vanua?"

He reaches back and slaps his upper thighs like a bird clumsily flapping its wings, in perfect mimicry of Tombani's habitual gesture of exasperation. His face is almost against mine and his necklace dangles free. He stares at me as though I were stupid beyond all hope. His breathing rattles through his congested nose in mounting fury.

Then, sighing exaggeratedly, he stops spanking himself and clasps his hands behind him while he begins the painfully patient explanation in a chanting tone of voice that sounds so insulting when his grandfather assumes it.

Tombani calls me to Vanua for the feasting and dancing of death, Veedlie intones, his wiry, nasal voice rising and falling in a monotonous cadence. The unmated males who are beginning to be pubescent have gone to hunt the wild pig, all except fat Oai who is now to be mated and who has no spirit left in him for pleasure.

"Fat Oai doesn't want to be mated?"

Veedlie recoils and spits to the side with such revulsion that the vein at the side of his neck swells and pulses. The monotonous chant is replaced by a rapid staccato stream of language that fills the cove with sounds like a monkey's chattering. I can understand little except that nothing is so terrible as mating, that a man has to make babies, and each time he lies with a woman he loses some of his manhood, and that is zagata, no good. He spits the word zagata out with such a violent turn of his head that a streak of saliva glistens across his cheek from his mouth to his ear.

"If he doesn't like it, why does he do it?"

"No one likes it," he cries in an agony of explanation. "But everyone must do it when the hairs come on the body. Everyone is mated, and if you do not make a baby from one rain's end to the next, you are zagata, tabooed and driven into the forest never to return to Vanua."

"But it is good to lie with a woman," I protest.

"Taeega!" he screams. "It is bad, bad!" His eyes glaze over like Tombani's and become inhuman. He spits again and makes a pathetic gesture, drawing away, covering his genitals tightly with both hands and hunching his shoulders forward defensively as though he were protecting his manhood from even the idea of its ever being shared with a mate. His gaze wanders fearfully up toward the towering palms, making me feel ashamed that I have frightened him with a truth he can probably never understand. The grotesqueness of our situation makes me even more ashamed. Here I am, an elderly man and father, arguing with a child who cannot be more than five or six years old about the goodness of sleeping with a woman. Past habits of thinking make the scene appear almost depraved, but to Veedlie there is obviously no shame in it, only outrage that I should be perverse enough to think such a thing could be "good" when everyone knows it is "zagata." They marry then, without any desire for it, considering manhood synonymous to sexual potency, seeing the act of mating as evil since it makes man lose some of his manhood, but necessary in order to prove his potency by producing children. Not to have children would prove sterility, which is a disgrace sufficient to ban him from society for the rest of his life.

"I go to Vanua for Maigna's death and for the feast to celebrate fat Oai's mating?" I ask, looking into his agonized face and turning the words around to make sure that I have understood correctly, to determine if the marriage is not, after all, the real reason for the feast.

"No!" he shouts, almost sobbing, "for Maigna's feast."

"Good," I say, reaching up and patting him on the cheek.

"Thank you," he barks. He turns away from my touch

and stalks toward the fire, his body in a tremble. Wrapping another navundi leaf around the shell, he lifts it from the fire.

When he deposits it on the ground beside me, I see that a thick, greasy substance has risen to the top of the water. It catches rainbows in slithering streaks of color. The child lifts the scum off with a twig, leaving the water clear, with no sign of the sea slug in the bottom. He tosses the refuse aside and steam-smoke hovers around it until it cools. I rub some of it between my fingers; it is soft and greyish and leaves a film on my flesh like chicken fat.

Veedlie stands beside me and pours the warm liquid from the shell into my hair, drop by drop, with one hand, massaging it in with his other hand. My head begins to itch and I reach up to scratch it and feel the sparse matted hair full of thin suds. We are washing my hair! When it is soaked and rubbed to Veedlie's satisfaction, he pours the remainder of the liquid on my beard and repeats the process. I am more than ever mystified. Are they that fastidious — that I must be shampooed head and beard before attending the feast? Veedlie leaves me and sets off at a jog trot for the river, returning in a moment to bring fresh water for rinsing the soap out. He makes the trip seven or eight times. The stuff leaves my hair as clean as any shampoo I have ever used and takes the wiryness out of my beard.

"We go now," he announces when we have finished. "We go to Vanua."

"Do we come back here?"

"No, kulangu," he says, wiping sweat from his forehead with his hand. "We stay in Vanua."

We are really going, then. I cannot understand anything about this. Why, if they care so little for me, if they think me so inferior, do they do all of these things for me? Is it merely to have more sport with me? No, they are cruel perhaps, or at least feelingless, but they are not subtle enough to savor torture. And after all, Tombani speaks to the children in much the same tone he uses with me. I have been certain that they would not care whether I lived or died, and that has been a killing knowledge, but if they do not care even whether their own parents live or die, at least I am not singled out for special contempt.

Dampness evaporates cool on my head and back as a breeze stirs through the cove. Getting heavily to my feet, I go for my possessions cached in the brush. I put on only my shoes, for my feet are still too tender for jungle walking, and wrap the rest of my things into a small bundle in the coat.

Veedlie leads the way into the underbrush. Before stepping through the parted bushes, I turn and gaze back at the beach where I have lived so many weeks. Nothing except the abandoned coconut shells and the faint smoke haze from our dying fire gives any indication that this spot has ever been inhabited. I swallow back the peculiar nostalgia that rises with the realization that my living leaves so little trace on the land, that nature reclaims instantly what she shared with me for a time, making my human passage here seem utterly futile. But this is immediately compensated by an underlying thought that provides strange liberation, strange pride: the satisfaction of knowing that I have been able to live so stripped of possessions as to become part of nature, so stripped that when I move I leave no evidence of having been here and take nothing with me — for none of these things I carry are necessary to my existence. I could toss them into the ocean and walk naked to Vanua and nothing would be greatly changed. I am carrying souvenirs of my past into my future, nothing more; and that past is being gradually bent and twisted and made strange to me in recollection as the strangeness of the present assumes its own normalcy.

The child moves ahead of me at a pace that amounts to a jog trot for him and very fast walking for me. No wind touches us in this forest where tree trunks are many times larger than my body and where daylight is so diffused that no trace of the sun appears through the black dome of foliage. Gnarled roots extend like gigantic snakes in all directions, forming an interlacing series of ridges beneath our feet, threatening to break our ankles with every step, and vines grow everywhere, draped from tree to tree like carelessly tossed ropes. Sweat is pouring from me after half an hour and my body feels as though it will explode with the pressure of generated heat. Veedlie's wheezing and my panting join with the jungle sounds of birds and insects. Distantly above, we hear the ceaseless roar of leaves, but those in view directly overhead are unmoved by any breeze.

Veedlie stops and tells me to wait here. Before I have a chance to ask him why, he stoops low and disappears into the brush. I can hear branches snap and his footsteps walking slowly away until there is only silence. I sit down on one of the protruding roots to rest.

Lifting my packet up, I wipe it across my soaked face. It smells of mould and security, and when I draw it away, the blue cloth of the coat is splotched black with my sweat. Every part of that woven cloth, each of those stitches, every button represents a link with a past that becomes precious. Will I ever see such things again? The bluish thread represents a whole world beyond this world which is NUNI.

The jungle encloses me as though I were in a small closet with miles of wall-thickness. There is not even enough air to evaporate the sweat that pours down my spine, and into the back of my pants.

I listen to hear Veedlie's slow return, realizing only now the desperateness with which I desire to get out of this closeness, and I think of those who are driven into the jungles in disgrace to live in this half-world of gloom for the rest of their lives.

"Where do you go?" I ask him as he steps out close by my side.

"Into the woods," he answers simply as he brushes twig and leaf fragments from his shoulders and stomach.

"What do you go into the woods for?" And then I see for myself from the traces left on him that he went to urinate. But why should he go so far into the brush — why should he go even out of the range of hearing? Surely no child his age would ever be modest about such a natural thing.

"Why do you go away to do that?"

He stops brushing and jerks himself upright. "You see?" he whispers in a voice of abject terror, drawing the words out from the back of his throat.

I am about to say that yes, I see, when I realize that he means to ask me if I saw what he did, and that since the language has no past tense, there is no other way to ask.

"No, I do not see."

"You hear?" His words are scarcely audible, trembling in his mouth, lifeless and mournful.

"No, I do not hear."

His shoulders relax in such a sag that I drop my pack and rise to my knees to keep him from falling. I grasp his shoulders and get to my feet.

"I wonder why you go so far to hide," I say gently as he leans against my leg and breathes with wheezing gasps.

"It's taboo," he sobs.

"What?" I look down at the top of his head with its white kinks of hair over the black crown.

"It's zagata!" he says with weak conviction.

"My God," I burst out in English, "not that too." I feel his body tense beneath my hand at the involuntary outburst in English, and continue in his language: "It is zagata to empty the body? But no, kulangu, it is good and very good."

"Zagata to be known. It is taboo," he says in a strengthening voice as his chest heaves with less violence. He explains to me that if someone catches you in such acts of the body, you are forever under his spirit and you are never again yourself and you are "dead without being dead."

"But what about the tiny ones," I ask.

He mumbles uncomfortably as though even discussing it might be dangerous, but I gather that children are not subject to these curses until they are tattooed.

"But if you see me?"

"I hold your spirit in mine."

"But I am not tattooed."

"You can walk and hide. You are not a tiny one."

They apparently do not tattoo the children until after they are old enough to control their functions, and the tattooing, which they call the "cutting," really has nothing to do with the curse, since I am not tattooed and still am subject to it.

"What about husband and wife knowing each other in this way?"

"Taeega," he says, shaking his head without looking up at me. "Never."

"What about parents and children who have been cut?"

"Taeega — never."

"What about the sick?"

"Taeega — never."

No one and no condition except infancy appears to be excluded from this taboo which is powerful beyond my understanding if I am to judge from the way it has terrified this child.

"Kalao." I command him gently, placing my hand over the top of his head and forcing it easily back so he is looking up into my face. He obeys with a smile. I smile back and he bursts into laughter that dissolves the fears of a moment ago from his face.

19

There is no air and walking has become stumbling through a blear of greenery, following the black form that continues to move about thirty feet ahead of me.

At first I think the sound is only the sighing of wind high in the treetops and pay little heed to it, but now it is a definite melody, floating bodiless to us, a weird and monotonous chanting that seems to go on without end, sung by a single falsetto voice of almost birdlike purity. I stop the rustling of my footsteps to hear more clearly. It seems to come from far away, from out of the very bark and rot of these jungles, a haunting, nightmarish chant that turns the sweat on my body to ice.

It is obviously nothing to fear, for Veedlie has not faltered in his pace, but the muscles in the sides of my neck pulse and I feel that even my breathing is held in suspension.

"Veedlie!" I call, recoiling at the harshness of my voice as it punctures the echoing thread of the chant.

He halts and waits for me.

"What is it? What is the sound?"

"It is Maigna dead," he answers, looking up at me imperturbably.

"What?"

"It is Maigna's woman, singing his death."

"Your mother?"

"Yes."

Again I am taken aback, first by the chilling cruelty of the chant and then by Veedlie's complete indifference. He discusses his father's death the way he might discuss clouds in the sky or the rising of the ocean's tide.

"We are near Vanua?"

"There," he says, pointing and walking on. I stare in the direction he indicates, seeing only foliage and tree trunks. Surely they do not live in this eternal gloom; no human could bear it for long.

We are coming to a place of dank smells. The earth beneath my feet seems less dark and roots develop faint shadows. Looking ahead I see that the foliage directly in front of us is silhouetted black against a thousand pinpoints of light.

Veedlie separates the brush and waits for me, his body vague behind inpouring rays of light that catch insects swarming between us.

The waters of a broad river flow by so fast they do not catch reflections from the distant opposite shore. Coolness seeps over my shoetops and reeds brush against my waist.

But something is wrong here. Opening my eyes wider, I search my surroundings to discover what it is. Sunlight sparkles on the water and the sky overhead is pale with the brilliance of noon, but something is wrong. The river is so wide I can see the full stature of trees on the opposite side; they tower to heights that give us the dimensions of insects. The underbrush rises in a solid wall of greenery directly out of the water.

Is it the chanting? No, the chanting continues, less ominous now that there is sunlight, but something about all of this is profoundly disturbing.

Veedlie stands before me, in water up to his calves, black in the midst of pale green reeds that are taller than his head. Pushing them aside with his hands, he lifts his legs high and steps forward, dripping mud and slime from his feet as he trudges out into the free-flowing waters of the river. I can hear the reeds snap and each splashing footstep he takes, and I realize that the water's silence is the thing that seems wrong. To look at it, one would expect to hear a cascading roar, but it slides by so silently that I have the impression I have lost my hearing. I wade out after Veedlie, listening to the sucking, bubbling sounds of my shoes being dragged from the mud, and to the cracking of reeds in my pathway.

Beyond the marshy shallows, soft mud gives way to a smooth river bottom of shale or gravel. The water glides past me cool and full of powerful tuggings that threaten to sweep my legs from under me. Ahead I see that the child has abandoned any effort to walk and is swimming at an angle against the current. Worried what I will do with my pack if I have to swim, I hoist it above my head to keep the book pages dry, and brace my legs far apart to bend over and drink. The water is up to my armpits, green but clouded slightly with swirling sand particles that hide my feet from me. I drink through the filter of my floating beard, and then lower my head full into the water to cool it while holding the bundle above the surface.

Shaking the water from my eyes, I look back to see that I am almost at midstream and when I stand upright, the curling torrents reach only to my ribs. I turn and drag myself in the direction of Veedlie's splashings, as the water becomes shallower.

He is standing waist-deep at the edge of the bankless underbrush when I reach him, and I wonder how he will ever find the path again. His attention is concentrated on a spot and I follow his fascinated gaze to a movement in the brush. Three animals are sliding down a clay embankment, tumbling and turning as though they had fallen or been thrown. As the first one smashes against a root and bounces convulsively into the water, I see that it is a small crocodile, or at least some reptile that resembles a crocodile, about two or three feet long.

"We hurry before the mother comes," Veedlie calls quickly over his shoulder as the other two slither into the water.

He flounders, half swimming and half jumping forward to our right, and without hesitation finds the opening. Grabbing an overhanging branch, he pulls himself up on his stomach to a narrow footpath of red clay. I toss him my bundle and drag myself up after him.

"We hurry," he repeats gravely. Handing me the

bundle, he begins to climb the faint trail that curves drastically upward to disappear in the jungle darkness.

The ground is wet and slick beneath my shoes and the odor of rot is almost suffocating. Although Veedlie walks only a few feet ahead of me, I frequently lose sight of him on the narrow, brush-lined trail, and I must carry my packet on top of my head or against my chest to make any headway.

The path becomes so steep and slippery that we must pull ourselves forward from one tree or bush to the next, bracing our feet against roots to keep from sliding back. In this kind of traveling, I begin to appreciate the value of nakedness, for my clothes are a severe encumbrance and the bundle is a nuisance.

The chanting floats about us, seeming to come from all directions simultaneously, but as we gain the top of the hill and stand up to catch our breath in this cocoon of greenery, the voice becomes definite and its purity is lost in proximity. It is like some endless animal ululation in such a high falsetto that my own vocal cords ache in sympathy, but the melody does not change. It seems to waver in mid-air in some minor-keyed undulation of notes that nevertheless appear to be definite. It is as primitive as the land about us.

The path is a red streak leading downward at a dangerous decline for perhaps twenty feet. Veedlie leans forward and peers toward its bottom for a long time.

"No serpents," he says sitting down and sliding to the bottom, like a child in an amusement park. His seat has left a glistening path in the slimy clay. I follow his example and almost bump into him. There is little black left visible on him. He is painted the color of clay. My beard is clotted with orange nodules and my pants pull heavily at my hips with this new weight.

I stand in amazement to think that Tombani has gone to all this trouble every morning to come and torment me. This is a long and disagreeable journey, and certainly hazardous if there are snakes and crocodiles about. It does not seem possible that a man would go through this each morning and night, especially in the company of children.

The gloom is less profound here, although we can still not see the sky. The path is clearly defined through a grassy plateau five or six feet wide, and the chanting is much clearer and more hideous.

The path curves sharply to the left and then back to the right in a large S formation and we are unexpectedly on an open bank not far from the river. To our left, across the deep and narrow ravine that has become the river's watercourse, I see a small, open pasture with yellow flowers catching the sunlight full in their pockets and glowing against the green cliffs of background jungle. It is apparently a natural meadow, for there are no tree stumps to mar its level serenity.

Veedlie trots forward through the trees to a pool directly in our path. It joins the river, but is separated from it by a barrier of logs through which the pool's water seeps in a thin waterfall. The difference is total between the two. Water from the pool rolls down into churning brown waters of the river, but the pool itself is absolutely still, shaded on all sides with trees that form a canopy over it. I can see no sign of habitation, and yet we must be almost on the village, for a faint haze of smoke hangs under the trees and the chanting is loud and immediate.

Veedlie climbs down the grassy mound and jumps feet first into the pool. I watch him rubbing the clay from his body and see an orange cloudiness spread out to discolor the green clarity of the water.

Leaving my bundle on the bank, I sit down and begin lowering myself into the pool, but the shock of coldness makes me draw my feet back. It is far colder than the river and I guess that it must be refrigerated by underground springs. Realizing that I will never have the courage to go in gradually, I hold my breath and topple forward, forcing myself to relax from the violent change; and after the initial shock, the coldness is a return to the greatest comfort I have known since being on this island.

Veedlie finishes bathing and crawls up the bank where he squats waiting for me under the shade of a vine-covered tree.

When I join him, he points solemnly down the beaten trail and announces that Vanua is here. Thick tree trunks frame the path, and all I can see in the high slot between them is a bend in the trail and what appears to be the corner of a bamboo hut through a thickening haze of smoke.

Now that I am so near, I want to put the moment off, to delay taking those last steps that will lead me to Vanua. A few feet away, I see a tree fallen across the watercourse to form a natural footbridge over the river that rushes past ten or fifteen feet below. The bridge joins this side with the open meadow which lies now in yellow tranquillity, so calm and beautiful that I am reassured. Promising myself that I will spend much time in that field, I turn and join Veedlie on the path leading into the compound of Vanua.

20

The odor of smoke perfumes the open space as we pass along the side of the first hut which blocks our view of the rest of the village. It is a low-slung structure with walls of woven bamboo and a thick roof of thatch that descends from a high center down to about three feet from the ground. At first glance, it looks somewhat like an elongated straw stack. But the thatch is not hay. I pinch some of it off and it crumbles in my hands. It is interwoven palm fronds, long dried from the sun. The chanting comes from inside this hut, and I can hear all of the rasping notes, all of the gurglings and bubblings of the human throat through the thin woven walls. It is the hypnotic voice of a woman, endlessly intoning the music of eternity, neither sad nor gay, but inevitable.

Veedlie passes beyond the shadowed corner and sunlight strikes his shoulders and white hair.

When I reach his side, we stand together as I stare at the deserted scene before me. Other huts, some larger and some smaller, but all approximately like the first one, can be seen in a vague circle nestling under trees at the edge of the forest, placed without any apparent plan and facing in all directions around an open space in which there is not a sprig of grass. The earth here is black and swept so clean that not even a leaf can be seen on the hard-packed surface. In the very center, two huts stand isolated side by side. One is merely a thatched roof supported by poles, open on all sides; its twin is walled in with a full door facing us. White smoke floats up gently from the center of its roof where there must be a large opening of some sort.

Veedlie explains that it is the fire hut, the cooking hut. The one other hut with a full door is only a few feet to our left, where, Veedlie tells me, Tombani lives.

All of the other huts have a different type of opening, more like a conventional window than a door.

"But where are the people?" I ask, staring about to see perhaps thirty or forty of these dwellings visible in the fringes of the forest, all of them appearing to breathe life.

"The people hide themselves," he answers simply.

The strange stillness, broken only by the lonely screaming of Maigna's woman and the natural sounds of the jungles, stirs uneasy tensions in me. I feel that many eyes are watching our every move, judging me, deciding on me. Do they feel resentment? Are they curious? Do they approve? But as we begin walking across the open compound, a hint of relief counters the tensions, for the scene is not somber at all, but rather neat and cheerful with its brilliant sunshine and the colorless harmonies of earth's blackness mingling with jungle greens and the soft greys and tans of bamboo structures. The place seems to have a double nature, vibrating with the unknown threat of savage hearts hidden from view but probably watching, and at the same time with a peculiarly innocent charm, for this scene looks as though it might have been lifted directly from the pages of some child's book of forest lore.

We angle across the compound to a hut almost hidden in the trees. It is an old structure with stained walls and a roof of thatch that is almost black.

Veedlie grasps each side of the windowlike opening and hoists himself up to climb over the sill and drops down inside. Raising my leg high and hunching my shoulders I step through the narrow opening into a dark hole of stench: the stench of soured sweat, of mould and ashes and permeated smoke; the stench of strange flesh and strange hearts; the stench of all that is primitive. I lean back with my seat propped against the window sill, breathing the fresher air from outside as my eyes accustom themselves to the obscurity. At first it is only a black hole, like the inside of a cave, for there are no other openings, but gradually I begin to discern details. A central beam runs from front to back immediately over my head. Standing, I can touch it with my upraised arm. Attached to it are smoke-blackened poles slanting downward to each side to join the walls only three feet above the ground. On top of these slanting beams, I can make out the rough exposed underside of the thatched roof. Stepping forward, I stare above me. The side beams are attached to the central beam by bark ropes wound around several times at each joint and tied. Through the layers of grime, I judge that these beams are unhewn branches or trunks of small trees. The room is narrow and long, a little larger than the bathroom of our home. The tightly woven walls let in a faint lattice design of daylight from the outside. There is no furnishing of any sort except a small mat in the rear corner.

"You live here," Veedlie announces, preparing to climb back out the window.

"Alone?"

"Yes," he answers.

"But whose home is this?"

"It is Maigna's," he says, perching on the window with his hands holding to each side and looking back over his shoulder. "When Maigna is dead his woman goes to live with fat Oai."

"But you tell me Oai is taking a mate."

"He is. They live together, all together."

"Is fat Oai's home like this?"

He twists his head further around and gazes about the room as though he had never observed it before. "Like this," he affirms gravely.

A snort of hopeless pity explodes in my nose as the scene of Oai's wedding night, with his mother sleeping beside him and his new wife, stirs up protestations within me. Deciding I would never understand or make myself understood in this realm, I let it drop without further questions except to ask Veedlie where he will live.

"I go to live with fat Oai."

He drops out of sight to the ground and I approach the window to see where he is going.

"You wait. You stay here," he admonishes, waving me back away from the opening. "You sit on the ground and wait."

I step to the side and gaze after him as he drifts nonchalantly across the deserted compound to the full door of Tombani's large hut. He shakes his head as though he were speaking to someone inside, shrugs his shoulders, scratches at his ribs and then strolls away with his stomach sticking far out and his back arched, stopping before the first hut we saw next to the path, the hut from which the death chant rises like smoke to cover the village. I watch him clamber up the front and through the window out of sight.

Alone for the first time in my new home, I turn about to absorb the sense of security it gives, but again the past throws the present out of perspective. When one moves into a new home, there is much to do, possessions to unpack, furniture to arrange, rooms to become acquainted with. I am gradually made aware of the light weight in my hand, my total possessions wrapped up in this bundle. Walking toward the left back corner, I kneel over the mat and place my pack beside it. And I am moved, and this is my home.

I stretch out on the mat, which is woven rather thick in a lattice pattern, large enough to provide only a half-mattress for my head and shoulders. Reaching up, I touch the ceiling's low edge with my fingers and dust drops down in my face. It is very still, very warm in here, and the smells in this corner become unbearable. All of them seem to be concentrated in the mat beneath my head. I carry it to the opening and, leaning across the sill, I stand it up against the outside wall in the sunlight to let it air out.

There is still no movement outside, nothing to betray the presence of other life here.

When I draw back from the window, I notice that it has a door of woven bark attached to a frame of straight branches which swings back into the darkness against the inside wall on leather thongs. It appears to have some sort of latch made of bent wood on the closing side. When I pull it forward, an object clatters out from behind it into the room, and I reach down through a cloud of dust to pick up a heavy spear, almost as long as I am tall, with a head made of sharp bone. I examine it closely. The bone point is grey with stain and dust, attached to the shaft loosely with bark rope. The realizations, the constant affirmations of their primitiveness stagger me. I return to sit beside my bundle and wait for what must come next.

My head nods forward on my chest and I breathe the reek of the hut's past, intimate, somehow gay and tranquil. What have these walls and floors known? — what bodies, what hungers and pains, what passions and revulsions, what bewilderments. It looks as much like an animal den as a human habitation, warm and dusty, of the earth, inevitable, full of the wisdom of ages of ignorance.

Darkness falls over the ground between my feet and I look up to see a tall, gaunt figure stepping through the opening.

"Tombani?"

"Yes, kulangu," he answers quietly, impersonally, going to sit in the back right hand corner opposite me as others darken the doorway and climb through. Fear of the unknown throttles me to an upsurge of nervousness that makes my knees shake in the circle of my arms.

The next man brings a smoking object and lays it on the ground at my feet, then takes his place against the wall next to Tombani.

"What is it?" I ask, but no one answers. Others come as black silhouettes in rapid succession, lay their smoking objects before me and go to sit facing me against the opposite wall, until that space is filled and they form a row in front of it. The smoking objects are stacked as high as my updrawn knees. They give off a faint odor similar to that of baked potatoes, but they are many times larger than the largest potato I have ever seen.

When all of the men and boys are in and seated facing me, they fill every inch of space on all sides. Light from the window outlines their heads and shoulders but their faces are black splotches. Straining my eyes, I can perceive no expression on any of them.

All movement dies to absolute stillness as though they were statues. I cannot even hear their breathing. Outside, the death chant insinuates itself into every crevice of being, and I can see the sunlight playing on trees across the compound.

After a few moments, I hear Tombani's voice from the corner.

"Eat," he says simply.

"Now?"

"Now."

The trembling diminishes for a moment. If they are offering me food, they probably have no sinister intentions, but why do they sit here and watch me in such complete silence?

I reach over my knees and lift one from the stack. Its

soft warmness weighs heavy in my hand. Biting through the jacket I chew on the meat which is as tasteless as the unseasoned potato it so resembles in odor. It seems to be not a potato, but some root, for the flavor has a sourness that is slightly nauseating. I swallow the first mouthful and bite into it a second time.

"Betel," Tombani commands in the same quiet tone he used in addressing me, and the halted activity of a moment ago relaxes into rustlings and breathings as attentions are distracted from me.

Betel nuts are passed around, but none is offered to me. I continue to chew my food and watch them in fascination. This is some sort of ceremony, obviously. The air is enlivened by their naturalness as they begin to eat the betel nuts, but almost immediately it becomes so loud that the death chant is drowned in the immediate crunchings of teeth against the betel meats. Almost as soon as the betel nuts have been popped into their mouths, they produce two or three containers made of large bamboo sections, and I watch them as those nearest me dip straws into a fine powder, bring the straws to their lips and dip them back into the bamboo containers again and again before passing the container to the next man. This is followed by an ordinary branch with leaves on it. After taking as much of the powdery stuff from the bamboo shoots as he wants, each man lifts the branch to his lips, bites off a piece of the bark and chews on it after passing the branch to the next man.

"Eat," Tombani says, and I realize that I am sitting here ignoring the food in my hands as I watch this betel ceremony.

"Eat," Tombani admonishes again, and something about the way he says it strikes my brain with the live shock of memory. Are there not virtually thousands of stories telling how an outsider is received into a tribe by being offered food? — gifts of food to show him that he is accepted? The memory returns full-blown, like the forgotten face of some past friend. But I remember also that you are rejected if you insult them by refusing to eat all of the food offered you. The small portions brought to me on the beach were only to keep me alive; they were not the ceremonial offering that this is.

I look at the pile before me and desolation settles over all of my senses. I, who have lived on a starvation diet for weeks, cannot possibly eat these many pounds of food. I feel like lying back and making no further effort. After all the tortures and torments I went through leading up to this, now, at the very moment when they seem to be finally accepting me, when I may hope for some peace in my life, I must fail this test and be rejected again as nothing more than a worthless chunk of human debris who has insulted them by refusing to eat their offerings.

I am full after the first one, but I continue eating, slowly, forcing my mind to work, hoping to find some way out. Shoulders that were highlighted dull before are glistening on all sides of me. The strong, sour odor rises again, and I am sure now that it must come from the betel chewing.

Outside I hear the clear bright call of a bird, and I look toward the window with longing to be out of here, already accepting and looking forward to the idea of returning to my cove on the beach, an outcast, to give up and lie forever in the shade, no longer caring what happens to me.

How can they expect anyone to eat all of this? They are cruel beyond belief, building up a man's hopes with an initial gesture of kindness and then slamming him back to despair with this impossible demand.

I have eaten six or seven, and the stack is still as large as it seemed at the beginning. There is nothing to do except face defeat. I no longer tremble. I no longer care. Let them do what they will. I pull up my knees to bury my head in them, but my belly is so full I cannot stand the pressure and I lower them again. My stomach's grumblings can be heard loud above their chewings and lipsmackings, and I swallow back the startings of nausea.

"Igoi mazutino," I hear Tombani's voice, calm and taunting, asking me if I am full.

I react from my torpor. Something about the suavity, the unction of his gentleness outrages me and I wish I had words to hurl my resentment at him. Instead, I say that I am sorry but I can eat no more.

My voice shames me, for it hides its resentment not in courtesy or humility but in an overlading of fear. I pretend I do not care, that my voice is the voice of someone who doesn't give a damn any more, but that is not true even to me. I cannot hide completely the submerged cringings of fear at what they might do to me if I spoke in the liberation of my bitterness.

Light is again shielded from the doorway as a general movement starts up and converges over me in the new darkness. I draw back into the corner, my sweat-slicked shoulders sliding across the bamboo weave and lift my hands to ward off the unknown.

They are stooping at my feet, ignoring me, picking up

the remainder of the food and dividing it among themselves. One of them drops a root back to the ground and wrings his hand, groaning that it is burned; and chuckling flutters through the entire group. I lie here numb with astonishment, in a puddle of my own sweat.

"We go now," I hear Tombani's voice, weary as though he were almost asleep.

Straining my shoulders and back, I inch myself up to a sitting position. "You go," I answer as I have been taught to say.

They step through my door and out into the compound without taking any further notice of me, leaving me sitting here in stupefaction, shaking my head against the upsurge of vomitings.

I must think of something else or my stomach will continue its slow rise into my mouth. I close my eyes and listen to hear their voices outside, natural and unconcerned, sounding like the voices of all the people on this earth, sounding like any street in any city heard from any window. I am back in a world that is somewhat akin to the world I have known — the world of man, no matter how primitive — the world that tells of man's appetites and his needs. I am no longer exposed to the stark language of nature. I can hear voices of men and women and children. I am in a home, in my own home, and living, breathing, mortal humanity surrounds it.

I bask in the drifting emotions, the long-forgotten emotions of security and privacy that are inherent in these smoked walls and roof, in this hiding place that is my own protected world where I can be myself in a way that is impossible out in the open world, where I dare to expose myself in all my hopes and dreams, where I can rest and find my courage, where I can someday hope to remember in all of their sharpness, in all their keenness the sweet details of my loss, my other life, my wife and children, without the throttling desolation that the slightest thought of them brings me now. I know that when I can remember those private things closest to the sources of my life without being ravaged by the pain of their loss, but rather being sustained by what I possessed, then I will be safe. Outside, I hear the activities of life, of mankind surrounding me, and for now that is enough. I am filled with a vast and sacred tenderness for all of humanity.

I climb slowly to my feet, careful not to jostle my stomach, and drag myself to the window. The jagged line of early afternoon shadows stretches out from the other side into the compound, throwing huts into speckled obscurity that is given a bluish tint by the hovering smoke.

Several women are spreading giant green banana leaves in a long row on the ground in front of the cooking hut, while others wander in and out its door.

The sunlight is full against the front of my hut, burning in through the opening on my stomach and hands, raising the temperature inside to dizzying thickness.

Should I go out? Am I expected to remain here? The woman still fills the air with her chanting, but no one pays the slightest attention to it. A group of men are gathering to seat themselves under a large tree that covers the alleyway between Tombani's hut and the one close beside it. Everything moves aimlessly, slowly in the many activities of the compound. The atmosphere is unmistakably festive.

I stand indecisively, clutching my stomach as sweat

dribbles out of my beard. If I stay in this oven, I will be sick. Perhaps they consider me one of them? Perhaps I should act as they do, get out and wander about in the open as though I belonged here as much as they do. My mind wavers. After the success of being accepted into the village this noon, I am paralyzed before the fear of doing something that might now sour them against me. Sticking my head and shoulders tentatively through the window, I wait for some reaction. Beyond the low eaves of fat Oai's hut, I can see a portion of the path leading toward the pond, and the pond evokes an image of irresistible coolness shaded from this sun that falls in slants against the side of my face.

I step out into the pocket of heat reflecting from the front of my hut. Some coolness of evaporation immediately brushes across my forehead and shoulders, even though no leaf stirs and the smoke hangs in motionless layers.

Although I am obviously seen from all sides, they do not interrupt their activities, do not stare; they ignore me completely. With my senses tuned to a high pitch, ready to tumble back inside if the natives show any reaction, I take the long step over the mat I have put out to air and shuffle slowly around to the side, noticing out of the corner of my eye the ragged descent of my thatched roof; first from above my head, then from my shoulder downward, giving me an enlarging view of tree and bush beyond, until I stand at the corner where the waist-high eaves sweep upward in a slanting plane extending back to the underbrush a few feet away. I wade into the brush, thinking I may circle unobtrusively behind the huts and come out on the path leading to the pond. But progress is impossible. Sun-warmed leaves suck at my sweating flesh and gnats swarm up to block my passage.

The sick taste of nausea has parched my throat. I must get to the pond. Do I dare strike out across the compound? No, it will attract less attention if I make my way along in front of the semicircle of huts on this side.

Warm stuffiness puffs out from each of the hut openings as I pass, and each time the odor is not what I expect to smell. These are not the usual reeks of humanity; there is no hint of the grosser odors of waste, of garbage and excrement and urine that always accompany community life. A humid sourness of betel and smoke and coconut gives the atmosphere a faint odor of lye soap that is neither pleasant nor unpleasant.

I glance obliquely through the openings into interiors that are beginning to be illuminated by the sun's reflections. They are like mine, about the same size, each with its bare dirt floor and sleeping mats, some with coconut shells and other rubble lying about in corners. In one of them, a black child sitting on the floor looks up at me as I walk past.

It is a relief to be walking, a relief to be out in the open. Reassurance trickles haltingly through me as my hut becomes more distant and no one pays me the slightest heed. Only fat Oai's hut lies between me and the path to the pool now, and my stomach goes ahead of my body in its dreams of lying in that coldness and drinking until comfort returns to health.

The nerve-shattering chant grows to intense loudness as I walk along the side of Oai's hut, muffled only slightly through the walls. I listen to its strange combination of serenity and inevitability intoned in a hideous animal voice and my footsteps falter to approach it any closer, dreading to walk past the opening from which it pours forth. To my right, almost directly across the compound, my sun-blazed hut appears small and faded through the smoke. As I step around the corner, I am facing the angle of Tombani's hut only a few yards away.

The sun falls at a tangent across the front of Oai's house, which faces north. I withdraw into myself and take the three steps that place me directly in front of the raw outsweep of sound which halts me in confusion, with the desire to cover my ears with my hands and run. My head turns, drawn to stare through the sun-brightened door frame into a dark jumble of bodies inside.

The pool, the sunlight, the thirst and discomfort swim confusedly to the background as all of my attention is magnetized to the highlighted view of a skeletal woman kneeling back on her heels in the harsh glare before the open door. She sits with her knees pressed together, her thin arms rigidly straight and her hands cupped over her kneecaps while she weaves slowly from side to side in a wide arc of motion that contorts her body from the waist up. Her back is curved so far forward that her empty breasts undulate freely like twin pendulums almost brushing her knees; but her head, with its white crown of dyed hair, is thrown back on stretched neck ligaments as though she were in a profound trance. I gaze into her uplifted face, following its slow snakings from side to side. Her closed eyes are black orbits staring blind, and her cheekbones protrude in violent sharpness beneath the tattooed shine of her flesh. She sways endlessly, rhythmically, hypnotically, a thin black figure, sweat-sheened in dramatic spotlight against the shadowy background of the hut's interior, fascinating me with pity and terror as she hurls her chant through the framed opening to the skies above.

The pool, the sunlight, the thirst and discomfort storm to the foreground of my consciousness and pricklings scamper across my scalp as I catch myself staring openly into the door. I turn quickly, half expecting to find myself hemmed in by scowling faces converging to accuse me of the unknown guilt I feel so strongly. But nothing has changed in the compound. Scratching my head against the spread of the itching, I hurry around the side of the hut and into the path, now shaded, but with an air so thick, so torpid I must gasp for breath.

Before I have reached the first turn, a new voice wails out, cross-cutting the death chant and clashing against it at intervals. The itching returns to pepper my entire body. Is this call about me? Are they commanding me to turn back? What have I done? I do not know, but the sense of my own guilt persuades me that I am somehow at fault.

Facing about and walking slowly toward the side of fat Oai's hut, I concentrate my hearing on the words shouted by the new voice, attempting to separate them from the accompanying chant.

"Maigna greets! Maigna greets!" I hear with a relief that sends heaviness to my legs. Stepping from the path, I see that the whole village is responding to the call. Beyond the hut wall, I watch them amble forward leisurely, unconcernedly, like a crowd gathering for a speech.

I edge around the corner and stand close to the side, feeling the eaves slant upward across my buttocks. A youth, very black with an enormous paunch curving out over pro-

truding genitals and with rolls of fat across the small of his
back is calling through cupped hands in all directions as he
twists the upper part of his body without moving his feet
which are planted wide apart.

"Maigna greets! Maigna greets!"

This must be the one called fat Oai. As he turns his great
head toward me, our glances unite in that strange communication that can occasionally be so poignant. His eyes,
large and grave above his cupped fists, reveal such guilelessness I cannot imagine their ever assuming the inhuman
glaze I have seen in Tombani's or even Veedlie's, whose
whole expression appears pallid and lackadaisical compared
to the peculiar nobleness of this lad's bearing and gaze.

He lowers his hands and I am taken aback. He is nothing
but a child now that I can see his full round face. From
his name, I had pictured him as a gross, stupid-looking adolescent, but he cannot be more than thirteen or fourteen
years old despite the largeness of his frame and the burden
of his unnatural fat.

Villagers are gathering around us in a sun and dust con-
glomeration of bellies and breasts, but my attention cannot be torn from fat Oai; it centers suddenly in the rami-
fications connected with the idea that this youngster will
be forced to take a woman to his mat while still scarcely
in the fringes of puberty. Perceptions graft themselves vividly to my imagination, muffling the whisperings and
breathings and shufflings of humanity that surround me as
I think of the loveless act he must fumble through this night
with a girl who is probably as convinced as he that it is
repulsive and evil. Bringing it to bear on myself, I realize
how I would have recoiled from such raw intimacy when I

was thirteen and how I would have been sickened and distorted had I been forced prematurely into this type of defloration.

He looks at me with unclouded brown eyes, eyes devoid of curiosity, ignoring the crowd and concentrating on me, infusing intelligence into me through no spoken word but only through his bearing and gaze until I am moved to profound pity for him, for he is too young, too young to be married. Every fold and every pore of his sweating body radiates the mysterious luster of innocence, some intangible aura that shouts loudly of his virginity, staunch and unknowing, highlighting his hulk with the same sweetness and freshness proper to the unripened flesh of all children everywhere; and I am certain that lust still slumbers latent in the secret crypts of his bloods and muscles and that his fledgling mouth has never tasted the salts of desire.

"You poor child. You poor child," I hear myself mumbling in my beard in English as I think how strange it is that merely seeing him has given me a new knowledge that completely alters my fatted arguments of this morning when I outraged little Veedlie by insisting that mating is good and very good. But we were speaking of two entirely different things — I understand that now — for this is not mating but rather a form of violation perverting a natural instinct by predating its fruition, like forcibly delivering babies when they are six-month fetuses instead of allowing nature to take its course. Perhaps if he were prepared to look on mating with childish enthusiasm, as an adventure or a game, he might rollick through it without damage and strut about proudly the next morning, but even that encouragement is denied him, if I have understood Veedlie.

I think of him struggling through the midnight revulsion, seeing it as evil, doing it under obedience to their traditions; probably souring forever the concupiscence that would eventually have leavened his body to the sanity of robust desires.

Fat Oai does not respond to my smile, but somehow he seems to acknowledge it with a brightening of his eyes. Then, facing the crowd, he draws himself up to full height so that his dyed hair comes almost to my shoulders, and stands in a self-conscious pose, casting sidelong glances at me, as though he were doing all of this to impress me.

With the suddenness of some cue I have not noticed, a concerted scream surges up from all throats, overwhelming the guttural whine of the death chant and causing my head to jerk around on surprised neck tendons. Men, women and children face the door, their mouths open in braying, their features betraying no emotion.

Veedlie's grinning face bobs through the opening and he perches, balancing himself on the door sill for a moment before dropping to the ground. I watch him land clumsily and wobble on his heels to right himself beside fat Oai, and I can hear a general softening of amusement in the screeching as vague smiles appear on the faces of the crowd. Facing them, he scratches his eye and opens his jaws to join in the new upsweep of wailing.

I catch his attention and motion him toward me with a nod of my head, wondering if I should make some pretense of adding my voice to this ceremony. The other villagers are cutting their eyes from little Veedie to me as he sidles across the hut front in full sunlight, holding his head erect and his mouth open in jubilant bawling.

I part my lips and manipulate my jaws silently the way I used to when pretending to sing hymns in church.

Is this bellowing supposed to express grief? If so, it is not very serious grief, for they are glancing out of the corners of their eyes at one another, flickering their eyebrows and jostling their shoulders in the same secretive gestures I have seen in so many classrooms when children were trying to stifle their gigglings and conceal their devilment from the teacher.

They look at me without expression, with neither friendliness nor animosity, and without curiosity, but blankly, the way one looks at a man walking down the same busy street in any town. Are they that dead? I would have thought that if my color and beard did not arouse their curiosity, my clothing might, but they observe me as though I had been here forever.

The concerted outcry ceases as unexpectedly and abruptly as it began, leaving an aftermath of rustling stillness that is as dense as deafness. The food lies heavy in my stomach and my limbs are weighted with the tiredness one feels after emotional upheaval, after attending a drama or concert that has strung the nerves to twanging tautness; and somehow I feel safer than before, safer now that murky and mournful evocations of eternity have died with the chant, allowing us to forget the unknown repercussions of life and death in the illusion of this sunlit world of reality.

But the sensation of safety is nullified when I look up. Two women stand apart from the group a few feet away. The one is a full-breasted young mother with an infant boy riding in a saddle of sweat on her shoulder. I am not given time to observe her more closely. She fades before the commanding magnetism that draws my attention to the withered old hag beside her, who stands tiny and hunched with her chin resting on gnarled hands which are crossed at the top of a tall branch staff. She consumes me with her jeweled gaze. If it were not for her long empty breasts flapping down below the crease of her abdomen with their elongated nipples pointing to the earth like purple sticks inserted in the flesh, I would take her for a shrunken old man, for the tufts of her bushy grey hair sprout far back on her head, leaving her forehead bald with its crossed lines of wrinkles and giving her a professorial air of intelligence that clashes frighteningly with her savage appearance. Her eyes are inhuman in their phosphorescent brightness, like the animal glaze I should imagine in a tiger stalking its prey as she stares at me with such intensity I must look away.

"Who is she?" I ask Veedlie, placing my hand along the side of his face and turning his head back so that he looks up into my eyes.

"Who?"

I nod toward the motionless crone. His brown eyes roll downward to look at her and then back to me.

"Rauka."

"Who is she?"

"The strong one. The sorceress."

"What?"

"The strong one, Rauka. She drives bad spirits away. She gives the mates for mating. She cuts the little ones," he adds, pointing to his face and then to his genitals. I lean forward as he shows me three almost imperceptible V-shaped indentions on the sides and underside of his fore-skin, forming an effective circumcision against possible stricture. "And she keeps serpents in her hut which it is taboo to look upon."

"Where is it?"

"In the woods," he says, waving in a direction behind Oai's hut.

He babbles on, but I turn my attention back to Rauka whose toothless mouth folds in to give her a sardonic expression of puckering. From her hips down she is a skeleton, with legs that are scarcely more than flesh-covered bones enlarged at the knee joints. They are hinged to her pelvis in such wide separation that I can see a top-wide triangle of background between her emaciated thighs. She scrutinizes me unwaveringly, with a communication of dead insolence and fascination which I cannot answer, under which I feel helplessly blighted.

"Is the other one her daughter?" I ask Veedlie.

"No, she's somebody else," he replies, turning toward the door through which an older youth is emerging with careful steps, faltering beneath the burden which he balances on top of his head with both hands.

As fat Oai lumbers out of the way, allowing the newcomer to advance, I see that the bundle is only one end of a long object, tightly wrapped in wide overlapping strips of bark that is still wet from having been made pliable in water. A second youth, carrying the other end, manipulates his legs through the door bringing the burden into full view. It is unmistakably a body, being carried out feet first. The physical contours are neatly traced with woven bark ropes tied at the ankles, knees, waist, shoulders and neck.

"Maigna?" I ask Veedlie.

"Maigna," he affirms pleasantly.

A hush settles deep within me, perceiving the presence of death and I catch myself unconsciously reaching up to remove my hat before remembering that I have none. The crowd shows no reaction. From the corner of my eye, I notice that Rauka has not moved, that she continues to ogle me.

Maigna's mummified figure is rigid, as though a pole ran the full length of its underside, for it is carried atop the heads of the two boys, with no other support to prevent its buckling. Their hips sway with graceful effeminacy as they swing toward us under the burden.

I step around the side of the hut to give them room, but when they turn the corner, the space is so restricted I must lean backward over the low eave to allow them clearance. Some inner demand for respect embarrasses me; some remnant of former emotions forces me to lift my hand discreetly beneath my beard and place it on the soaked flesh over my heart, lowering my head and saying to myself: "Peace eternal grant him . . . " I hear the boys' quickened breathing and bushes scraping against the other side of the shroud in the scorching stillness as Maigna's body passes before my nose. It exudes a fragrance of wet straw, the scent of a hayfield after an August rain. I am struck with the neatness of the wrappings at this close range, as though he were bandaged from head to foot in an expert dressing of stiff buckram gauze. The bushes spring softly back into place as the carriers jostle forward on hips of oil.

Something nudges me in the thigh and I look around to see that others are falling in line and that Veedlie is trying to push me ahead, patting my hip as one would a horse's rump to get him moving. He tugs at me to precede him down the path behind the body, to lead the cortege.

I step in behind the carriers and Veedlie marches at my heels. Glancing back, I note that the rest of the villagers are following single file. The hag, Rauka, and Tombani are hidden from view somewhere back there.

My thoughts flow back to conventional funerals, to the mournful hush surrounding them, to the eternal calm of funeral parlors and the plush discretion of hearses — to the intolerable pall of sadness over all of it; and I contrast it to the festive brightness of this day, to this parade wherein a half-naked white man leads a group of naked savages through brush. And later there will be the feast, the celebration.

Arriving at the pond, the two pallbearers step out onto the fallen log that forms a footbridge across the ravine of the river's course, connecting this side with the open meadow. Sunlight catches crystals of sweat on the shoulders of the youth in front of me, highlighting his sinewy muscles as he weaves confidently across the narrow bridge.

I glimpse the pond longingly, promising myself a drink and a bath later, and hesitate long enough to slip off my shoes before venturing onto the tree which is barkless, slick, sun-white above the brown river-rush below.

The two carriers trudge toward the shadows at the far edge of the meadow, leaving a faint trail of bent weeds and flowers. Dried stems from past seasons burn into my feet and I sit down to slip my shoes back on. Thin yellow buttercup petals, made luminous by the sunlight, brush freshness against my cheeks in the burning stillness. Veedlie threads his way through them to my side.

He bends forward, a black shadow against dazzling yellows, and plucks one of the blossoms for himself and another which he solemnly presents to me. Others follow his example, bending forward and straightening up, each of them holding a short-stemmed flower to his chest.

Even on the flat vista of the meadow we continue to advance single file, passing the ragged perimeter of shade where highlights become dull, where blossoms lose their radiance and where scalding humidity seeps out through jungle fissures to envelop us in torpor.

Maigna's body has been deposited on a mound of earth scooped out beside the shallow grave, moist earth filled with bits of grass and straw. An expectant stillness tenses the atmosphere as the hag Rauka shoulders through the crowd and stalks, with surprising agility, to the edge of the grave, dragging her staff along the ground beside her.

For some reason, I am certain that I will hear weeping start up from the motionless group, and I scan them uneasily, half turning, waiting for something to happen. At this close range, I have the impression I am looking into tattooed black masks, not human faces, masks with yaw sores around their eyes, stoic masks, cold and feelingless.

Men and women intermingle, living bodies, living sexes with mask faces; but it is the women who fascinate me, for they are both transparent and indecipherable. They do not wear the teeth necklaces I have seen on some of the men or any other adornment. Only the youngest mothers and pubescent girls have breasts that make any pretense of standing out; the others hang limp and flat over their ribs, and all of their abdomens protrude slightly with the arch of their backs, no matter how skinny they are. Although they are naked and sweating and more female than feminine, there is an instantaneous communication of reserve that nullifies lubricity more thoroughly than if they were clothed in full Victorian tea garb. They resemble the very earth that spawned them, so untouchable and disinterested that their movements seem more akin to the tides or the winds in the trees than to human actions. Their faces remind me of a roomful of discarded lamps, loveless, unlighted by illusions and incapable of lighting illusions in others, dulled by dusts of resignation, to an expression of long-suffering behind their tattoo. Have they ever experienced even animal ecstasy? — even the basic gratification of rut? Could they abandon themselves to pleasure and yet be — ?

The nasal whine of Rauka's voice, so cracked and thin it no longer sounds human, intones the beginning of the familiar death chant, wavering between the fundamental tone and a repeated note a minor third above it, then returning in a guttural bawl that is not allowed to die as the crowd join their voices in a caterwauling that renews the melody; the women in piercing falsetto, the men in bass and tenor unison, giving an impression of bagpipe harmonies. Eyes are reduced to slits, but there is no swaying, no elasticity — all is harshness and rigidity. The men chant flatly, never changing the monotony of their tones either by loudening or softening them, but the women's voices rise and fall from full-lunged shriekings to moans, producing a strange alternation, now as though they were accompanying the male voices with their whisperings, now as though the men were providing a background for the wailings.

How long will they chant? If they continue as long as Maigna's woman did, I will never be able to hold out. The music evokes unwanted realizations in me, realizations telling me that although I led the cortege and have apparently been accepted into their life and now stand in the midst of them clutching my flower, I am more a stranger here than I was when I regained consciousness that first morning on the beach. I am flooded with the hopelessness of my total lack of communication with them, with their eyes and hearts and souls and bodies. And yet my heart struggles out to them, searching them for some sign of affection, for some sweetness, for some companionship. Only in fat Oai have I discovered the sympathy of a glance wherein something was understood.

Turning, I see Maigna's woman, lounging with crossed arms at the back edge of the crowd. Her eyes, dry and dull, stamp her with an expression of complete boredom. Fat Oai stands beside her with his head lowered as though he were studying his vast belly. Behind him, I discern, over the band of yellow flowers, the distant woods and the smoke haze of the compound of Vanua.

Oldness becomes a part of me, as though it were a necessary ingredient of the moment; oldness is in the focusless desolation that rises like vapor above all these things; oldness is in the dribblings of sweat that sting into my eyes and salt the corners of my lips; oldness is here in the outpuffings of my stomach that make my pants too tight; oldness is in the slicked hairs and flesh around my navel; oldness is in the folds and tissues, in the multi-veined nothingness of my groin where potency slumbers unaroused since the crash; oldness is fed into me with the chanting, telling me that when a man has no one to hang his life to, he dies within himself and warning me not to die that way, not to die as these loveless beings have died in a moral and spiritual existence that makes mortal death, not living, the occasion for celebrating.

My mind is revolted and turns away from the savage immersion into death. I seek deliberate escape from its desolation in simulating pleasure, by the building of sensuality against the castration of despair in that secret way of lonely men in lonely places who diminish their loneliness by looking at women and offering themselves the hidden solace of improvising daydreams of sweetness and passion with them. Glancing sideways, I single out a young virgin, heavy-breasted and thick-hipped, to appraise every pore of her body as one would that of a woman one desires to seduce in imagination, to visualize leading her into the brush and caressing her, kissing her, making love with her. My gaze sweeps over her breasts and belly and shoulders and buttocks in an effort to stir my own blood from this lethargy of isolation, in the hope of nullifying my oldness with some sign that will reassure me of youth in passion; but my interest wanes even as I seek to inflame it.

Shifting my attention away from her, I listen to the eternal coilings of the death chant and feel my shoulders sag in the private disappointment of a man whose belly has failed to reassure him, disheartened that I have not experienced those amiable chafings of virility that can offer such unique consolation to the middle-aged.

I close out the scene about me and wonder how many others, approaching my age, seek the poignant reassurance that I have sought this moment through images calculated

to test vitality within the bloods and muscles and organs of
our bodies? — not from lascivious motives, but rather as
one would check his strongbox to assure himself of his
material reserves. It is a part of dreading barrenness, dreading death, fingering for the pulses of life, and needing to
feel the sensual stirrings as proof that we are still supported in our lives by reserves of potency; cringing, in
what private anguish, from the final profession of impo-
tence that will brand our flesh as rubble and announce to
us our future incapability of exploding nerves into ecstasy
and life into being, of proving to ourselves the dignity of
our complete manhood. Whether the act is ever to occur
again is no longer the important thing; no — all that comes
to matter is the knowledge that potency feeds vitality into
our bloods and muscles. As long as it does, we can rest in
well-being, whole in the certitude of our competence, our
vigor, our fullness of humanity — safe in the certitude that
we are not barren . . .

The chant flags in mid-air, dwindling away like gnats
disappearing into shadows. I gaze at the delicately organized cup of yellow in my hand, framed in the red wrinkles
of my thumb and forefinger and the grey curlings of my
beard. Thank God the chanting is over.

From the shrunken hole of her mouth, Rauka declaims
words in a sexless, metallic voice. Her sibilations rise and
spew about us, echoing back from the wall of trees, a constant flow of sound without clarity. Only fragments detach themselves from her gummings.

"We are placing you in the open sunlight where
you — "

But it is impossible to follow her as she blabbers something about the dead man's having the companionship of two yellow butterflies in the day. I make no further attempt to catch her words until finally she slows to very definite pronunciation with: "We leave you in sunlight, and we go back and wait in shadow."

Little Veedlie is rubbing his forefinger across his sore eye and openly yawning when Rauka stumps down the mound and flings her flower into the hole where Maigna will be laid. All attentions are focused to her frail body. One of the carriers peers at her, his hand absently scratching beneath his testicles, until she nods her head violently forward showing her almost bald crown. He stoops quickly in obedience and slips a bark rope beneath Maigna's shoulders while his companion slips one beneath the knees.

The crowd watches in that strange suspension of time that marks the close of all important ceremonies. Nothing moves, not a leaf stirs; the air is thick and rancid of nature and of bodies. I bend my head far back to see that the sky is blanched with the sun's incandescence above the towering silhouette of the forest in whose shadow we stand.

When I look back, the two carriers are facing one another at each end of the grave, straddling the hole with their legs planted wide apart. Their arms are pressed in against their ribs and bent at the elbows with the forearms up in front of them. Biting into the black flesh of each hand, the tan windings of the rope ends descend to cradle Maigna's body which dangles between their knees. Muscles quake violently in their arms and legs as they brace themselves and begin lowering the body by lowering their hands.

Again the hush of finality sifts through me, touching perceptions of eternity and floating them upward in a cloud of infinite nostalgia as I watch the mummified figure sink gently from sight into the earth in a silence so vast, so unifying that I am filled with peace. All of these people are reacting to its powerful communication, stilled before the eternal mystery and showing reverence for the solemnity of this homage to Maigna and to death. In a blurred view of the scene, I note that they are not moving: they pose in locked attitudes as though all of them were caught and petrified in the midst of dreams.

The shriek rips into the quick of nerves and a paroxysm of shock sweeps through my body, bobbing my head up. I see one of the carriers floundering, struggling to regain his balance as the earth crumbles at the grave's edge beneath his foot. Dropping his ropes, he sprawls forward atop Maigna's body. The added weight tears the ropes from the other native's hands and the foot-end of the corpse crashes into place while the boy steps back in astonishment, massaging his scorched wrists.

The crowd thaws from its frozen reverence into surprised chucklings that falter a moment before gathering impetus that swells monstrously to a full roar of merriment about my ears. Little Veedlie stamps his feet into the carpet of bruised flowers and dances with delight, slapping his buttocks so enthusiastically that his own blossom disintegrates in his hand and showers yellow petals behind him.

The carrier scrambles into view, beams at us as he jerks his foot from under Maigna's body, and makes a great show of stepping victoriously from the grave. His antics rekindle the laughter to a screaming, thigh-slapping din while Maigna lies ignored in the shallow box of earth where he has been so unceremoniously delivered. I feel myself shrinking from this unspeakable desecration of hilarity as though it were contaminating, and watch them with revulsion as they begin parading past the hole and tossing their flowers on the body, so preoccupied with their giggling and chattering that they scarcely heed their acts and allow the blossoms to fall where they may.

Stepping forward, I bend over and place my flower on his littered chest where some of the earth crumblings have fallen. Little Veedlie dodges behind me to the edge of the circle to pluck a fresh buttercup for his offering.

I wait in exhaustion for what must happen next, but already they are striking out across the pasture, returning to Vanua. Since they ignore me and make no semblance of marching in order, I straggle behind, wanting more than anything else in the world to be alone for a time, to stop unnoticed at the pond and cool myself; to wash from me the heats of my body and the confusions of my heart in restful isolation. All of this has been too jarring to me, too rich in its newness; everything in me cries out to escape it for a while.

At the bridge, I see the last remnants of the crowd disappearing into the tree-framed pathway leading to Vanua. Afternoon shadows stretch to the opposite bank of the ravine, speckling the fallen log.

I squint back at the burial site where the two naked carriers are squatting beside the mound, shoveling dirt over the body with their bare hands, while Rauka, her chin resting on her folded fists, hunches over her staff, a mute skeleton contemplating their labors.

I turn aside toward the pond which nestles clear and

deserted, sparkling from a purity of underground springs that evoke the blues and greens of waters that are iced. With my last strength I deposit my shoes on the bank and allow my body to topple forward into the bashing coldness. Needles of shock flash through me. I float suspended in the frigid undersurface and listen to the unutterable silence of my heart while my legs settle downward with tortoise slowness. Time and movement fade into the relaxation of eye-closed numbness as I forget all other worlds except this liquid world where changes are balm to my body. Chill invades feverishness, shrinking flesh to tautness over my frame and seeping into the depths of my entrails. Without moving a muscle, I drift with the moment as my toes rake gently across the frozen pebbles of the bottom.

21

Without being aware that I have slept, I find myself awake. My vision is diffused in all directions around and about and beyond the face above me. Briefly, I glimpse the shaded underfoliage forming a high arbor above the black silhouette that peers intently down at me. A child stands in the grass at my head, hands on hips, bending far over me and gazing into my face. Through the muffle of drowsiness, I cling to one thought. I must do nothing to frighten this full-cheeked infant away. Smiling, I speak a soft greeting and move my eyes back in my head to see that it is a girl.

She ignores my greeting but lowers her head closer to mine, engrossed in the upside-down view of my face.

"N'gari kikiki daoka," she says in such childish accents

that I must guess more than I actually understand. And
I notice that her skin is smooth and fresh, that she has not
yet been tattooed and therefore has not been named, being
called simply "girl baby."

The grass is cool against my back, and I am glad for this
sleepiness that deadens my heart to the acute rise of hope
that the child inspires in me.

"You sit with me?" I suggest.

"I sit with you," she answers.

I stretched out my left arm and she hops around to the side
and kneels in the hollow of my armpit, sitting back on her
heels in the way of these women, with her knees drawn
together and her hands folded primly in her lap. Gazing
sidelong at her, I allow my arm to encircle her back. She
inches forward until her knees are pressed into my ribs.

And she is like any other child in the world, without
even the tattoos to give strangeness.

"You are pretty, child."

"You are pretty, Jon," she smiles, dimpling her cheeks
in a shy overcoming of timidity.

Seeing her and feeling her flesh touch mine with growing ease that is devoid of any hint of repugnance, I have
no doubts as to how I must behave. I am at home in the
world of childhood and all constraint evaporates from
my chest in the blessed relief of familiarity. I can be
natural with her, for she is like all children and with children there is never the need to fear the spontaneous intelligence of the heart.

"Do you want a name?" I tease, feeling authority and
liberation return to my stunted bloods.

Her eyes open in blank surprise and her head starts

forward in a movement of expectancy.

"Since you are no bigger than a finger, I name you Ririkinger."

Her hand flies up to my chest. I sense its faint weight through the thick mat of my beard.

" 'kinger?" she whispers.

"You," I say solemnly, "are not N'gari kikiki daoka. You are Ririkinger!"

" 'kinger! 'kinger! 'kinger," she laughs.

"Is that good?" I ask, drawing her close to me, fingering the folds of her feet beneath her infant buttocks.

"Good and very good," she explodes ecstatically, repeating " 'kinger, 'kinger, 'kinger," and thrusting her face forward to giggle into my beard.

Moving my right arm across my chest, I grasp her beneath the armpits with both hands and left her into the air, as I have done with my own children so many times. And like them she grins with elation and screams when I swoop her from side to side and dive her downward to kiss her on the cheek. The clearing is transformed into a world where all is guilelessness, all is innocence and gaiety, all is centered in the child's amusement, and in the unfoldings within man's withered heart when he becomes the child with no other change from childhood than the forgotten perspective of years.

"Oof," I grunt in fatigue, lowering her to rest on my stomach. Her tiny legs flail against my belt and she melts the crusts of stagnation within me with her gaze, clear of the cautious dregs and full of that expression of unreserved joy that is reserved to the eyes of infants.

"You," I announce with mock majesty, "are Ririkinger."

" 'kinger!" she sings, planting her fists on my chest and rising up on stiff arms. She puffs her jaws out in imitation of my pompousness.

"You are pretty, Ririkinger." I slap her behind as she tumbles forward against my chin.

"You are pretty and very pretty, Jon," she says with sudden drowsiness, and I feel her muscles turn to mush almost instantly with sleep. I cradle her body to me in a rocking motion from side to side as my nerves absorb the gentle nourishment of peace.

"She is woman."

My body convulses in spasm at the unexpected whispering. My eyes fly open and I am staring into the rage-distorted face of Tombani. I clutch the child to me as he transfixes me with his slitted glare.

"It is taboo to touch female," he purrs cunningly, tainting the atmosphere with subtle viciousness.

"But a child," I protest, stupefied. Surely he doesn't think I would defile —

"She is female!" he bellows, stepping over my head in a fleeting perspective of underthighs and wobbling genitals. He sweeps the child up by her arm and flings her through the air to one side.

I plant my elbows furiously in the grass behind me, rising up in defense. The child thumps to the earth with a breathless grunt that becomes a deep inhalation, then a scream. Tombani tenses over me, lifting his club into the air. His dripping lips curl away from his tushes and he weaves over me with an insane leer on his face that throttles all intelligence within me. I wait, unable to move, sickened by the raw horror of viewing feverish eyes in which there is no hint of mercy. And a sudden devastation of light floods my insides with the certitude of death. The sky above is infinitely blue, trailing scattered white clouds with underpuffings of grey; two sun-pinked cockatoos float serenely from tree to tree in the stratospheres beyond.

All of it is intensely real, lifted from the context of time into the timeless motion of a dream until his club trembles and arcs toward me with the full sweep of his body. The movement obliterates my paralysis and I flounder to one side as his leer wells to enormity before my eyes. The clap of wood against bone reverberates through my head, and the child's screaming is abruptly silenced. The skull-cracking pain sears into my brain, cross-cutting nerves to the quick of agony and then shifting to numbness. My head lolls painlessly to the side, but I have the impression that I am terribly hurt. I feel myself sinking downward, sinking into mists. Saliva bubbles from the corner of my mouth and the sinkings gather momentum, hurtling me through nothingness.

22

The odor of smoke is strong in my nose. I am looking at the ground-level of the cove through a veil of red stipplings. My eyelids close again of their own accord. But the reek taunts me, biting into my nostrils, holding me to consciousness when all desires float to the return of nothingness. The smoke clings to me, full of the reastiness of burning hair and pork, making me want to vomit.

Senses arouse themselves in the panic of nausea. If I vomit, it will kill me. The effort of paroxysm would obliterate me.

Perceptions are distant, but amplified in distortion to every sense, like loudspeakers in an auditorium.

Buy seats, only a nickel, one nickel to hear water gurgling from the pond. No, not worth a nickel, Lord.

There was a princess bruised by a pea through seven mattresses. The walls of my brain are separated from the world through seven thicknesses of mattress, but odors and sounds ricochet through the auditorium, bruising me. Thickness, all is thickness, mattresses are thick and Bibles are thick, night is thick and loneliness is thick, Rabelais is thick and Aquinas is thick, and God there is thickness in good bread and God in sunlight — but no, banish quickly the sunlight, the hidden vision of the eye recoils from brightness — thickness then in autumn greyness, kind to sight, and God there is thickness across bare backs of women and in the splendid glutens of their wombs, and there is thickness God in the pursed lips of shame — but no, banish quickly the pursed lips of shame, the hidden vision of the soul recoils from pietism — thickness then in wholeness, God, but hell, son, what you call wholeness I just plain call immoral and I'm preaching about that this very next Sunday — do you ride this bus often?

Yes sir.

You go to school somewheres?

Yes sir.

Me, I run a Bible College for young boys and girls about your age. Turn 'em into preachers to carry the Word out to the peoples of this fine country.

Yes sir.

You a pretty high-type boy, son?

Yes sir.

Don't drink or smoke or nothing? — keep yourself clean like God means you to?

Yes sir.

Got your share of problems, I guess?

Yes sir.

Don't fiddle around with the body? — keep the temple holy, eh?

Yes sir.

Awful nasty business young boys fall into these days, smoking dope, vandalizing, screwing around with girls.

Yes sir.

The Lord said to be mild and be temperant — that don't mean smoking dope, vandalizing and screwing, does it? I tell my students, like Saint Paul says — do you want to hear what I tell my students?

Yes sir.

Well then stop looking out the window and listen.

Yes sir.

That's a nice boy. You about sixteen, ain't you?

Yes sir.

That's when the devil starts working in your body.

Yes sir.

I tell my students — if you can't stand the devil torturing your manhood, get married — God allows that if you're too weak to be clean. I guess you're hoping to get married some day, son?

Yes sir.

Well, that's all right, that's okay because God says you can do it without condemning your soul to hell if you're too weak to resist the devil of the flesh. That's okay but it can be a nasty, nasty business. It can take you away from God without you hardly even knowing it. You just go and get lovey-doveying around with a woman and the devil puts fire in your unspeakables and you turn into a animal. I always say the angel flies right out of your heart. Do you think a man with fire in his unspeakables thinks about God? No, he turns his back to God.

He goes about his sinning and forgets God even exists. He can't be doing things like that and at the same time lifting up his soul to heaven and saying 'God be with me during this act,' now can he. It makes you blush to even think about it, don't it?

Yes sir.

So, even though God permits it, you're turning your back to Him every time you do it, ain't that right. That kind of thing can be nasty, believe me. Do you know what the books say about it? Course you don't. Well, here, lean over. I ain't ashamed to tell it to the world at the top of my lungs, but on a bus ain't the place for it. Do you know what screwing is rightly called?

Yes sir.

God calls it fornication. But you know what they call it in books? You just look it up in the books, in the dictionary or in Roget's Thesaurus. They call a male fornicator a libertine, a rake, a debauchee, a loose fish, a rip, a rakehell, a fast man, a gallant, a seducer, a lecher, a satyr, a goat, a whoremonger, a deceiver. And they call a female fornicator a courtesan, a prostitute, a strumpet, a tart, a hustler, a chippy, a broad, a harlot, a whore, a punk, a streetwalker, a Cyprian, a piece, a frail, a demirep, a wench, a trollop, a trull, a baggage, a hussy, a drab, a bitch, a jade, a skit, a rig, a quean, a mopsy, a slut, a minx, a harridan, a wanton, a Jezebel, a Messalina, a Delilah, a Thais, a Phryne, an Aspasia, a Lais, a concubine, a mistress, a fancy woman and a white slave. And listen to what they call the act — you know — the animal part of a man: impure, unclean, dirty, not be mentioned to ears polite, immodest, shameless, indecorous, indelicate, indecent, loose, obscene, bawdy, pornographic, concupiscent, lickerish, rampant, lustful, carnal, lewd, lascivious, lecherous, libidinous, erotic, ruttish, salacious, Paphian and dissipated! How do you think it makes God feel to see a young man like you, all of our fine young men and women, turning to Satan sprinkling their seeds wherever he tells them to? Do you ever listen to any of these lewd stories your friends might whisper in your ear?

Yes sir.

You mustn't listen to them. I used to but I conquered that when Jesus came into my heart. Now, if there's anything I hate, it's smut . . .

Gnats swarm in thickness at my ear. The face of a fattish older Reverend Mackay swirls through thicknesses filled with all of the virtuous connivers; and God there is thickness in the clottings of my chest. Smoke fills the thickness, holding me to life, holding me away from nothingness.

I reach up to brush gnats away. Fingers touch a scabbed knob behind my left ear. I feel it through my fingertips, not from inside through my head at all.

My cheek is on my right arm. The green odor of grasses mingles with smoke. I lick my lips and taste grass stems.

Rolling over on my back I hear someone else groaning through my lips. It mingles with the thunder of rustling grass and pulls a wall of migraine down over me.

The brook trickles. If I could get cold water in my belly, on my head, enough to calm these hurricanes of dizziness.

Slowly, easily, sitting on the grass, I scoot down the bank on heels and hands like a spider crawling.

My feet slide on mud and dangle in. The pain of coldness against arches sends other pain spinning. Not daring
to look down, I stretch my arm out. Palmfuls of chill
bathe my face. I sip from my cupped hand, again and
again. I toss it up and allow it to dribble down over my
head and shoulders, bathing the wound until the scab
softens.

Leaving my shoes wherever they may be, I rise up stiff-
necked, cautious, ready to sink back to earth the moment
nothingness returns. But my vision clears on the fat odor
of scorched pork.

I hobble rigidly, each step a carefully planned stratagem,
in the direction of the path.

What will they do to me? I stop against a tree as liquids
boil up in my skull. Do they think me dead? God. There
is no place else to go. I could not walk more than a few
feet.

Ligaments are drawn to strainings in the back of my
neck. All of this for touching a female! God. I will not
stand for it. If they continue to treat me this way, I will
leave. If Rauka glares at me, if Tombani torments me! —
I will leave. But now I must return to my hut and rest in
quietness. There is no place else to go. In the belly there
are knowledges that the brain cannot prove. The wrong-
ness is there. I will die if this continues — die in the belly
if not in the brain; die as these wretches are dead.

I round the corner of Oai's hut and stagger to sit on the
doorsill. Shadows from the opposite side stretch almost
to my hut. I will wait here, wait until I see what they
will do to me.

The compound bustles in brilliance. Nothing is brilliant,
but there is brilliance in the air, festive and smoke-strin-

gent. They sit, walk, crawl, toss, wallow on each side of the banana-leaf spread, eating food from it while other food is carried out through the door of the cooking hut. I am in shadow, but there is no hint of breeze. Will I ever be dry again? — dry of these incessant sweats.

Long rays of sunlight, blue with turnings of smoke, blare across the compound's dusk, barring the view of jungles beyond.

They ignore me. I push myself away from the door and shuffle barefoot across the packed earth toward my hut.

Picking up my mat, I ease myself inside where dust particles swim in a raw glow, a red and spacious glow, a glow of the savage. I kick the mat out straight and kneel to lie on it, pausing to stare back out the door for a moment. I cannot distinguish Ririkinger in the turmoil of festivities, but I see Tombani, sitting apart with his back to a post, smoking a tiny clay pipe. He gazes in my direction, probably seeing my sunlit face and shoulders in the door frame. Bracing myself, I attempt to glare him out of countenance, to pierce the barrier of smoke, to salvage my self-respect with this defiant glowering. He contemplates me absently with an expression of great gentleness and sympathy, his figure radiating the serenity of age. My sight dims from somewhere within me in vague embarrassment and my attitude seems suddenly childish.

The sun parches my face and I melt into weakness, lowering myself, with my hands gripping the window ledge, until I am lying back with my head on the mat in a furnace of golden light that smells of coconut sourness and burnt hog, waiting, waiting for something, listening to their laughter and shouting . . .

23

"Come, friend."

His voice is distant, mingled with the pale ocean of my beard.

"Come, friend."

A ragged toenail scrapes against my rib, catching in underarm hairs. How long did I sleep between the first call and the second? I brush the foot away and abandon myself to the pressure of drowsiness.

"Come," he insists, and I recognize the childish voice of Veedlie.

"What do you want?" I ask, without opening my eyes.

"You do not eat."

"I am full and very full."

"You eat."

"I am sick. Go away." His toe grates into my armpit again, and I open my eyes to the silver glare of twilight.

"You come, kulangu," he says again, with no inflection in his voice. "You eat betel. Fat Oai takes his mate."

"Does fat Oai ask me?"

"Fat Oai asks."

Strange gratification awakens me to the courage to move. There was something in fat Oai's glance after all, something that makes him request my presence at his marriage. I climb to my feet, dumb with a headache but touched that I am wanted.

Following Veedlie through my door, the freshness of evening air settles over my shoulders. In the somber light of dusk, I see that all vestiges of the feast have disappeared and that the earth is once again swept clean. Against the background blackness of the forest, the inside of the cooking hut glows full of the pinks of an invisible fire. I stand still, stretching myself to full height and inhale the balm of jungle stagnation, cool and moist, dampening the foul after-odors of the feast.

A shadow crosses the compound, hurrying from the cooking hut to Oai's hut where the villagers are gathered.

He arrives before we are half across the compound and I watch him drop to the ground and blow sparks from the punk he has carried. A flame crackles in green wood, expelling a column of thick white smoke straight into the air and lighting the undersides of bellies and flanks and breasts that mill around in the half-light.

Little Veedlie leads me around the group to a point near the opening of fat Oai's hut where Tombani squats on his haunches against the flickering wall.

The old man glances up at me, his eyes reflecting fire-light and removes his pipe long enough to say: "You sit here, friend," patting a place beside him on the ground. His voice is soft and cordial, with no undertones of apology, but simply as though nothing had occurred between us earlier. In my dullness, I reach up and finger the bruised lump which fills the cup of my hand, wondering for a moment if I have not suffered the violence in a dream. He replaces the tiny pipe between his teeth and pats the ground again. Shaking my head in bewilderment, I squat beside him and lean back against the retained warmth of the wall.

Behind us, the hummings and screechings of night crea-tures and the croaking of frogs begin to float out from the jungle. The fire of green twigs, perhaps symbolic of puberty, pops loudly and shoots its sparks in all directions. Rauka parades toward us with her long staff and I see the giant silhouette of Oai trailing after her.

The crone plants herself directly in front of us, facing the crowd and all motion ceases in the firelit semicircle. Fat Oai and a girl stand together before her, the three of them forming a triangle. Faces are stoic, expressionless in the firelight. I watch the flames through the wide opening between Rauka's legs.

Without moving her feet, and without speaking, she turns the upper part of her body toward fat Oai, who steps forward so close that I can hear his dolorous breathing. He raises his left arm and she places a thin armband of braided bamboo around it above the biceps, weaving the loose ends together with rapid manipulations of her fingers. Then she turns from him toward the girl, whom I cannot see; but from the writhings, I judge that she is placing an armband on her also.

"What is she doing?" I whisper in Tombani's ear, my voice cold with the reticence of our recent violence.

"She mates them," he answers, turning his head to speak quietly to me, but keeping his eyes averted to the ceremony. I draw back from the bitterness of his breath.

The crowd relaxes into fidgetings as Rauka secures the girl's armband and steps back away from her. Tombani rises to his feet with a grunt.

"We go," he says down at me, nudging my elbow with his knee to urge me up. Irritation throbs into the ache of my head at the gesture.

"It is finished?" I ask, pulling my arm away from his knee.

"It is finished," he says, his voice assuming the resonance of something profoundly final, more like the announcement of death than of a marriage ceremony. The hush taints the atmosphere, felt from the hearts of all, a longing, a sadness of accomplished pain.

Rauka turns, glares down at us and hurries past the fire into the night. She is followed by the jostling backsides of all the other women except Oai's new mate, who steps over the door beside us, a spectre of loneliness.

Oai stands motionless in the firelight, his head lowered, his gaze indrawn in his own isolation as no man speaks to him, no man laughs and pats him on the back and congratulates him. The other males are ranging themselves in a large semicircle extending from the sides of the hut in an unbroken line around the front, sitting cross-legged before the fire and facing the open door.

Peering above their heads, I see the shadowy figures of women disappearing through the gloom into their huts, leaving the compound deserted except for our firelit circle.

My pain, my fatigue are blanketed as my attention becomes absorbed in the black hulk staring dejectedly into the flames, and I am drawn to speak to him, to say some encouraging word in his ear.

All of the men are in place except Tombani and me. They give off an aura that gradually penetrates to my intelligence, an aura not of rawness or severity, but one transformed by portents of pity, of sympathy, swelling in poignancy when young Oai stirs himself and waddles to the door of his hut and climbs inside. I squint after him, squint at the black hole as the door swings shut replacing it with a barrier of solidity, alive with dancing reflections from the flames.

A movement at the end of the circle attracts my attention. Betel nuts and branches and the bamboo shoots are being passed around. Tombani's grip closes around my elbow and he shoves me toward an empty space near the center of the circle.

"Why do we stay here?" I ask, pulling my elbow away from his clutch.

"To keep evil from entering," he answers glumly, nodding toward the closed door.

In the earth-bound simplicity of his words, I am stirred with a first hint of real sympathy for these men. We do not sit here in celebration, there is not the slightest trace of ribaldry; no, we form a circular wall before Oai's door to assure him that evil will not get past us to threaten him this night. Expressions are sober with understanding, sober with the duty we perform sitting out here helping the children bend themselves to an awesome conformity demanded of life. Rauka's gummed words come back to me: "We leave you in sunlight, and we go back and wait in shadow." And in the waiting, all obey the commands of living, the shadows of existing.

Tombani shells a betel nut and pops it into his mouth, folding the fibrous husk and laying it on the ground between his thighs.

"You take betel," he says through loud crunching.

I obey, choosing one and passing the rest to the thick-lidded man on my left. He accepts them without smiling, without looking into my face.

"We stay here all night?" I ask Tombani, peeling the nut and tossing the husk away.

"No, when it is over we go."

Veedlie has jumped up and retrieved my discarded betel shell. He holds it between his hands and brushes it vigorously up and down on his teeth and Tombani explains I must use the fibrous inside as a toothbrush, to clean my teeth. Little Veedlie hands the salivaed shell back to me, and I imitate Tombani, placing it on the ground between my thighs.

"Eat," Tombani commands impatiently, his brows lowering over the shadows of his eyes. I drop the large kernel into my mouth and bite down on it. Bitterness freezes my jaws for a moment, but I chew until it crumbles, filling the space between my lips and gums with fragments that have the taste and texture of green peanuts.

Tombani is dipping a straw into the bamboo shoot and bringing it to his lips. He tells me it is poki, a fine powder made from pulverized sea shells and that I must take only enough to sweeten the betel or it will blister my mouth. I dip the straw into the black hole of the shoot and feel it contact softness. The powder begins neutralizing, not sweetening the sourness in my mouth, and I bring it to my lips on the wet straw several times until the bitterness has turned into a flow of bland saliva that must be swallowed in tricklings.

"Keura," Tombani announces more amiably, handing me a tree branch. When I hesitate, he tells me to bite off some of the bark and chew it up with the betel and poki mixture in my mouth. I place it to my lips, feel the wetness of others' gnawings and tear off a strip between my teeth. Spicy fumes fill my mouth and nose with a coolness that burns, and I see that it has turned the contents of Tombani's mouth blood red. A dry scorch is clamped over my ears and cheeks as I swallow and chew in a movement of my jaws that becomes almost hypnotic. Senses are thrown into a tangent and concentrated as the fire begins to separate in my vision with the rise of fever to my face, becoming two fires and then fusing into one and separating again in a constant swivel of fusion and separation. Reaching up, I pat my cheeks with the palms of my hands. My jaws react as leather, stiff and nerveless. I move my head on the creaking ratchet of my neck, toward Tombani, who is watching me closely, and his face separates into two and flows back together again as the fire did. Drunkenness rises up, rolling in vast clouds through my brain.

God forgive me. I'm getting drunk at a funeral. No, a wedding. I'll do something wrong and get bashed in the head again.

"Are you all right, friend?" I hear Tombani ask.

"I am dizzy."

"It is betel."

"I see strange things."

"It is betel. Things dance. Sight dances and tongue dances and head dances."

It is like bolting a bellyful of whiskey on a hot day. I cling to reality with intense concentration.

"You like?" Tombani's voice penetrates an underthrumming of deafness.

"I like," I say too loudly. "It is good."

"You have enough?"

"Yes."

"You tell legend?"

"What legend?"

"Legend." He smiles in double images of kindness. "The tongue dances and legends are told."

His information is late and far away. I think, with tremendous intelligence, that I must tell a legend, but only the grossest images come to mind. I must not, I tell myself firmly, I must not tell grossness. I must not mention woman.

A legend is being told. The first native on the right, an elder, scoots on his behind up to the fire and speaks in a chanting tone of voice, not singing, but speaking his phrases in cadenced monotony.

. . . *goes in full day to the top of the great hill where bushmen live, goes alone, and at the top of the hill he stops and sees below the cliff a serpent in curl. He gnaws through a branch and takes away the leaves with his hands and bites through its croppings with his teeth until he has a pole with two legs.*

Pain streaks through my ear, but I am grinning, swallowing back the urge to ask: "Pardon me, kulangu, but whom are you speaking about?" Cheapness, all is cheapness within me, cheapness wells up and abounds in my private night.

. . . and he holds the pole before him and leaps from the cliff, burying the pole legs in the earth on each side of the serpent-head, with such force the branch pierces his side. Then he takes the live serpent and carries it to Rauka who places it in her basket to guard us against the bushmen. Each day she puts fire to the snake to make it hate, and when it hates she shows it the head of the bushman she keeps; and one day we know she sends the serpent back to the bush and the serpent finds a bushman and hating him for the burnings, kills him.

That's a noble and dull damned story, I think, swallowing back words as blood warms to tempest in me, and we are telling legends wherever men are gathered, but not legends of snakes. A party of men sitting around and drinking and telling legends always of ass, always gurgling and giggling, somehow sure that laughter is good and makes the legends good until the white-bellied ones come in and sneer and call it cheapness. Cheapness, they make it cheapness, the whited ones. What is good, you call cheapness, Reverend Mackay, with your shame and your platitudes. Our great struggle, friends, is to overcome our lower natures. Overcome, hell. And where is it so low, and how is it so low? Overcome? No, cover up, Reverend, cover up ass in your cheapness.

And here and now — no ass and no cheapness — stars are out and when you look up they separate and draw together in swarms. The sky's full of them, God, full, close there, spread out over the treetops.

What's he talking about? I focus on his fire-streaked face, on his chanted words, earthbound and guttural, eerie in the night, tying heaven to earth.

. . . and the bushman comes and takes his child's head away and Maigna waits for him in the night, waits for him to return, waits sitting against the wall with his boar spear. He hears the noise in the night and he rises to his feet and waits for the door to open and he pushes his boar spear through the bushman's body, and in daylight he carries it to Rauka who takes the head from the body and smokes it for her hut, tying it to the ceiling, and Maigna drags the body into the river for the gators to eat.

I wonder what fat Oai and his lady are doing in there. Looking up at the blank door which pulsates with my heartbeat I feel myself grinning again; but the grin fades once more in my loathing for this thing that I have become. Is it the betel? — the concussion?

Concentrate, I command myself. Concentrate and seek to revive right feelings. Think of the night and the lonely, lonely world behind those latticed walls; and let compassion crowd out the cheapness.

A giant moth sweeps into the light, fluttering silver above the flames.

They take their turns, narrating their endless legends of heroism which has no other motivation than duty. All of it is duty, all acts and all emotions foreordained by the sterile compulsion of duty, never of pleasure or desire or free choice, making all things that would be nourishing in freedom become tasteless because of their slavery to elemental nature. What will I tell them when my turn comes? Will I tell them about the great heroes of history and fiction? Will I slump to the earth and be dead drunk before they get to me? Will I invent some legend about love and translate it into their language? Yes, love — the unknown chemistry the ghost mystery of this land.

You do not know love, and yet you see its faces all around you, for love has many faces. Love is first in the movements of things which cannot feel and which cannot reason but which are given inclinations by their natures. In this love a tree loves the air, for its nature inclines it to rise up in the air, and the pond loves the river, for its nature inclines it to unite with the river.

And again love is in the senses of things which can feel and smell and taste, and man has this love and animals have this love, for it is the inclination of the eyes to love what they see as pleasurable, to love beauty; and it is the inclination of the ears to love what they see as pleasurable, to love silence and sound; and it is the inclination of the body to love what it sees as pleasurable, to love food and drink and air and reproduction and all other things that nature demands for it.

And again love is in the spirit of things which can reason, and man alone has this love, for it is the inclination of the spirit to love what it sees as good, to love thoughts and ideas and truth. And the appetites of these loves are many, for there are the sense appetites in animals and man and the rational appetites in man alone, so that human love is both of the senses and of the spirit.

And there are three kinds of human love, which are love of yourself, which is a good love; and love of friendship, when you love someone because he is good and because he loves you in return, which is a better love; and love of benevolence or kindness, when you love someone for himself alone and not because of any good to yourself, which is a higher love than any because it makes you grow out of the boundaries of your world and into the boundaries of his world.

And of all the faces of love, the causes are only three, which are knowledge, for you cannot love that which you do not know; and goodness in the loved object, for love is a movement of the appetites toward that which it sees as good, and you must see goodness in an object before you can love that object; and likeness, for loving yourselves you love most that which is most like you.

And the goal of love is union with the loved object. And this is the difference between knowledge of a thing and love of a thing. You can see and know an evil thing without seeking union with it and therefore without its harming you, for in order to know a base thing, you must raise it up to your level as in order to know something sublime you must lower it down to yourself; whereas when you love a base thing you go down from your level to unite with it, as when you love a sublime thing you are raised up above yourself in an attempt to unite with it. Love always seeks union with the loved object, as the moth seeks union with the flame; and in the appetites of the senses, this object is pleasure and in the appetite of the spirit this object is goodness. The sunlight of your lives comes when both of these appetites are satisfied, when the spirit sees as good that which the body sees as pleasurable.

But when the body insists in a pleasure which the soul

sees as evil, or when the body rejects a movement which the soul sees as good, then there is cloudiness in man's humanity. When the senses experience pleasure, they desire to repeat the experience regardless of whether the experience be good for the man or evil for the man, for the senses do not reason, do not know right from wrong; and if the spirit does not step in and forbid the body to repeat an evil act which gives it pleasure, the senses will move the body to gain the pleasure again and again until it grows from the weakness of a thin strand of bark into a habit which is stronger than your strongest woven rope, too strong even for the spirit to control. Therefore, if the body must have a pleasure which is not good for the man, the goal of the body will be fulfilled but the goal of the spirit will never rest in satisfaction, and there are forever clouds within you. The moth there — its senses love brightness. The pleasure of brightness is not evil, for if the moth fluttered around the brightness of sunlight on a wet leaf, it would remain unharmed; but now it will dive into the flames because it has no reason to tell it that the brightness of the flames, which are its pleasure, are in this instance its destruction. Around the leaf, the pleasure would be the same, but it would not be an evil to its body since there would be no danger of death.

It is the same with man. Once the body experiences the pleasure of physical ecstasy it desires to repeat that pleasure as often as possible. But the body cannot reason, the body would feel the same pleasure whether its partner be the man's wife or his sister or his grandmother. You draw back in horror from such a thought because your spirit can reason and tell you that the pleasure is an evil with his sister or his grandmother because it is against all of nature. But these things which are evil give the very same feelings to the body's senses as the pleasures of union with one's wife, which is seen as good by the spirit because it is right according to nature. The pleasure is no less when it is seen as good by the spirit, and then there can be sunlight. You do not see this, for you think that it is evil for a man to lie with a woman, so even though his body may know pleasure, there will be cloudiness because the spirit sees it as wrong. But it is not wrong. You say that it is zagata because when man is losing his semen he is losing his manhood, but it is man's nature to lose his semen, which returns to fill his body again with new strengths of manhood through all the days and nights of his youth. Such goodness you see as the moth diving into the flame, but it is rather the moth circling around the sunlight on a leaf. If it is good for the river to flow into the sea, which is its nature, and if it is good for navundi to bear new fruit for our bodies, which is its nature, then the spirit must see as good that which the body sees as pleasurable in mating, for it is man's nature to lie with woman and to care for the children she produces with him, and if man loves the woman, then the appetites of his body will be satisfied in pleasure and the appetites of his spirit will be satisfied to tell him that it is good, and both his body and spirit will rejoice in sunlight. So the spirit must tell the body which of its pleasures are like the sunlit leaf to the moth and which are like the flame. But what the spirit tells the body must be real or man will hate those things which nature provides as both pleasurable and good and love those things which are pleasurable and evil. What Oai does tonight is both pleasurable and good, although he is too young for it, but because his spirit tells him a lie, tells him it is evil, he hates what he should love.

But all of these majestic truths are voiced to the accompaniment of another simultaneous image wherein one part of me strolls through the halls of some pagan castle where thousands of women loll on couches and on the floors, beckoning to me, and I am smiling cordially out over a sea of breasts and arms and thighs, trying to decide which one . . .

A mulch rises up to fill my throat as night returns to its single vision of trees and firelight and earth and shadows. Why this sudden upsurge of emotion? God — is there not enough reason for it? Yes, but why now? Why at this moment? I don't know. I want to go where there is quietness and lose the present and the past and the future, erasing for once the delusion of strength and age and beard that urges man to become dry-eyed and crusted as the years move him away from childhood. No definite thing causes this welling up. Only some distant burden of futility wherein my words have contrasted a truth to the terrible reality of this world of Nuni where man is merely one of a group of mournful slaves to elemental nature. "If fat Oai does not make a baby from one long rain until the next, he is driven into the jungles forever . . ."

Mumblings within me counter the mumblings outside. A legend is droning through the greater darkness and my own inner mumblings have the cumbersome bulk of vividness that sometimes comes with drunkenness, dragging my head down as I bury my eyes agains the knobs of my knees. Must I become like them to exist? Must I learn to despise fat Oai if he does not produce? Must I learn to bash in the head of a man who touches an infant female? It is too late and I am too old to change the setting of my heart. How, then, am I to bring back the focus of hope? I know what would do it, but that cannot be found here. A kiss would do it — not the kiss of passion — God no, in such extremity, passion is a luxury — no, the kiss of repose, the kiss that pours the substance of affection into the heart, the kiss that allows the heart to replenish itself with enough health to dilate back to normal.

Tombani touches my arm. I lift my head and look at him with pink coals capturing the corner of my eye. After a long moment's hesitation I reach out to receive the betel he drops into my palm, feeling my body bend my will in some great callousness. If not the kiss, I tell myself, then the betel. If not the strength of softness, then the tough weakness. I bluster, overriding objections within me. How close am I, with this betel, to the new solution, the unexpected solution — the escape route of drunkenness — knowing a familiar premonition of caution and knowing too that the end of such a route is even greater blackness. But with betel all of this can be dulled. With betel there are promenades in palaces of orgy, taking me away from hardness and insects and the grit of dirt beneath my bare feet. With betel there is numbness.

Slowly, and with infinite regret, I allow my thumbnail to pierce the outer shell and begin peeling away the husk, aware that Tombani has handed me my own private hell, aware that if I take this one, I am sacrificing the sunlight for the swamp, for I will take many others and forever in the building of habit; but if I interpose my will and throw this one into the night, the chain will be broken and I can then freely choose to take others or not. But a mosquito drones loudly between me and the stars and my belly puffs out its demands for escape.

Biting down into the betel, I turn to take the poki shoot from Tombani, relieved that the struggling is over, relieved that I have opened the doorway to illuminations. Now I can become one of them, for are not all slaves brothers? Only the masters differ; I a slave to my own appetites as they overcome the controls of my will; they, slaves to the laws of the winds and the tides and the times, the laws of nature — and we will be united in the two slaveries which produce the same effect . . .

Night closes in, a summer night of frogs and birds and dampness from the woods, swimming in brilliance and full of nameless temptations. I watch the moth swooping toward the flames, and it is my brother, going irresistibly to its pleasure. But no, it veers away and flutters off into the night. It did not go to its destruction! My heart swells within my chest, filling the cavity until I can scarcely breathe. Desperately I try to spit the betel out, to follow the moth away from the flame.

24

Rain is sifting gently over my body, strumming against the earth and rustling in the trees, pulsing to the fore and then fading away, pulsing and fading. I must move, but I am too wonderfully comfortable to make the effort.

I listen to hear the voice of legend, to hear frogs and nightbirds, but the world rests silent beneath the muffle of rain.

I open my eyes to view illumination, to view flames, but the world rests somber beneath the burden of night.

The heavens are a movement of lightning diffused behind low clouds, lightning flickering constantly without sound, pulsing and then fading away, pulsing and fading.

In moments of green glow, the world is sheathed in perpendicular rains and the forest is a black mass of silhouette.

Placing my hands in slosh, I push myself up to a sitting position and comfort leaves me to neck stiffness and head stiffness, pulsing and fading.

Strumming modulates to splashing and I hear the louder thump of drops through the dome of my skull. Silent lightning highlights the black hole of fat Oai's door, open now. It is over then. It is over and they have returned to their huts, leaving me where I lay.

No longer the stridor of smoke, no longer the reek of fat. I inhale the freshness of ozone, the purity of washed air, beginning the convoluted journey through pulsings and fadings to my feet and to marchings and staggerings. My hut is there, standing out green in lightning and disappearing from the world in blackness. It fascinates my gaze, flickering off and on.

I weave through my door and sink to the mat, listening to bubbling quietness. The rain is far away, silenced in thatch, pulsing and fading, pulsing and fading, God . . .

25

The pressuring needs of my body drag me from sleep, winding me through coilings and clawings in long paths to wakefulness. There is foulness in my mouth and foulness in my head and risings of foul digestion in my throat.

Beams and underthatch detach themselves from obscurity. I get to my feet and turn to the sunlighted opening where the hut's shadow throws its triangle on the earth before me.

Each step reverberates a clangor through my head, but the world is alive with freshness across the rain-washed compound. Morning sun gilds huts and foliage across the way, outlining them in sharpness. No puddle remains unabsorbed in the damp expanse of compound. The earth speaks to me through my bare feet, first in dryness and then in dampness as I step into the square before my door where the rain has blown in.

Where are my shoes? I cannot go far enough into the brush to hide myself without my shoes. I peer back to darkened corners of the inside while a faint spiraling of memory insinuates recollection into my brain. They must still be at the pond. Yes, I left them there after the scene with Ririkinger, after the bashing.

What happened yesterday? It is a strip of overlapping hints, a confusion. My brain is a thick muscle this morning, unflexed to recall, and all events simmer in vagueness; but the sun pours across the land in morning jubilation and birds transform its brilliance into songs. This is not the moment for worrying about yesterday. Earth and nature and humanity take decisions from man's hands and brains, telling me I must carry my body into the brush. I will go behind my hut where the foliage is dense and risk being seen. And what if I am? The observer will announce haughtily: "I find you in taboo. Your soul is now mine and you are dead to your own soul."

And I will smile and say, "Very well," and forget it.

As I step through the opening, nine women are marching single file from the pond path into the compound, carrying heavy packs of bananas and coconuts and leaves on their heads. A young man, carrying nothing but a long boar spear, leads them and another, similarly armed, brings up to the rear.

They amble toward the cooking hut, all ages, all sizes, the one following in the footsteps of the other. They balance the bundles atop their heads and glide smoothly, erectly, their arms to their sides.

The earth is sponge-softness beneath my bare feet and

the sponge-sweetness of morning absorbs acids from my heart as I pick my way through brush around the rear of my hut. Leaves fling their globules of rain in stipplings of chill against my bare flesh.

"Kulangu?"

I recognize Veedlie's voice calling from the front of my shack.

"Wait, kulangu," I answer.

When I return into the open, he is sitting before my door, his tiny fist buried in the socket of his sore eye in a frenzy of rubbing.

"Taeega, kulangu," I exhort, and his hand drops down on his belly. He looks up at me soberly, his sore eye closed and twitching, with an expression of resignation that is as old as nature. It is comic in the painful and touching way of such things, and the fullness of my sympathy goes out to this child who is in this moment so ageless.

Bending forward, I hold his face between my hands and tilt it up to the heavens to examine the sore where a crusted scab has been partially dislodged. It does not appear infected, but the scab is very thick, as though layers and layers were added to it through constant scratchings.

"Can you cook some water?" I ask.

He answers that he can, but stares at me with such blankness I must summon authority from my emptiness and command him to bring fire here, and a shell of water wrapped in navundi leaves.

While he is gone, I return inside my hut and kneel before the bundle of my belongings, searching until I find the stained white square of cloth that was once a handkerchief.

Activity and the delicious undercurrent of talk attracts

me quickly back to the door where I see that fat Oai is kneeling over a bundle of sticks, scooping through the wet surface of the earth to grey dust beneath in order to lay a fire. Others are gathered around Veedlie who is the center of some intangible excitement.

Holding the back of my neck, I step out, cringing from the hangover pain, and drop my handkerchief into the shell of cold water Veedlie holds between his cupped hands.

Expressions of wonderment and uneasiness are cast from eye to eye around the circle of men and boys, and I glance above them to see others gravitating toward the smoke of our fire, drawn to us from all directions; and it occurs to me that cheapness is resurging in my actions, that I am adding flourishes to my simple hope of treating Veedlie's eye, and that all of this is obviously taking on the aura of a mysterious ritual to these simple hearts.

Fat Oai crawls on hands and knees, gathering small rocks into his fists and placing them around the rim of the fire dugout. I look across the compound toward Tombani's hut and the scene immediately above the flames becomes liquid and wavery through the invisible up-flange of heat.

Taking the shell from Veedlie, I arrange the thick wrappings of navundi leaves and place it over the circle of rocks to boil. The curious group swells as I ease myself to the ground. They follow my example, sitting cross-legged on all sides and beginning the betel ceremony. No women approach, however. They remain in their distant occupations, idling in door frames or wandering in and out of the cooking hut.

A perceptible breeze flows southward from the jungle, enlivening the morning with an undertone of gaiety and comfort that makes the betel appear repulsive to me at this hour. I lean back against my hut, relieved not to desire it after my torments with it last night.

Fat Oai lumbers away from the blowing smoke, lifting his arms to his forehead. His lips drip redness from the betel he has already chewed this morning.

"You sit with me," I say directly to him. He weaves drunkenly, gazing down into my face and I understand that he is attempting to hold me in focus. The tender eyes of yesterday are bloodshot and glazed today, altering him from a splendid youth into a blubbery savage. I pat the ground and he eases his bulk down beside me with a cautious grin, a timid and somehow searching grin as though he were trying to remember me from some distant time, a touchingly childish grin in the face of a brute. He draws up his knees and rests his elbows on the clotted mud of their surface so that the fingers of both hands are locked together in front of him and stares down at his paunch. The wedding band digs deeply into the lardy flesh of his biceps, every woven strand visible at this close range.

I am about to speak to him, to say something kind to this dead-eyed child, when the sizzle of boiling water is born on the silence. I glance over to see flames licking out through holes between the rocks, burning the navundi leaves black and drawing thick white smoke from them. My handkerchief has ballooned out over the cup, like bread dough that has risen out of its container.

Pulling one of the longer branches from the fire, I snuff

out its flames against the wet dirt, break off the charred segment, and poke the handkerchief back into the water.

We wait in a silence of holiday vitality as they observe all actions with fascination, continually turning and nodding half understandings to one another.

My head begins to concentrate its pain into the lump behind my ear as their betel fumes join with the blowing smoke to permeate the little amphitheater before my hut.

Tension becomes tangible when I fish the steaming handkerchief from the water with my stick and wave it slowly back and forth to cool for a moment.

"Come, Veedlie," I say, caught up in their mood of melodrama and wishing now that I had known there would be an audience, wishing I had done this in private. What will Rauka think? Despite myself, I am adding little touches of showmanship that turn this simple operation into a hinted sorcery before their amazed eyes. Is it not probably taboo for anyone except the rauka to perform cures?

Veedlie, with that expression of simultaneous pride and terror that is so universally the property of children, plants himself staunchly before me and fingers his teeth-necklace.

"Lie here," I command, indicating the ground to my right as I fumble the steaming handkerchief into a square of four thicknesses.

He hesitates, ogling the vaporous white square and digging nervously at the yaw beneath his left ribs with his thumbnail.

"Come, kulangu," I urge gently. My words draw him from his fascination and he sinks down beside me, allowing me to guide his head into the pillow of my lap.

His face puckers with dread as I lower the soaked cloth, and although he does not whimper, his abdomen tenses to rigidity when the heat touches his eye, and his heartbeat throbs visibly against the drum of his flesh.

Naked bodies sit cross-legged on all sides, black against the background of morning foliage. Their shoulders are hunched forward and they are so engrossed in what I am doing that their chewings have slowed to unconscious ruminations. Two of them are leaning far to the side to see around fat Oai's body. All eyes are glassy from the betel, but in the intensity of their interest, the thick masks of savagery have been stripped from their faces to reveal expressions of groping concentration, of struggling communication; benign expressions I have not encountered here before — like those of a classroom of drunken students listening wall-eyed to a lecture on major logic.

Supporting Veedlie's head with one hand, I press the cloth over his eye with the other. A tremor jars his body and I look down to see that water dribbles from the corner of his eye across his cheek and into his ear. I mop it away with a swish of the handkerchief, leaving a glistening streak on his face. His eyes shuttle with every movement, following the whiteness, and it occurs to me that these people have never before seen a white cloth — that they have probably never seen an eye given the simplest treatment and that my activities must be akin to magic in their minds.

Veedlie's body relaxes from the initial shock as I apply the compress again and again until the last trace of scab has melted away and the wound is clean and neatly centered without suppuration or blood to form a new crust. Some antiseptic or salve might be all that is necessary, but

I have no knowledge of native herbs, no fats or oils from which to create a salve. For a moment I am tempted to use urine for an antiseptic, but I decide against it: if they recognized it, they would be outraged to think of applying taboo to a sore.

"You stay with me," I say, patting his side to tell him it is over. "You do not touch and I cure you."

He clambers to his feet and runs his fingers lightly over the smooth welt, as one might proudly examine a scar after an operation.

I douse the handkerchief in boiling water again and hang it over the door frame to dry as natives walk up to gape at the wound and at the miraculous cloth that wrought the cure. I tell myself that if I can keep the flesh around Veedlie's pock soft and clean, and prevent the itchiness of scabs from forming, the yaw may well dry and heal of its own accord.

Fat Oai drags his belly across my outstretched legs and pulls himself up to kneel with his hands on the door frame, not touching the handkerchief, but staring at it and bending forward to smell it. Others lean over him from all sides, their normal heads dwarfed by the massiveness of his, and yet — here against my nose — his profile is that of a little child.

The stench of their betel-soured closeness draws the tendons of my neck tight as I stare out through the cage of their legs, resisting the temptation to brush the mealy texture of mud from their knees. Instead, I push against their legs, hard enough to make them open a hole through which I crawl out into the open air.

Veedlie is gazing heavenward, allowing two elders to

contemplate his yaw, his cheeks puffed out smooth with pride. I call to him to accompany me to the pond for my shoes, determined to keep him in sight until the sore is cured so that I may watch him and discourage him from scratching the eye. Now that I have made such a spectacle of the treatment, it occurs to me that if I do not succeed, their contempt for me will be boundless.

Natives are drifting toward a table of giant green na-vundi leaves, spread on the ground from the door of the cooking hut almost to Tombani's hut, when we round the corner returning from the pond. Veedlie sidetracks into his hut and rejoins me with two coconut halves and we walk to my hut to leave my shoes before going to join the villagers for our meal. The men sit on one side of the leaves and the women on the other. I have not yet seen men and women mingling in any community activity.

Before we have taken our seats on the ground, the sour-ness of the root and coconut odors cuts my appetite, but Veedlie stoops and fills his shell with dripping handfuls.

I dig my fingers into the warmness of a white and green concoction I have not eaten before, and brace myself against the taste, but when I bite into it, I am surprised to find it good. Taking it away from my face, I study it more closely. It is a thick pudding or cake, made by alternating layers of the small green unpeeled bananas with layers of coconut meat, wrapping them in navundi leaves and cooking them. Its blandness revives my appetite and I eat with good hunger.

As I reach for another helping, I am struck by the com-plete impersonality of these people. We are physically close, with arms underreaching arms, with bodies rubbing against bodies, and yet it is as though none of them recognizes the presence of another soul here. Each is totally immersed in the business of eating. No one speaks. There are no sidelong glances, no spontaneous smiles and noddings of the head. We sit and lounge and stand in a jumble of humanity, like animals at a trough.

And always — I realize — I am searching the crowd, searching for something. I admonish myself to forget them, to be as they are, but my attentions go out to them, studying their faces —

a woman there, with thick betel-stained lips and a strongly modeled face that would be handsome in another setting, stops chewing long enough to bite at the corner of her fingernail and spit the fragment over her shoulder — studying their bodies —

fat Oai there, sitting cross-legged like some enormously fat oriental god, his flesh sleek and full, his black paunch creasing at his thighs and hanging down to a vast circle over his mud-caked genitals, but holding his body square and erect, with one hand cupped over his knee, gazing blankly.

And always I look this morning for that which fills me with dread — the frowns of Tombani or Rauka; and that which fills me with hope — the smile of Ririkinger; fearful now that something may have happened to the child, that she may be punished for allowing me to touch her.

As they finish and get to their feet, they leave imprints in the soft dirt, imprints of knees and toes where the women have sat, imprints of buttocks and ankles where there have been men. Others are constantly joining the group to make their own imprints, to dig into the foods for their turn. They favor the root mixture that is so detestable to my stomach and scarcely touch the banana and coconut cake I am eating.

There appears to be no set time for meals and no call to announce that food is ready. It is scarcely midmorning and we are being served. They come to it as they get hungry and leave whenever they are satisfied.

Ririkinger appears across the navundi spread with a group of girls. I wave to her, but she ignores me as though she has never seen me, and I suppose that she has been forbidden to recognize me again.

But when she has planted her tiny knees in the imprint of a woman's knees, she glances over to me with an open smile that allows me to see her teeth.

"Ririkinger," I say softly. She lowers her head timidly, her jaw wrinkling out with delight and peers secretly at me from under her infant brow. Primly she fills her shell with food.

The sun and hot food raise sweats on my body and the ache behind my ear throbs through my skull. I stifle a belch and rise to my feet to go where there is shade.

Veedlie tells me to follow him to the open shade hut where it is cool.

Rejecting the impulse to nod cordially to the other eaters and say something polite, such as: "I certainly enjoyed the meal," I cover the knot behind my ear with my cupped hand and follow Veedlie's strut around the end of the leaf spread.

Easing myself down on one of the mats beneath the open hut, I feel its retained coolness from last night's soaking and inhale the sweetness of wet bamboo. Veedlie, holding his shells against his chest with one hand and pressing on his groin with the other, announces gravely that he is "going into the brush" and will return to rest with me afterward. I warn him not to touch his eye, but the food has produced its heavy narcosis in me, insulating me behind a wall of drowsiness from caring whether he scratches or not, insulating me from everything except the urgent need to succumb to slumber. With my arm folded under my cheek, I watch him trotting on his shadow toward his hut at the far end of the compound.

A fly is crawling across my lips, dragging me from the fringes of unconsciousness with a snort. It drones into the air, sluggish and glistening with green highlights. Time has been suspended, but if I have slept at all, it has been only a moment, for I can see the eaters beyond the stained supporting pole of this hut, bending over their food. Ririkinger's sun-ridged spine shines with sweat at each protruding nodule.

Tombani appears, crossing from sunlight into shadow to join me. Through drugged senses I watch him and listen to the fly's insistent buzzing, in a growing fury of irritation. Now I will never be able to rest. The old man shuffles around my feet to my back, clutching a tiny clay pipe between his withered lips and carrying a wilted palm frond before him.

Turning over on my back, I squint up into his eyes which glisten dully, yellowish and clouded.

"Sleep, kulangu," he commands as one would command an animal, without kindness, without humanity.

He nudges a mat into place with his foot, squats over it almost to the ground and falls back on his rump with a grunt. Holding the palm frond in both hands, he waves it slowly over the full length of my body.

"It is good," I mumble, grateful beneath my constant upsurgings of resentment at his manner of speaking to me.

His mouth purses over his pipe and he does not deign to answer.

"It is good," I insist, my scalp prickling with determination that he shall reply as he has demanded that I always reply.

"It is very good," he concedes unconcernedly, his words accompanied by an exhalation of twist smoke that is carried back into his eyes, provoking tears. He shakes his head and raises his face to the thatched ceiling above us, blinking out tears that roll down his tattooed cheeks. In all of it, I see a white-headed patriarch weeping above the constant movement of the fan, and my drowsiness becomes pity and tenderness for the sight. The double row of listless green daggers swishes over me.

26

I awake in the turmoil of nervousness, staring into Ririkinger's eyes and feeling her infant body wriggling on my stomach. Her eyes are open and her mouth coos in a half smile, and for a moment she is my own Cindy, long ago, crawling into bed on Sunday morning to play with me. But senses return in fear and astonishment, telling me simultaneously that I am in danger of being clubbed again, that the child is like all children in her response to affection, and that she is not alone. I am overwhelmed with infants who crowd giggling around me, crawling and pretending to sleep between my legs, at my sides, under my armpits. Their naked bodies suffocate me, bathing me in sweat, but I feel the bombardment of fulfillment in my heart.

Ririkinger pulls at my beard and squeals " 'kinger,

'kinger, 'kinger," proudly, as though she were showing her name off to her nameless companions.

I search the compound for danger. The village bakes beneath full sun, deserted of life. Little Veedlie sleeps curled up on his side on the mat Tombani occupied, and the palm frond lies where it has been tossed, drying in the sun, each daggered leaf crisping to a sheath.

The children pretend to be sleeping, with close-lipped smiles on their unmarked faces. From somewhere within me I hear chuckling filter through my beard and their bodies are brought to live squirmings once more, as each seeks a more favored place.

"You are pretty, Jon," they begin chanting, repeating the phrase from all angles until I tell them to be quiet for fear of arousing the adults.

A movement around the corner of the cooking hut attracts my attention and I kiss Ririkinger quickly and drop my head back to the mat. If it is Tombani returning, I will snore, pretend I am asleep. Nerves rattle in my chest and I hold my eyes tightly closed, feeling muscles relax on all sides of me, listening to the immediate hush of the children.

We wait, all movement dead except my loud snoring, wait in the upbuilding of tensions as footsteps pad slowly in our direction.

"Go," Tombani's voice mumbles from a few feet away, calmly as he spoke to me at the pool yesterday.

I concentrate on my snoring, waiting for something to happen. Nerves and muscles tighten against me from the children's bodies.

"Go!" he screams, his calloused foot thumping into

Ririkinger's body. I feel coolness where she has been lying, and a miniature hurricane of movements beneath my legs and armpits as other children are kicked and driven away.

My snoring continues to rasp above whimperings and cries and my body is locked in rigidity against quakings of dread as I wait for violence, wait for the club, wait in fear and outrage.

Rise up and kick him in the belly, my heart urges. You are stronger than he. Rise up and possess your rights as a human, your rights to the love of children, but the knot on my head swells to fill my consciousness and my snoring hypnotizes me as the children's snivelings fade into the distance; and despair spreads its leaden weight through my stomach. All that is right, all that is human is taboo. If I move to counter it, I am clubbed. The body's fears paralyze the soul's actions to rightness.

I hear the crackle of bamboo and open my eyes to see Tombani sitting against Veedlie's back. The old man keeps watch over us, his face in repose, mild and kind as he begins peeling a betel. I must not hate him so, but in the swimming aftermath of tension and disappointment, he becomes the cause not only of my loneliness, which is bad enough, but even worse, the cause, too, of my cowardice, driving me to be ruled by the body's fears rather than the heart's hungers. In some distance of perception, I know that he is turning me into the animal the rest of them are, nullifying the sum of my past existence, nullifying the habits of past experience, turning me back into a thing that I am not, through the pressures of the body's fears. I stare into the old man's benign face, rested and full of complacency. Could he ever understand that he is constructing a prison around my soul? No, he acts, and his actions produce actions within me that are dragged to a level of cowardice, and it is self-loathing which severs me from my manhood.

When midafternoon sun has almost reached my mat, Rauka's call breaks the droning silence. She is standing in the bushes near Oai's hut, leaning on her staff, crying in the monotonous repetition of a beggar: "To the water. To the water. To the water."

Veedlie rolls over, rubbing sleep from his eyes and Tombani raises his kinky head to gaze dully about him, struggling to open his lids against betel heaviness that puffs out the flesh beneath them.

"What is it?" I ask, pulling myself up to a sitting position with my hand on one of the supporting poles and feeling sweats dribble downward beneath my beard.

"We go to the pool." Veedlie yawns.

I get to my feet and step around Tombani, who is lost in his betel dreams, sitting in a trance. Taking Veedlie's face in my hands, I examine the wet flesh around his eye. It is open and clean.

"We go," he says, shaking Tombani's shoulder. The old man unwinds himself, his stare fixed and unmoving, and we straggle out into the sunlight. Others appear through their doorways into the compound and gravitate toward the pond where Rauka continues to call. All walk or stumble as in great drowsiness, and I wonder thickly if the food is not somehow drugged.

White cloud banks billow up in massive grandeur behind Oai's hut toward the east, and a stronger breeze stirs the treetops, but the earth is dry and hot beneath my bare feet.

We join the crowd at the path, ambling along behind sun-flecked shoulders. Tombani precedes me, bent in stupor, his club hanging from his hand at his side. No one speaks, although there is a vague pleasantness in the sounds of splashing water around the curve of the path.

The pool is obscured from sight by a mass of naked bodies beneath the canopy of thick overhanging foliage. I observe mud-streaked bodies slide into the cold waters, gasp with shock, rub themselves briskly for a moment and climb back out on the bank, clean and refreshed. The entire village appears to be bathing at the command of Rauka, and the change between their drugged and worn appearances when they go into the water and their fresh and relaxed features when they climb back out becomes a change in the atmosphere as talk springs up, as laughter bursts forth from the group of men and cacklings from the women. They bathe together, helter-skelter, keeping the pool full of black heads, but as soon as they are back on the bank, they drift toward groups of their own sex.

The water is completely muddied when we step into it, but none of the chill is lost. I notice that Tombani's eyes are gathering focus, that the cold water is bringing him back to reality.

Squatting in the milky water, I allow my head to sink below the surface, and in the relief from lethargy, there is relief from despair. I hold my breath and massage my scalp with all my force, and in the darkness, it occurs to me that Veedlie should not have his head under the water, that the filth will infect his eye.

My pants drag at me when I crawl out, full of bulkiness and cumbersome. Would it make the slightest difference to them whether I wore them or not? Why, in such a world, do I cling to a useless habit of modesty? It would be much more comfortable to cast them aside; but something within me forbids it. Perhaps someday I will bring my habits into conformity with good sense, but for a time yet, the lingering remains of my former self must be respected.

Already the tone of the village has changed when I turn from the path. Men are gathering in the shaded alleyway between Tombani's hut and the hut next to it, sitting with their backs to the walls facing one another; the infants run toward me. Ririkinger grabs my hand, screaming delight as others crowd around. She swings on my arm as though it were a rope, drawing her feet up into the air and shutting her eyes tight. I bend to the side and lower her to the ground with great gentleness while the other children grab me around my legs and struggle along beside me with each step I take. Their screams fill the compound with laughter, and I look up, understanding nothing. Women are observing me with broad grins on their faces as I proceed toward the circle of men. Why should they club me one afternoon and laugh at my predicament the next?

Weighted down with these infants, I am about to turn back into the woods and play with them when Rauka stalks across the compound, blathering insults, and drives the infants away in a rage. She sneers at me through a drool of betel and I feel my mouth drawing to the tightness of resignation. She storms away, still shaking her head and talking to the earth in a loud voice.

"Go to hell," I mutter after her as the women bend double with paroxysms of laughter — adding freshness to the torpor of the day. For a brief moment, when the children were clinging to me and when the adults were enjoying the sight, this might have been any place on earth. For a moment there was naturalness.

Glancing toward the cloudbank which is building upward in rolls of clean-cut whiteness against the blue of the sky, I go to take my place in the circle of men beside Tombani's hut, drawn there by a desire to belong, drawn toward the betel dynamism.

But first, before I begin to see double and think double, I must bathe Veedlie's eye once more.

Crossing my path, a child steps from the shadows and wanders toward the group of other children. His face is horribly lacerated, as though someone had carved every inch of his flesh, and it is swollen beyond any possible recognition of features.

I take my seat beside fat Oai and nudge him, pointing to the mutilated child, and ask him what has happened.

He explains, bending his head toward mine, that the child has been cut by Rauka three days now as all children are cut before being given a name; and that the cuts are packed with blue mud from the pond to make the designs beautiful.

Talking with fat Oai, my first impression of him returns. Now that this morning's betel has worn off and the bath has revived him, his eyes and his manner express a simplicity and an innocence that cut through all barriers of background and unite us in an understanding that would never be possible between Tombani and me, or even between Veedlie and me. I feel warmed and somehow com-

forted by his presence, as though some noble security lay
in his heart, as though he could be trusted. An intangible
movement of friendship draws us into easy speech, into an
unmistakable delight in one another's presence. Perhaps
his hulk gives the impression of solidity to his character,
perhaps his obvious suffering before he was mated, perhaps the fact that he, too, because of his abnormal size,
is different from the rest, is a stranger, an outcast from
normalcy. I think, listening to his childish voice and feeling the growth of affection for him, of Montaigne's reply
when asked how he explained his sublime friendship with
Etienne de la Boétie: "Because it was he, and because it
was I"; words written in the tower of an ancient French
château, brought to life in the black folds of this giant
savage where I sense the potential of great humanity.

The fire is brought, the water heated and the men watch
while I hold Veedlie's head in my lap and treat the eye in
repetition of this morning's performance; but I pay little
heed to it in my preoccupation with fat Oai.

"Why are the children not named until they are tattooed by Rauka?" I ask him. Veedlie opens his mouth to
answer, but Oai's voice dominates. He speaks with such
childish eagerness I cannot follow each word, but I end
up understanding that so many children die from the
cutting that it is considered a needless waste of time to
bother giving them names until the parents are certain
they will live to carry them through life.

"Who are the bushmen?" I say quietly, dipping the cloth
back into the boiling water.

"The bushmen live high in the hills," he answers stonily.
"They are evil."

"How, evil?"

"They come in the night to the fresh-water villages and they kill and carry our heads back to their bush villages. They tie them by the hair to their ceilings. Their huts are filled with heads of fresh-water villagers."

"They come often?" I ask in disbelief.

"Not often."

"You have seen them?"

"Yes."

"Where?"

"On trails in the woods. And by the high river. They are little and their flesh is never clean. They are filled with evil spirits."

"Do they come to Vanua?"

"At night sometimes to take heads."

"And what do you do when they come?"

"The rauka keeps snakes in her baskets and she makes the snakes hate the smell of the bushmen and when they come in the night, she puts her snakes in the path and when the snakes smell the hated bushmen they strike them and kill them."

"Do you find the dead bushmen's bodies when they have been killed by the snakes?"

"No." He smiles slyly, almost whispering as his eyes dart around the circle.

"How do you know the snakes kill them?"

"Rauka says so. Rauka knows," he whispers again, warning me with his eyes that I am not to speak of such things further. Turning, he takes the betel and passes it to me. I tell Veedlie his treatment is finished, and lean back against the woven bamboo as men crowd around him once more to examine his eye.

Selecting a betel for myself, I dump the remainder into the outstretched palm of a youth to my right.

While some of the men continue examining Veedlie, I reach above my head and hang my handkerchief to the low eaves of Tombani's roof, inserting the corners into the ragged thatch.

One of the men to my left has scooted out and sits facing down the alleyway, beginning to narrate a legend to which no one appears to be paying the slightest attention; but the word "Maigna" causes me to glance at fat Oai and concentrate on the tale of his father. The legend concerns Maigna's battle with a shark in the reef waters, and from his language it is impossible to place the time of the story or the time even of Maigna's existence. This man whom we buried yesterday is simply no more today. He has entered into the world of legend which is timeless in that it is always narrated in the present tense.

Thinking over Oai's answers about the bushmen, I wonder how much of them are true. I have seen no evidence of mountains, but then it is impossible to see distances in this jungle or on the beach. I cannot believe that it would be possible for Rauka to train snakes by tormenting them and then making them associate their torments with the sight and smells of a bushman's head; why would they not more obviously associate their torments with the sights and smells of the woman who was tormenting them? And since rauka is the name given the sorceress and is also the word for sorceress, it must also be the name of all past sorceresses; and since the language has no past tense, these things might have been true generations ago and only sound contemporary through the uses of the dialect.

Men are taking their places against the opposite wall as the betel is passed down that side. The narrator continues his chanting of legend. Tombani is the last to squint into Veedlie's eye; and as I am biting into my betel, he steps between my outstretched legs and bends forward with his hands locked behind his buttocks to scrutinize my drying handkerchief, studying it for a long time through the up-drifting smoke from his pipe. He inches closer with no concern for the fact that his lower belly and groin are almost in my face, forcing me to turn my head to the side to avoid contact with them.

Betel sourness stabs at my jaws, and I reach to the side for the poki shoot which fat Oai places in my hand. Tombani backs away and goes to sit opposite me, his face relaxed as though in scheming contemplation, eying me with a faint smile.

I bring the poki straw to my lips again and again, swallowing sourness until sourness becomes blandness, until myopia begins its pulsings and fadings in my vision.

Greater shadow falls over Tombani's smug face and my head wobbles to the right to see that the compound is no longer sunlit. The heavens are a dense movement of grey clouds, a balm to sight. Women and children fill the open space with a bustle of activity, sweeping the black earth with palm frond brooms until no trace of debris remains to detract from the impression of neatness that makes this compound irresistibly attractive. A funnel of white smoke pours up through the roof of the cooking hut, carried strongly toward the woods behind it by a breeze from the west.

Glancing around me, I wonder if the men ever do anything except go for their meals and spend the rest of the time sleeping and eating betel. Food is plentiful, the women prepare it; there is no apparent commerce of any sort, no possessions beyond their crude spears and an occasional necklace and the coconut-shell eating vessels. What in God's name do they live for? What goal is there other than death? What goal to stir them to high points of achievement and low points of failure — to punctuate this eternity with any emotion other than monotony of waiting? — to give meaning to the passing of time? And yet they arrange time in their own instinctive ways, suiting the activity to the peculiar climate of the hour; for there seems to be nothing much in the morning because the morning is naturally alive and gay with its own freshness; indolence through the hottest part of the day, stultified by their foods until the community bath in the pond revives them to the particuar calm of midafternoon; and later, when dusk breathes melancholy from the jungle depths, there is the mutual huddling against beginning night, the betel, the legends. Their life is strangely organized to fill the dangerous hours with activity and companionship and to leave the naturally pleasant hours as they are.

Lips that have been purple become glistening vermilion and grins appear on faces made vapid by drunkenness. I focus my gaze on little Veedlie who lolls glassy-eyed, a sleek-bellied midget against his grandfather's bony ribs, puffing casually on Tombani's clay pipe.

In the distance, whirlwinds twist treetops in sudden agitation and the slow drumming of thunder accompanies the intoned legend, withdrawing us into ourselves and withering the day to autumnal nostalgia, weird nostalgia, the nostalgia of empty grinnings and boredom. It seems that I have been here forever, that I have always known this world somewhere in my heart, that I am more native to it than to a land of parks and paved streets and neon signs and watches and clocks and time signals and daylight saving and weeks and months and anniversaries . . .

The scattering motion of rain jerks me back to my senses. It is advancing in a crystal wall across the compound. The world scurries before its shimmering onslaught, full of black legs and outcries as women and children dash for shelter, full of laughter and shouts as our alleyway becomes a crowded passage of men bumping against one another in the rush. I stare at the howling onsweep as it marches toward us, swallowing up bodies in its folds. A current of chill air strikes my face and I straggle to my feet in confusion. My handkerchief is ripped away. I run to retrieve it and ram it into my pocket as the day blackens to the garish twilight of storm.

Tombani is tugging to lift the inert body of a completely drunken Veedlie when the downpour clatters onto rooftops beside us and sweeps through the alley on east winds. Fat Oai bumps me from behind and herds me with his bulk around the corner and into the open door of Tombani's hut. Tombani follows with the dripping body of his grandson flopping across his arms.

Standing in the doorway, trees to the left are dimly visible through sheets of storm. Rain lashes in, wetting my pantlegs and chilling my bare feet. I step away. Oai and Tombani are attempting to balance Veedlie's limp body against one of the inside supporting poles, and howling with laughter as the child sags from side to side.

This hut is much larger than mine. The front half is separated from the back by a series of upright poles buried in the earth and bracing the central beam of the ceiling. Behind them, in the dim interior, I see a mass of humanity, probably members of the old man's family, seated on mats.

I ease myself to the ground, leaning against one of the poles in the middle where I can look through the door out to the grey turmoil of storm.

Tiring of their game with Veedlie, Tombani and Oai allow him to crumple over on his side with his head almost touching my leg and come to sit on the ground near me.

"Are you a rauka, friend?" Tombani asks, his voice scarcely audible above the storm. He speaks with such simplicity, so calmly that I am sure I have misunderstood.

"What?"

"Are you a rauka? You cure Veedlie. Are you a rauka?" he says patiently. The question floods my brain with the astonishment of unsuspected hope. Rauka is powerful here. If I were a rauka, they would respect me and my entire role would be changed. I lean forward, swallowing the fullness of betel saliva, and peer through the gloom into the old man's eyes to see if he is serious. He wears the same speculative smirk as when he contemplated me so slyly before.

"Yes," I mumble, manipulating my tongue through thickness to clarity. "I am rauka."

Fat Oai's body flounders away as though some force had jerked him under his arms.

"Then you are female," Tombani croons, his lips protruding into a pucker on the word daoka, his eyes closing to slits of craftiness.

"But no, I am male as you know I am male," I laugh, glancing at Oai who shrinks from me as though I were leprous.

"Rauka is always female," Tombani insists gently, drawing up his knees and locking his arms around them.

"You see from my face that I am male," I argue.

"Rauka can change face," he taunts. "Rauka has many faces. Rauka is always female."

"You know I am male," I shout. "You see from my voice I am male."

"Rauka can change voice," he snorts. "Rauka has many — "

"What are you doing?" I roar, my voice distant to my deafened ears, as he cradles the club to his chest.

"It is taboo for rauka to sit with male," he explains with feigned patience. "You are rauka, you are female, you sit with males."

"Rauka is on the other side of taboo," I blurt out. "You know rauka judges taboo, not patriarch!"

"No rauka sits with male."

"I am male rauka. It is good and very good for male rauka to sit with males," I say through drunkenness as he staggers to his feet and steps in front of the door. Rain splinters against his legs and his face is lost in obscurity above me.

"Can rauka change sex?" I bellow up into the darkness, raising my hands to protect my head. He hesitates. Wind blows splattering against the bamboo wall.

"No rauka can change sex!" I insist.

After a long moment, Oai whispers from the corner, *No*, almost at the same moment Tombani says *Yes*. I plunge into the momentary rift of doubt.

"No, show me the rauka who can change sex. Male rauka always has manhood, female rauka always has womanhood."

"Rauka always female," he argues.

"I am rauka and I am male."

"You make babies with your manhood?"

"Yes."

"Show me. Show me babies."

My hands drop hopelessly into my lap. How can they understand that there are other worlds when even the word *world* means nothing more than this island?

"They are out there," I say, gesturing toward the forest.

"Bring them to me."

"I cannot."

"They are no-good?"

"They are good. They live away. Across the water there are other nuni. I do not drive them into the woods because they are no good. They live away," I explain through the hoarseness of despair. "They are not no-good, they are good."

"You cannot show me," he gibes triumphantly, and I hear the sharp intake of Oai's breath.

I roll, flinging myself away from the expected blow, knocking against Veedlie's head.

"Rauka can change body," he hisses, bending over me.

"No, no she cannot," I say in final desperation, seeking to focus my sight on the beams above me, watching them pulse and fade.

"Why do you cover sex in Vanua?" he says tentatively, obviously searching his brain for truth. "Because your sex is womanhood one time and manhood one time?"

I bring my dancing sight to rest on a long split in the

beam overhead, but my senses splay in all directions, going to the sound of rain, going to the air's crawling dampness, going to the smells of sweat and betel permeating the earth beneath my head. I am aware that his voice has changed beyond the barriers of racket in my head. The idea of attempting to explain why I wear clothes makes me concentrate on fighting my way back to my senses.

He steps away, silhouetted against the dull light from the door, and I see he holds his club to his side and not over his head. His voice is thick with authority and severity, like a father speaking to his son when he commands me to expose myself.

Oai lumbers from the shadows and the two of them stand above me in the drizzling silence. I lie motionless, feeling Veedlie's wiry hair against my bare thigh, attempting to trundle my cumbersome brain into line. I must think and God it is impossible to think when the jagged crack in the overhead beam pulses and fades, pulses and fades. From somewhere in the back of the hut a child begins to whimper, a single thin tone repeated again and again. I roll my eyes wearily back in my head, but can see nothing.

"All males must take mates," I hear Tombani's canting begin as a whisper and take strength, as though he were speaking in a trance. "If you are male and not no-good in your manhood you have a mate. Show her to me. If you have no mate, you are female rauka in changed body or — "

"I am male rauka," I bellow as outrage boils up in me from the irritating cadence of his words, from the image of myself lying here exposed, arguing with a man who appoints himself god of all judgment. "I prove manhood in making babies. I am male and it is good male rauka sit with males and cure their sores." Pushing myself up into a half-sitting position I glare into his face.

"It is good," the old man sighs, seemingly taken aback by my rage, or perhaps only tiring of the dispute. He steps across my body and into complete obscurity at the back of the hut where the infant still sobs. "You go now," he urges gently.

I reach to pull my pants up, worn with drunkenness and tension.

"You hide manhood to make you woman rauka," he observes from the darkness.

"No."

"If manhood does not change into womanhood, why do you hide it?"

I step out of my clothes and wad them into a bundle under my arm.

"Is that good?" I ask, stepping toward the door where rain pelts my shins. "Now all may see from my cures that I am a rauka, and all may see from my body that I am male."

"It is good," he concedes grudgingly, his voice weak with uncertainty.

I catch the door frame and hesitate long enough to get my bearings, for my hut is invisible behind the glinting downstreaks of greyness. I slosh out into the deluge, followed a short distance by the child's muffled wailings, and then nothing except rain.

27

Tombani has spread the contagion of doubts about me, raising a subtle barrier that shuts me out of their lives.

Why?

I do not voice the question. It springs through betel numbness and is there in my ears without my ever saying it.

My floor is a soft paste of mud. Each morning it dawns clean, but then it storms throughout the afternoon in endless twilight.

Ririkinger — there is the hope. I sit here passing the time fashioning dolls from bark and coconut husks, dolls I hope someday to give to her. For now, I cache them and wait. She smiles at me every morning when I go to pick betel from the bush behind Tombani's hut, for she lives in the ante-hut adjoining his and is somehow related to him. But for two days I have not seen her.

The others appear to accept me as a rauka. Each morning they accompany Veedlie to my door, and each morning I treat more and more of them for their yaws as they see Veedlie's now almost cured. But in accepting me as a rauka, they no longer accept me as a man. Rauka Tataolagi stands at a distance, her chin resting always on her folded hands over the top of her staff, glaring silently at me throughout the cures. Veedlie and fat Oai ignore me. When I command, they obey, but without the easy reactions of companionship they showed me before.

A man can do anything but beg for that which must be freely given — some recognition that he exists and is known — and I have begged even for that, and it is a bitter and destructive thing to do. I begged for it when I was driven by rain-filled twilight to go and sit alone with Tombani one evening, not speaking but eating betel together. I beg for it every mealtime when I stand naked above the spread and wait for someone to make a place for me to sit, and always end up carrying my food back to my hut to eat alone.

My hut and my betel, my scraps of bark and husk for making dolls, my glasses and my scattered pages of *Great Essays* . . . How many times have I read these few remaining pages? — only to absorb words that have no meaning for me. I sit on the mat in the mud, with light from the door falling over my shoulders, adjust my wobbly glasses and read, and words are taken into my brain from a world I can scarcely believe was ever mine. Words of Montaigne and Sainte-Beuve, phrases of Swift and Shaw, making no more impression on me than the rustle of rain except when they strike coincidence in a truth I am now living.

"*Well!*" I read in a paragraph from Pater, "*we are all condamnés as Victor Hugo says: we are all under sentence of death but with a sort of indefinite reprieve — 'les hommes sont tous condamnés à mort avec des sursis indéfinis': we have an interval, and then our place knows us no more.*" Other sentences follow, a jumble of print on water-stained pages. Someday, I tell myself, I will reread all of these things carefully, and I will invent words comparable to these in the language of the savage, for that is the great frustration. When there are no words and there must be living with the language, the living and the thinking are delimited to the capacity for expression. How can there be a plea for justice when the word itself does not exist? How can there be right reasoning when the word *reason* does not exist? It is as though all past knowledge, all past needs were nullified through their nonexistence in the language. *Kindness, charity, generosity, affection, sweetness,* these things appear as fragments of instincts, never clarified and made solid because never communicated even to the brain.

I know that I must wait, but there is no time for waiting when the afternoon turns dark, too dark to see the book or the dolls, and I must sit here in mud and escape the past and the future in betel dreams until there is nothing but the great calm of now, the mollusk numbness.

28

I bite into the betel nut's bitter kernel and try to forget the child in the corner. From time to time she babbles her pitiful pleas to the shadows. With the back of my hand I wipe saliva from my lips. Myopia floods mind and vision quickly and I must force my eyes to focus on Tombani who sits motionless, ignoring the infant. Rain has slowed to a faint mist and the last light of day sifting in the open door silhouettes the old man's skeletal figure.

Why?

But no, I wrinkle my forehead, shutting out the question, refusing to beg again for what must be given if it is to have any value, waiting for Tombani to speak, waiting for him to show some sign that at least he tolerates my presence. Others lounge away from us there in the bog of slush at the back of the hut, near the child.

"Why? Why Ririkinger?" I hear some part of me daring to ask, while other parts cower in their separate cells.

Tombani's eyes open wide in puzzlement, and I realize he does not know I have given the child that name and must think I am asking: "Why? Why finger?"

"Why her?" I say, nodding in the child's direction, cherishing the frail interest that enlivens me.

The old man, his protruding lips dripping betel juice, stares at me in scorn; then, shrugging his shoulders, he explains that the matriarch, Rauka Tataolagi, will begin the cutting tomorrow. She will open small designs in the child's face with a sharpened bone and pack them with blue mud from the —

"I know how it is done," I hear myself mumble, thinking of the mutilations I have seen on the swollen faces of the other children. But not Ririkinger. God — her flesh should remain smooth and soft. I shake my head against remembering Oai's explanation that they do not give their children names until after the tattooing because so many die from it.

Beyond the door, to my right, twilight filters stagnant through wet jungle foliage. I chew my betel and glance at other villagers, vague shadows in the early evening as they wade humming across the quagmire of the open compound and disappear into the safety of their huts for the night. Sitting here, a cross-legged bundle of beard and nakedness, I reach up and feel the bruised lump, raw and tender, above my left ear. Wind shudders high in the tops of trees and there is the subtle movement of night descending on the jungle.

I try to keep my eyes averted from Ririkinger, wishing

now that I had resisted the temptation to seek Tombani's companionship against the lonely dusk; but again and again I catch myself peering past the supporting pole into the gloom of that corner.

Her hands are bound above her head with strips of bark to a stake driven into the ground. Her body hangs listlessly, scarcely supported by buckling knees. The screech of a nightbird echoes through trees, quickening me to reality. Why should they bind her like this? Surely she would not run away. For a moment the blank daze of fear dissolves from my chest as I lick my lips and turn to Tombani to ask him for mercy for this infant. But the movement causes pain from the lump on my head to shimmer through me and chokes back my words. *The end of that route is even greater blackness,* I hear from retained memory. My shoulders sag forward and the betel is not enough to make me unconscious of my shame.

"Keura," is all I can say. Tombani's arm detaches itself from the shadows and he places the twig in my hand. I brush mud from a spot and tear off the bark with my teeth, chewing grit into the betel and poki mixture. I am driven to it, driven to sink into my betel dream and forget the child — my child — in the corner. But no, she is not my child. I want to forget that child and all children as I forget everything else.

My head droops forward while I chew and swallow, waiting for the familiar betel numbness to turn me into leather. No one speaks. Through the thin back walls, a single cricket livens the air with its presence; its warm sound in the desolate evening. Cricket on the hearth — God — an old home full of autumn fire in the hearth, full of the smells of waxed furniture and dinner's lingering aftermath, and the chirping of a cricket on the hearth. The scene is abstracted into calico and warmth and a rose-cheeked infant lying on the floor in the gross pleasure of food's digestion, reeking of decency and security and livingness. The child looks at me and smiles, safe in her regard for me, and I smile back down at her and reach out my foot to poke at the bottom of her shoe in a gesture of reassurance.

The pole bites into my cheek through the tangle of whiskers as my head falls to the side, and I tremble with the chill of mud beneath my seat. Far away there is a jungle listening to all the live things. Here, close by, there is a cricket. Cricket on the hearth, full of cheer, awakening old instincts, long dead, returning them to pierce the thick shell of forgetfulness. I am here and now. I am in the presence of the infant Ririkinger, hanging from the stake, but I am also in the presence of my own Cindy, long ago, sick and feverish in a bed of white sheets. But I am another John Harper, a different John Harper, hovering over her bed, my hands suddenly too large and clumsy, not knowing what to do with them. I fold them across my lap. My beard scratches, turning back on itself in the hollow of my throat, and I am floating in the world of double images, myopia, floating through images that shine with life, counterpointing the *then* and the *now*. It is Saturday night — God — and I am polishing the boys' shoes in the kitchen while Susie irons Cindy's dress for church tomorrow. It is Sunday afternoon in the amusement park, with the carrousel music and the orange and raspberry and lime snow-cones and the children's sticky fingers being wiped on my handkerchief. Strange — God — strange, I see them only as children, not as the adolescents they have become, and yet I loved them no more then than I do now, love their adolescence, love their . . . I am listening to the cricket with such concentration it is nullifying the present, turning me back into the other John Harper, completely different from this betel-drugged derelict who sees all things through watering eyes and who trembles with anguish, like a child, before the infinite reaches of loneliness.

Time and betel dulled the sharp edge of memory until tonight when palaces of orgy are replaced by a cricket on the hearth, when a swollen-bellied black child becomes my own white child of long ago.

I raise my head and focus on Tombani through the blear. "Damn your filthy soul," I mutter in English.

He grunts. My cheeks burn with an upflushing of fever and I carry my belligerence into dialect. "Why do you bind her like this?"

The old man bends forward and stares at me, with that expression, sometimes so poignant, that knows nothing of ignorance. His explanation is the monotonous chant of derision, but the night, the wetness, the inseeping hush of drizzle alters his tones into whispered softness.

"The cutting is painful. The pain kills one so young. To save her from the pain, she is kept on her feet and awake for three days and three nights. When time is ready for the cutting, if she is still alive, she sleeps and feels nothing . . ."

His voice joins with the silence without seeming to have ended the sentence. He lights his pipe of twist with a coconut punk which turns his face orange and glows through his silhouetted fingers when he blows against it.

A mosquito drones close to my ear. I wave it away and concentrate on the approaching drunkenness.

It is getting too dark to see. Tombani grunts a command and young Veedlie detaches a handful of twigs that are suspended from the ceiling on a bark cord to keep them dry and brings them over to light a fire on the floor between us. I stare at the sparks as he blows hard, his face close to the earth, holding the coconut husk against the kindling and working with it until the entire underside of his face, chest, belly and thighs is outlined in the brilliant brushstrokes of firelight.

From the corner, a whimper floats to me, thin and fragile, a flower born of silence. Tombani does not react in any way to it; he stares serenely at the play of firelight on the stained weave of the walls. My glance shifts to Ririkinger. I can see red flames, caught in tears, rolling down the mute child's cheeks. My own child lies in a bed of white. The white image of the white child fills me with tremblings of pain for the black child. Reality strips away its mask and flaunts its rawness to my brain, telling me how she will hang there all night in mud up to her ankles, surrounded by bodies that sleep, that snore, inhaling the foul accumulation of smoke; hanging there alone and perhaps flickering out.

"Let me have her," I hear words from my lips, distant words and cracked, harsh words and sobbing. My head flops up in my total astonishment to hear what I have said. Tombani's thick eyebrows lift. He exhales a cloud of twist smoke through his nose in a snort, as though such an idiot request did not merit even so much as an answer. I sit stunned by the radiance that flashes through me. They care nothing for their children. It would mean nothing to them. Radiance returns the words beyond my volition to torment my lips, pouring forth on the impulse of my own salvation — not so much for her as for myself.

"Let me have her," I plead, my voice steadying itself on the focus of some distant hope, some giant hope. I can feel myself sinking, sinking into the swirling vortex of nothingness, held to the time and the spot by the magnetism of that faraway hope. I listen to drippings from the eaves into puddles beyond the smoke-fogged door, to the silence of a drying drizzle. I listen to Tombani's feet suck through the mire as he pulls his knees up in front of him; and I watch all things in the magnificent assaultings of radiance; I watch the uppuffings of turbid smoke from the fire, watch pink reflections on his knotty shinbones. His face twists into a smile around his pipestem and his eyes glint a thousand subtle understandings.

"She must be cut," he answers softly.

"You filthy pig," I whisper, stupefied by his callousness. "You filthy son of a bitch," but my words are in English, mottling emotion, parroting courage; words symbolic of a man, uttered by a ghost. Cheapness scores my intestines with unbearable clarity, the cheapness of cowardice.

Abruptly Tombani's mood changes. He closes his fist around the tiny bowl of his pipe and removes it from his mouth, spitting vermilion saliva into the mud between his bare feet. Outside, the rain has completely stopped. The old man points to the door, his arm casting a dislocated shadow on the woven wall behind him and tells me to get out.

I pull myself up against the supporting pole, determined
to stand my ground. Soupy mud from my buttocks trails
down the backs of my legs. I falter again, hating the faltering as some strange moral debasement. Through layers of
smoke I locate the black hole of the door. No, I must stay
here and protect my Cindy. I struggle away from it,
struggling back, hating the strange debasement that drags
me toward the black hole.

"Let me have her."

With a flick of his hand and a belch he dismisses me.

Betel saliva fills my mouth. He has gone too far in his
derision. *I could step forward, but why? I could roar my
bitterness down at him, but why? I could take my Cindy
from him by force and surprise, but why? — and flee with
her into the jungle, but why? I could vomit out this trembling, no longer trembling of fear but of idiot debasement,
but why? I could raise my arm and strike out and there
would be magnificent liberation from the debasement and
the cringing, but why? I could, but there is the white wall
of my own pain, the unknown consequences, the unknown
payment. They would kill me.*

The body, then, holds and the soul must accept its
greater pain through fear of the body's lesser pain. New
redness settles into old whiteness. Without looking back,
I plow through the smoke and out the open door: grief-
stricken no longer for the child, but for the defeat of the
father, my own defeat.

Night air is clean against my face. I stop and lean against
the soaked wall of the hut. Washed night is a well of immense purity and gentle approach. I inhale the purity
in gulps and I am inhaling my own reproach. The clean

gives remorse to the unclean. I mourn the loss. I mourn the vividness of my realization, for I was close to the victory of the soul over the body's fears. I would have won if my body had not been ligatured by fears of pain, of death. This prison of cheapness, of cowardice, unbearable to the soul, would have been destroyed by the one grandiose gesture I could not make.

Placing one foot before the other, I shove myself outward from the wall and stagger toward my hut across the compound. Later, later I will win, but I know that there will never be a time later except in greater difficulty, and that will come only when the driving despair to escape the prison goads me beyond myself toward the ultimate cowardice of annihilation, not the noble ideal of freedom.

On all sides, sodden huts cluster in protection from the jungle beyond. Water rushes over logs blocking the pond from the river. I look up to a clearing in the sky, to a pool of fledgling stars surrounded by rolling cloudbanks that are lighted at the edges by an invisible moon. I brush my hand across my eyes and the heavens become distorted in myopic grandeur, with two outlines for every image. All of it accuses, every sound, every health of savage movement, every animal movement in the jungle, every odor, every star, every silvered puddle — all that is good on this earth. I am accused by universal goodness this night, and it turns me into a solitary chunk of loneliness.

It must be escaped. Crickets burden the stillness with their tinseled raspings. I want to close myself away from night's purity, to fall asleep, not to rest but to be rid of consciousness.

Inside my hut, I bolt the door with my heavy boar spear

and stand listening to the heartbeat that throbs in my ears. Numbness creeps across my forehead, dulling thought. I allow myself to sink to the earth as dazzlement rolls over me. Why? This is not the betel. *Let me have her.* But no, it is not that either. Let there be at least no such lying to myself. As long as there is truth, the splotch of hope can remain. Now, the dazzlement fills me with the vertigo of hope. I must not pretend that I am experiencing the noble grief of a father over the fate of his child when it is really the grief of my own debasement. I cried "son of a bitch" but in a language no one could understand, and with cringings.

Loneliness fights numbness like a duller light fighting blackness. I must get this straight in my mind. There must be no hiding of my real grief of debasement beneath the noble grief for the child, unless the noble grief can become the real, dominating and hypnotizing. *Let me have her.* I have not drowned the needs of my heart in betel drunkenness. Let the nobler grief persuade. Let me sink into it until it fires my soul above my body's dreads. Let me think of the child at the stake, of the long night alone for her, of the mysteries within her veins and organs that may never know another night.

A humming catches overtones in my brain. It spins, gyrating, building slowly, mercifully driving out thoughts. I turn on my side, drawing up my knees and cradling my paunch in my hands. Outside moonlight fades to gathering mists within me. The humming builds its crescendo, ever louder, like some giant mosquito gone mad inside of my head.

Mists and moonlight. Mists and sunlight. Light trans-

piercing prayers. Shafts of light bursting through the roar of insects in my brain. Cockatoos floating white against blue skies, full of screechings from tree to tree, and the expanding chest of a white man, not cowering, but holding the child high on his shoulders and walking full of pride, carried forward on the flow of tons of heartsperm, tons of soulsperm, tons of spiritsperm, slashing out and crushing with great dignity and greater tenderness, pushed onward by his strength; and then a raised club, a leer and mists forming before the eyes and a sniveling sun glimpsed through a veil of red . . .

Mists swirl and I roll in my drunken dream of power and intense liberation. The humming accelerates into cheapness. *Everything is on sale today, everything cheap.* The humming comes through the loudspeakers of the cheap sale and people are listening to it, waiting for more band music while they finger the cheap objects and the cheap coins in their pockets and speculate *Is it worth a dime? Everything costs so much. I'll take this child at the stake and this crude little hemp-and-bark doll, and that gold locket over there and five or six —*

The confused thought blasts through with such force that the humming in my brain stops abruptly. I am not sure what I will do as I drag myself up and jerk my pants from the overhead beam. Concentration centers on standing upright while I fish through my pockets. And outside in the silence, no other sound but the cricket's thin chirping —

I drop my pants to the mat and turn about slowly, trying to locate the door in the stippled blackness until I see a frame of moonlight seeping around its edges.

I throw it open, showering my belly with water. Moonlight filters through trees into puddles. I must not think, must not let it accuse me until I can stand beneath it without guilt, or lie dead beneath it, but sweetly, without cheapness. I stagger across the compound, closing out the the desire of panic to turn me aside, wishing for some reason that I had brought my glasses.

Reflected firelight dances in liquid brightness on the mud before Tombani's open door. Placing my left hand on the door strut, I step inside.

And I am staring through a choking fog of smoke down into a face blank with astonishment.

"Let me have her," I command in a voice of wavering authority. "Let me have her. I'll give you this." I swallow my heart and hold out the locket by its thin chain.

Tombani's eyes dilate and fix on the golden disk while he unwinds himself and rises slowly to his feet. In the background, behind the supporting poles, other members of the family stir and look toward us. My glance shoots to Ririkinger. She hangs motionless, suspended from her frail arms like a black tear. Her head lolls forward on her neck in an attitude of death. The fire shifts into a dozen fires, and agony that I am too late crumples my insides. Before I can fall, a pain sears across my palm as the locket is torn away.

I lock my knees to hold myself up, squinting to focus my gaze on Tombani. I think how carefully I have kept it hidden from savage eyes, always going into the jungle before pressing the button that opens it, always looking about to make sure I am not being watched before taking out the faded snapshots of my children. Now, the locket with its pictures of everything I love in the world is clutched in the mud-caked hands of a man who would sit by and let a child die.

Without emotion I raise my fist high in the air and bring it down with all my force. The old patriarch crumbles like a decayed leaf. I rip the locket from his hand and stand above him reeling. I have done it. It is too late to turn back now. The fire is coming up to meet me. I am sinking. Regret and pity and the magnificence of absolution from my guilt of cowardice flame as I seek to retain my balance. I am squeezing the locket until tendons in my arm are rigidly knotted. The fire rises to consume all of my attention, the fire and the elongated navel of the gasping native and his little clay pipe which lies in the mud where it fell beside him.

A whimper softer than silence reinforces me, jars me back. I catch myself, holding to the supporting pole, and peer into the corner. Through the haze, I see Ririkinger's head sag to one side as her small hands clench and unclench. Smoke tartness, flame tartness fill my eyes with tears. I am staring open-mouthed when a movement to one side makes me turn. Veedlie is handing his grandfather the club of the patriarch. The child splashes back into the shadows as I transfer the locket to my left hand and wheel around. Tombani, clasping his club, is crawling to his feet.

I look through the smoke fog for the door, but my eyes delude me and everywhere I see the white child alive and breathing in the black child's pain.

Could Tombani ever be placated now? It doesn't matter. I listen to the child within me, to the child's destruction of cheapness, releasing me from the bondage of cowardice. I raise my fist above my head again. The old man ducks and crouches defensively. We stand across the fire from one another, a naked patriarch and a naked derelict, splattered with mud and greyed in smoke. I glimpse the reflections of scattered coals through the slits of his eyes. And then his eyes open cautiously in an expression of vague bewilderment.

"Let me have her," I urge hoarsely. "I'll give you this," extending the locket to him again. His shoulders tense and he holds out his hand, palm up. I allow the locket to dribble through my fingers on its chain and step back from the fire. Placing his club between his thighs, he lifts the locket to his face with both hands, glowering at it, smelling it, and then it is as though the expression of brute ferocity were suddenly stripped from his face to reveal his true expression of childish delight. Without taking his fascinated gaze from the glistening metal that reflects red spangles all over the hut, he nods brusquely in the child's direction.

"She belongs to me?" I ask, feeling perspiration detach itself and dribble down the diagonal crease in the back of my neck.

"She belongs to you."

I stare, full of open-mouthed incredulity as tremblings settle into exhaustion in my stomach, for I am no longer looking at the proud, scornful patriarch, but at a white-haired old man with withered flesh; an aged child with grinning betel-red lips over stained tushes, absorbed in the play of firelight on gold; his eyes bright orbits of wonderment as he cocks his head from side to side.

A sigh from the child brings me to my senses and completes my exhaustion. I move and act in automaton, incapable of assimilating my feelings. The fire's warmth touches my legs as I step over it and slosh to her corner. My hands are steady when I untie the soft bark liana that binds her to the stake.

She collapses into my arms and I carry her past the bustling knot of Tombani's family who ignore us in favor of the locket.

The night, then, is changed. The moon is low behind the trees, pouring through in slants to mottle the earth. As I trudge wearily home, I hear the old patriarch shouting to his villagers, calling for fires and betel nut to celebrate his new fortune, filling the compound with his jubilant voice.

All I can feel is the unbelievably light weight in my arms, and the surge of relief that she is safe and that some cheapness has been flecked from my heart, a relief so immense, so attached to the guiltless night and the guiltless universe that I am incapable of reacting to it except quietly, in stunned preoccupation. They run from their huts, preparing to celebrate as I ease myself over my door. They have new fortunes, and I have a child.

Soberness returns me from the pulsings and fadings of myopia. I deposit Ririkinger on the mat and massage her wrists. If there were tears left in me, the smallness of her hands would bring them to the surface, but now there is only the numbness of fulfillment, nothing else. When warmth returns to her fingers, I spread my coat over her and lie down beside her. A peculiar timidity makes me lie away from her, completely in the mud, with my hand resting on her shoulder. But she stirs and moves closer to me. I inch over onto the mat, cradling her head in the crook of my shoulder and allowing my fingers to explore her sleeping face. The flesh is soft and smooth, the way a child's flesh ought to be.

The two of us are alone in a world apart as the outside noises of celebration pour through the thin walls of our hut. An old man and a child. After the long loneliness I once more have a daughter to hang my life to. I lie here listening to the laughter and shouting and chanting; and watching the flickering specks of red and orange from the celebration fires that seep through the cracks of our hut and dance on the opposite wall. I lie here holding the child close.

29

The scratching of someone trying to force open my door brings me from profound sleep. Ririkinger is clinging to me for warmth. Easing myself away from her, I adjust the coat around her shoulders and go to the door.

The sunlight is a slap across my eyes when I open. A fury explodes beneath my chin, and Rauka, sticking her elbows into my ribs, seeks to climb over the opening and force her way past me into the hut. My muscles react automatically, almost in sleep. I bar her way with my arm and tell her to go.

Her lips cleave to her toothless gums in an insucking expression of rage and she throws her frail body against me. Her flabby breasts scrape against my wrist, as dry as leather.

Insults pour from her as she fights to get in to the child. Then, seeming to realize that she is not strong enough, she relaxes and her eyes grow large in frustration, arousing some long-forgotten emotion of compassion in me. I put my hand on her shoulder and turn her aside with great gentleness, but her head jerks back, glistening purple at the cheekbones, and she spits betel juice into my face.

Releasing her, I raise my mud-caulked arm and wipe at the spittle, telling her to go. She stalks away in such outrage that her thin legs seem on the verge of cracking from the force with which she plants them on the ground.

Behind her, behind all the activity of morning in this compound, the forest rises in a wall of intense greens, unbroken by other colors than the tans and browns of bamboo huts. Leaves stir in the trees and a light wind ruffles my beard. Puddles from the week's rains have soaked into the earth, giving the area a washed effect of neatness that is irresistibly cheering. The bluish haze of cooking smoke hangs delicately over the compound, softening shadows, softening all harshness into health. Naked women work together, sweeping away the debris of last night's celebration, spreading ashes from the fires in a wide area around Tombani's door in splotches of whiteness against the black earth. I watch Rauka storm in Tombani's hut.

I feel no urge to cross the compound. Nothing draws me to the betel bushes behind the patriarch's hut. I am drawn, rather, to the pond, for I am encrusted with mud from head to toe.

Ririkinger lies curled up on her side; her tiny hand protruding from the coat covering, is folded loosely beneath her cheek. I gaze down at her and wonder if she will ever

understand the miracle that transforms today from yesterday through her presence?

Not daring to leave her alone, I carry her to the pond
and deposit her on the grass while I bathe; and the day
with its quietness, its aftermath of uneasy threat from
Rauka, is transformed in this glade where I first met Ririkinger. All of my gestures are small. I feel little and hollow and lost, but there is no longer the taste of acid in my
heart. The open meadow, with its floor of yellow buttercups, dazzles midmorning with its freshness. Everything
within me echoes that freshness, like a washed vessel or
like ground prepared for planting. I am shaken with occasional tremblings, but they are no longer the tremblings
of despair — only the natural results of great upheaval.

Through the trees, I hear the call of Rauka, telling the
villagers to bathe, repeated again and again as a chant.

Not wishing to be here when they arrive, I hurry down
the path, through an arbor of speckling sunlight, toward
my hut. When I pass in front of Oai's dwelling, Rauka's
voice catches in her throat in the middle of her call. I do
not look in her direction, but pick my way along the most
solid portions of drying earth.

After the purity of outside air, the outpuffing humidity
of my hut repels me and I step back from the door.

I carry Ririkinger to the shade hut and place her carefully on one of the mats. Flies swarm about us in such
thickness I pick up an abandoned palm frond and sit here
fanning it over her body.

A movement across the way attracts my attention. Tombani is peering out of his door, gazing sourly around the
compound. He totters out, holding his hands to the sides

of his head, and shuffles toward the pool in a profound stoop. I stare after him, see him an old and faded man, and it is impossible for me to realize the fullness of my triumph: not the triumph over him, but the triumph over my hatred of him, melting now as he saunters toward the path, a living caricature of all the hangovers in the world. No, the triumph is over no one, none other than myself — the almost involuntary triumph when I was driven to dominate the body's fears at no-matter-what cost last night.

The laughter and chattering of bathers returning to their huts arouses me from my daydreams. Men and women and children, their bodies glistening black with fresh-washed wetness, stoop and dodge low-hanging branches as they amble alongside Oai's hut and enter the sun glare of the compound. They walk in shadow and light. They disappear through doors into their huts, into their own earthen divisions of flesh. Only they know their laughter. Only they know their touches. But in birth and in death their grimace is the same as the world's, and it is the same in joy. I observe them with the first warmth I have felt since Tombani clubbed me — no longer a complete out-cast from their lives, for another's breath enlivens the airs of my hut.

Ririkinger's steady breathing is interrupted by a whim-per and she throws her hands back to clutch at her cheeks. I kneel over her in the strange relief of movement and feel my stomach compress when I place my face close to hers. She squirms as though in nightmare, her eyes loosely closed in concentration on her misery and for a moment her mouth screws up to weep. I massage her abdomen, the way I used to do Cindy's, feeling its mud-gritted surface beneath my palm, until the muscles relax and grow soft in my hand. And all of the charity, and all of the acts I perform for her are given back into me, filling me with the sanity of self-respect in being needed, in caring for, in having some human life dependent on my giving. My heart, shriveled through being required to retain all of its gifts into itself, expands on the steady pulse of unfoldment now that its gifts may be shared.

Returning to the perimeter, Tombani takes his bearings, rubbing at his forehead as though it were hurt. With pond water dripping from his body, he shuffles toward me.

"It is no-good," he announces, holding the locket out and stepping under the shade hut.

I keep my hand protectively on the child's stomach and answer: "It is good and very good."

He illustrates how it is no-good by attempting to slip it over his head without unclasping it.

Getting to my feet I take the locket and tell him to bend forward. He places his grey kinks, full of water globules, against my chest. I open the clasp and fasten the locket around his neck, deciding that someday, on the pretext of working it for him, I shall flick open the disk and remove the pictures of my children. If I had not been so addled I should have done it last night. I look at the chain links nestling in deep wrinkles across the back of his neck. I have made a strange bargain, but one that, in some hidden way, is as satisfying as it is poignant: I have traded the most realistic vestige of my past — Susie's tooled gold locket with its pictures of my children — sick things in my heart now, intimating tragedy; traded that for the sanity of the future, have used it to buy myself a life. And I am com-

pelled as I draw my hands away from the clasp to leave
the photos where they are until the day when they can
become part of inevitability; when they no longer sear me
back from my ability to accept the inevitable. Then and
only then, I know in some inner harshness of wisdom, will
I permit myself to retrieve them.

Raising his head, Tombani pushes out his lower lip and
rolls his eyes downward to study the golden disk on his
chest. Unconsciously he fingers the knob above his right
eye where I struck him last night.

"You are hurt, friend?" I ask, moving his hand away
and examining a cut which has clotted to a freckle of scab.
The taut flesh around it has an unnatural sheen.

"Yes, it hurts," he whispers disarmingly.

"I am sorry, friend."

He edges Ririkinger away with his foot, as one might the
body of a sleeping animal and squats to sit on the mat in
a whirlwind of flies. I join him and pick up my fan.

For a long moment there is silence growing to uncomfortable dimensions between us as I wave the fan over his
head and Ririkinger's body. He sits with his head buried
in his upraised knees.

"Is it taboo to kill a rauka?" he asks finally in a voice so
thin I can scarcely understand him.

"Why?" I ask cautiously.

He raises his head and wipes the back of his hand across
his mouth in a universal gesture of uncertainty.

"Rauka Tataolagi says it is not taboo to kill male rauka."

"She is wrong," I say flatly, stopping the fanning.

"She says you make me do evil."

"How?"

"She says it is evil not to cut the child."

"Rauka Tataolagi is wrong. A male rauka is more powerful than a woman. I tell it that it is good not to cut
children and evil to cut them."

Again he wrinkles his forehead in puzzlement and then
raises his hand quickly to cover the knot. The corners of
his mouth drop and his bloodshot eyes look into mine beneath the diagonal of his hand and fill with tears in an
expression of childish misery. He appears tormented in his
search for an answer to what must be, for him, a complex
ethical problem, and I am certain that Rauka Tataolagi has
filled him with doubts and arguments.

He starts to speak, but closes his mouth and lowers his
head again into his arms and a long, grunting sigh escapes
his lips.

"You hurt, friend?" I ask gently.

"Yes . . ."

"I am sorry. Go to Rauka Tataolagi. She must cure
you."

"No. She says the hurt is an evil to punish me for giving
you the infant."

"She cannot cure such evil?"

"No one can."

"I am stronger then. I can cure it."

He raises his tear-streaked face in bewilderment and
opens his eyes blinkingly against the sunlight's midday brilliance.

"Rauka says the hurt stays in me until you are dead."

"Rauka says wrong. I show you she says wrong. If I
cure you, you know she is wrong and I am right. Does it
hurt only there?" I ask, touching the lump on his forehead
with my finger.

Wincing, he pushes my hand away and brushes his palm

across the top and back of his skull, telling me it hurts all over.

"Come. We go," I command, discarding the fan and taking Ririkinger into my arms. The old man struggles to get up. I place my hand under his elbow and lift him as one would a bird by its wing.

The earth, crusting under sunlight, burns into the nerves of my bare feet, sending its heat up into my ankles.

At my hut I tell him to wait while I climb inside with the child slung under my arm. Tepid mud sucks at my feet and insects swarm up as I squat and search for the handkerchief. Not finding it, I am driven to grab up the white splotches of my shirt and undershirt and escape from the swelter back into the open air.

The old native braces himself when he sees my white clothes. He steps back, grinning sickly and raising his hands, palms out, when I offer him the bundle to carry for me. I instruct him to bring fire and sticks and a coconut shell to the pond, and I hurry over the baked earth toward the path.

The glade is deserted, the muddied pool quiet and un-ruffled, and the only sound is the perpetual gurgle of water trickling over the log spillway into the river ravine.

Dropping the rags, I put Ririkinger down on the grass and straighten her legs into a comfortable position for her.

Clouds, like some slow-moving celestial surf, mass silvered greyness above treetops on either side of the meadow, altering the sun glare to mezzotints of thunder glare, touching all color with slightly brighter luminosity so that tree greens are tinted with lime, and shadows glow from hidden sources.

There is strange detachment in activity, a quiescent desperation of which I am hardly aware. I must relieve a man's pain, not only for him but for the future safety of Ririkinger and myself in order to gain every possible advantage over Rauka Tataolagi. All instincts and all knowledge tell me of the urgency of these things, but only the emotion of peace responds.

I intend doing nothing more than putting hot compresses on Tombani's feet and cold ones on his head in order to draw the blood from his head. However, there must be a certain display of complexity if I am to impress them with my abilities as a rauka, with my sorcery. Since the cure is one my square-faced Pennsylvania Dutch grandmother taught me, I feel almost exaggeratedly apologetic to her for thus posthumously attaching the taint of witchcraft to her defenseless and God-fearing character.

What can I do? — crumble some leaves in the water? No, that would be too obvious. I peer about me in the blistering stillness for something that might give me an idea, remembering the prescriptions of Paré from my youthful readings of his *Journeys in Diverse Places*, wherein the sixteenth century surgeon lauded the fine medicinal results he got from oil of lilies and essence of roses . . .

I cross the river's footbridge into the open meadow where I stand knee-deep in buttercups, their blossoms fresh and transparent as an exquisite girl. They are like Susie on a Saturday morning, radiant, fragile and yet vigorous. But there is no time. This is another life, a savage life and the delicate hollowness of Susie's cheeks is replaced by an image of the ruminating hollowness of Rauka's. With regret and a sense of brutalization, I tear yellow petals from their stems and bruise them, rolling them between my palms so they will not be recognized for what they are by Tombani.

I am stepping from the log near the pond, holding the soggy mulch against my beard, when Tombani, his eyes half closed in pain, drags himself toward me.

"Build the fire," I tell him as he plops, loose-jointed, down on the grassy bank near Ririkinger. "I go for navundi. Guard the child."

Ducking beneath the wilted leaves of an overhanging branch which has been cracked and dragged down by the storms, I strike out along the river path in search of a banana leaf in which to wrap the shell for boiling water. On the way, I cache my handful of buttercups behind a tree, at the juncture between two of its snake-rooted tendrils, feeling still an almost perverse aftertaste of guilt at having done violence to something so feminine.

Speckles of banana green, pinpointed through the jungle gloom, attract my attention, and I turn to my left from the path. The mud is soft in the eternal twilight of the forest, so soft I can make out another's footsteps leading toward the sunlit area before me.

Through the brush I see a miniature clearing which is enclosed on all sides by a wall of banana trees, broad-leafed and luxurious. No vegetation sprouts from the black mud of the tiny perimeter, now churned and drying with cracks in it, but a wretched lean-to cringes beneath the full blare of sunlight. It is so constructed, with a low shed roof of thatch, that I think for a moment it must be a privy with a full door at the left of the front side. A man my size would have to stoop almost double to walk about inside.

Something stirs beyond the door and I squat back behind the navundi screen. Gnats swarm beneath me, between my legs, giving a ring to silence as I watch through leaves. The movement gathers form from the substance of obscurity and assumes the cramped features of Rauka Tataolagi at the opening, her tufts of hair pointing outward in white cones above each ear. Dragging her staff on the ground, and with her head stretched out on her scrawny neck, she ambles into the brush at the side of her hovel.

I listen to her body sloughing against leaves until she is beyond my hearing.

Insects underline awareness of my nakedness, cumbersome and flaccid. I brush them away and rise up for a full view with my cheek touching the uplifted fingers of a banana stalk. The forest is silent, motionless; ropelike vines drape in and out of foliage. All of it waits in the suspension of some distant storm threat.

Crossing the few feet to her door, I place my hands on each side of the frame and bend far forward. Heat and dampness breathe into my face, full of flies, full of permeations of old smoke, old nauseas and old urines, full of rot and reast — the stench made more purulent by a contrasting hint of sweetness, like perfume on carrion.

Holding my breath, I glance about the cluttered interior. On a large mat, a young woman, her belly enormous in a pregnancy that must be almost immediately deliverable, lies spraddle-legged, snoring in a mire of sweat. The idea of her being brought to such a pest hole for her birth throes appals me.

The back end of the shanty, to my right, is a jumble of woven baskets piled on top of one another; and in the green-spotted obscurity above them hangs a silhouetted object so strange I am both driven to flee and at the same time drawn through the door toward it.

With my head retracted between my shoulders, I stoop and step over the sleeping woman's body into the corner, stirring up a vast activity of green glints as flies effervesce disturbance.

I study the object closely before perception of what it is confirms my suspicions and fades all other details into the background, obliterating sounds and odors when I come to realize that I am staring almost directly into the closed eyes of a head which dangles from the rafter on a two-inch cord of bark, the small and serene head of a young man, smoke-blacked and mummified, but not shrunk, not disintegrated. I am gazing in awakening awe at the symbol of eternity which changes the chemistry of all things — of my body, my soul, of the land and the time — slowly, almost imperceptibly, making of all things new things, and I am seeing a bundle, a leathery balloon, a ball, a thing that once lived and breathed and ate and drank and slept and roamed these forests, and most probably was intimate with violence; and yet all of that is dispersed and I am looking on blankness, on a blackened parchment where nothing of his living and breathing and eating and drinking and sleeping and roaming is transcribed, where nothing remains except a fragment of smoke-cured flesh sculpted into features to tell of the years of living that went into its development, and where violence is nothing more than surmise in this mask of repose, this mask of tranquillity.

I react without shock, without disgust, without sorrow — his face does not evoke these things. No, it evokes rather an ineffable calm that flows out from him into me, muting stridor to a quiet and secret tenderness for all that has its place in living; for the earth and its parts and the seasons and their parts, and the sweats and the flies; for every emotion, for every joy, yes, and every sorrow; for all that was once tied up in the making of this bundle; for all that is given me to live — even those dimmest and harshest things — in view of all that is suspended for him.

His presence communicates to me a shifting of knowledges wherein the logic of eternity once again supplants the logic of the moment. He makes me see that the tattered perceptions of my human condition, those perceptions that have led me into such anguish, must transform themselves around the same human condition — through a perspective of eternity — to lead me into joy; showing me that tragedy is not in the condition but in man's perception of the condition; that while I am heavy with years and suns and trees and storms, he is gone from years and suns and trees and storms — that while I must rake sweats from my eyebrows, there is only dust on his.

I close my eyes wearily, and when I open them again the vividness is gone, and I am gazing at an impersonal mask and seeing there nothing more than any other bundle, any other leathery balloon, any other black ball. It has dismissed me, I whom it never even recognized, to the new miracles of mud and heat, letting me see their conformity to the rules of all the older, more obvious miracles.

Flies are dribbling over my body and I am brought back to the moment and to the squalor, but changed now; heightened in tone to a dimension of benevolence, for I am seeing these things, smelling them, feeling them, living them, not in errant space, but as a part of the passage of time that will lead me to his estate; and they are rendered intensely precious because he dangles here at my shoulder no longer seeing these things, smelling them, feeling them, living them, no longer involved in the parts of time, but only in the whole of eternity. That which is out of all time, tells me of the miracle of these clacking cycles where all is zoned in hours, minutes, seconds up to that final fraction of instantaneity which leans against the wall of forever, that which is out of life tells me of the miracle of living — tells me that it is as black an ingratitude and as great a stupidity to cavil over any of the many-mooded conditions of time as it would be to cavil over the single-mooded condition of eternity. The reality of heats and smells, the buzzings of flies, the stained greys of bamboo return to the foreground of consciousness in that peculiar sharpness of detail summoned by moments of profound peace. Guarding the emotion, clinging to it as a gift of truth so intangible it might dissolve back into blankness, I turn and step over the sleeping woman, hearing my feet suck liquidly from the mud.

Half blinded by the slap of outside glare that makes trees look violet, I draw up short before the stooped blear of Rauka. I scarcely make out her features before my mouth is filled with the foretaste of nausea spurting up from my throat. Sinking to my knees, I pour out my insides against fissured crusts of mud, dimly aware that thin black legs are stalking away and almost immediately returning. The upblaze of reflected heat burns my cheeks and eyes. Her body swims before me, spangled and transpierced by shafts of light caught in my tears. I croak that I am sorry for having invaded her hut.

She props her chin against her staff and extends a wavery streak of arm to offer me a banana leaf. Wiping my mouth with it, I realize that to an onlooker I would appear to be in an attitude of obeisance, kneeling before her. When I am finished, I lumber to my feet and brush my forearm across my eyes.

"Thank you, friend," I say, my voice altered to a deeper bass by the acids of nausea.

Without giving the traditional response, she swivels slowly around the pivot of her staff, following my every move with eyes that glitter from heavily folded lids.

"Thank you, friend," I repeat, discarding the banana leaf at her feet in a faint gesture of defiance. Again she makes no pretense of giving the required answer. Her mouth is closed in a thin line of toothless gummings, creating pockets at each side of her lips. Her eyes dance above her delicately flared nose, constantly fluctuating between expressions of gloating and innocent amusement and hatred; all of it in a face so shriveled the wrinkles look as though they were inked into the flesh.

I cannot decipher her changing expressions. Is she enjoying this triumph of catching me in the taboos of looking on her hut and vomiting — that intimate act which presumably makes her the possessor of my spirit? But from the sparkle of intelligence in her buried eyes, I have the impression that she does not believe in such taboos any more than I, that she is rather reveling in the victory she can manipulate through the ignorance of others, through this complication of innocence which becomes first mystery and then guilt in the minds of those who cannot unravel the truth from the fabric of fact.

"Thank you, friend," I repeat insistently. Refusing to answer, she flexes her jaws in more rapid chewings that stretch tendons into a frame for the ribbed hollow of her throat.

We stand here, a bearded and aged white man and a shrunken and ancient black woman, both naked beneath the nakedness of the sun in a world no larger than this enclosed perimeter where all is baked mud and navundi, exchanging clothed emotions, testing strengths; and my confusion gathers itself into the focus of admiration for her, for I recognize in her something superior to the dullness I read on the faces of all others here; and I know I would experience a certain dejection if she weakened and deigned to answer, much as a general would if an opposing general were to show cowardice or falsity; and indeed, I am awakened to a brief hint of exultation that comes with the discovery that one is to be tested at his best by an enemy of stature; and I realize that this wizened crone is an aristocrat, an indomitable woman, but one of vitality and the irresistible charm of a certain toughness that makes her even more feminine.

And yet I am bewildered as to what this will bring. She is a person of too much quality to castrate an enemy, she would not degrade me by being lenient — no, she will, as she should, use my every mistake, my every fault to her advantage. She becomes immediately more formidable and more attractive; the consequences of mortal threat cannot alter the enormous sympathy I feel for her at this moment, a sympathy of union in our understanding of all these unspoken things. I gaze down at her and feel my own face relaxing into a smile, certain that we would be friends if circumstances had not contrived to turn us into enemies.

She leans on her pole, her head at the level of my chest, scrutinizing me, and her eyes boil up into vivacity as she disengages her hand from beneath her chin and reaches out in a rapid movement. Before I can react, two stinging tugs at my beard coincide with jerkings of her sinewy biceps.

Stepping back, I attempt to penetrate her expression, to read some clarification in a face puckered into a simultaneous smile and frown, and I think that there should be words that explain, words that would communicate understanding and warmth, words that would permit the wisdom of negotiation to arrest the ignorance of action. But the language is void of such nuances.

I hear myself chuckling as I gravitate toward the path by which I came, brushing gnats from my stomach. In a nearby tree the cicada frictions dryness into raspings that broaden silence, raspings that give tone to the time and the place and the woman — perched and static and bright.

"I go, friend," I taunt affectionately, stripping a banana leaf from the closest tree and waiting for her to answer. She is hunched over her staff, her lower jaw loose-hinged in chewings, her eyes fixed speculatively on me as though she were seeking to pierce my covering of flesh and hairs in order to evaluate the dimensions of my brain and heart. When she does not answer, I turn to retrace my footsteps toward the riverbank, carrying with me the image of the old woman in her statuesque pose which is nevertheless so animated, wondering at the mysteries of her life and cult as indicated by the misery of her hut and the head dangling above the baskets, wondering too if it is the head of the bushman the old native was describing in his legend. If so, the baskets probably contain the snakes.

Tombani is stretched out on his back beside little Ririkinger on the sloping pond bank, his eyes closed to a sky completely overcast when I appear back in the glade with the blossoms in one hand and the banana leaf in the other. Smoke from a small fire rises into the air between them.

As I step over him toward the fire, the patriarch licks his lips and swallows painfully, fingering at the disk of gold cradled in a pocket of sweat at the hollow of his throat. His eyelids separate slowly and he looks up into my face, his eyes glazed, not with the inhuman glaze of before, but with that most human of all glazes, the glaze of helplessness in pain, the glaze of suffering that flecks his charcoal pupils with a yellowish mottle.

Telling him to lie still, I wrap the banana leaf around the shell and place it on the fire, dusting in the buttercup petals. His eyes wall to the side in a daze of apprehension. Dropping my undershirt into the heating water, I kneel to soak my dress shirt in the frigid water of the pond, which is now almost cleared of the milkiness stirred up by the bathers. For an instant I see the unruffled picture of an old man, his sparse hair awry, his bearded features sketched in with peculiar softness, his eyes hollow and deeply sunk beneath the silvered outcroppings of his eyebrows, his face given fullness by the downpull of gravity. The image overwhelms me with its newness. It is the first time I have seen myself since the crash, and I am seeing here a stranger, coarsened and aged beyond all recognition, but also strengthened in traits, with a thick vein I have never before noticed tracing itself down the side of my temple. Beyond treetops in the water, clouds march majestically across the heavens, full-bulked and somber, until a drop of sweat from my nose detaches itself and ripples the vision.

I keep the stained wrappings as hot to Tombani's feet as

he can bear them and those on his head cold until tension drains from his body and some of the strain in his face is transformed into cautious delight which erases the yellow flecks from his eyes.

"Is it good, friend?" I ask after a time, continuing to change the compresses.

"It is good and very good," he mumbles, propping himself up on his elbows and turning his head gently from side to side as though testing his neck muscles. His face relaxes into blandness, mingling surprise and childish awe with the indrawn expression universal to all who experience something beyond credibility.

"You tell it now that I am male and rauka and more powerful than Rauka Tataolagi, who cannot cure you as I cure you," I suggest, kneeling over him and wrapping my shirt once again around his head. "You tell it," I pursue slowly, "that your pain is not an evil spirit that punishes you for giving me the child. I cure you and the child is still mine. So, it cannot be such evil that causes your pain. Rauka Tataolagi is a weak rauka. She tells wrong things. Is that so?"

"That is so?" he returns my question with a new intonation.

"That is so. You see it is so."

He leans forward, without answering, and becomes engrossed in the simmering water where yellow masses are revolving up in a circular motion from the bottom. He sniffs at the steam, holding the shirt edge up on his forehead and craning his neck forward.

"You tell it?" I ask again.

"I tell it," he answers simply, removing the wrapping and climbing to his feet.

"It is cured?" I ask.

"It is cured," he says, suppressing a smile that shows his brown tushes for a moment. "It is good, friend."

"It is good and very good," I answer gratefully, remembering Paré in dimness and my grandmother in dimness and the mummified head and the brighter dimness of Rauka's chewings.

"The rain comes," he says, cocking his head to listen to the slow approach of rustling through leaves. The distant cicada continues its raspings, telling of dryness as wetness gathers toward us.

I lift Ririkinger and carry her cradled across my chest, following Tombani toward Vanua. At the entrance to the path, he turns and smiles at me. I return his smile awkwardly, the meaningless way one would that of a stranger.

30

Ririkinger stirs on her mat behind me and sighs.

When I bend over her she squints her eyes open and studies my face gravely for a long moment.

"Ririkinger," I whisper.

She lifts her hand in the pure act of tenderness that exists only in a child or a lover, and caresses my cheek with her fingertips, smiling through puffed eyelids.

"Am I 'kinger?" she asks in a tone of awe.

"You are 'kinger," I say, lifting her up into my arms and kissing her cheek. Her tenderness vanishes into giggling as she writhes away from the tickling of my beard.

Through my open door I can see villagers parading past, gathering in knots around the banana-leaf spread, jabbering and laughing in their high-pitched voices.

Throughout the early morning meal I can discover no indication of disapproval, and I wonder if Tombani has told them of my cure. Ririkinger and I eat with the rest of the village, seated in the mud around the long spread of banana leaves. The child appears dazed but strong enough as she kneels with her buttocks back on her heels, prim and touchingly grown in her attitude, and we eat well of bananas, the root mush and what I judge to be crabs cooked in coconut milk. Several times I see people casting side-long glances at us, glances in which I can discern no hint of suspicion.

Some of the young men, squatting on my side of the mat, are speaking of going for a swim in the ocean. I ask one of them to bring me some sea slugs so that I may wash my hair and beard. He smiles timid agreement.

After breakfast, the children begin to converge near the shade hut. I whisper in Ririkinger's ear that I have some-thing to tell her, that she must return to our hut first, that she can play afterwards. She follows me obediently, pick-ing her way across the drier spots of ground.

Inside I explain completely, again and again, that she is now my child, that she is to live here with me and that if Rauka Tataolagi approaches her she is to run immediately and tell me. She nods her head that she understands, and appears enchanted with the arrangement.

Giving her one of the dolls, I lift her through the open-ing and watch until she is with the rest of the children, where it only takes her a moment to turn the doll into shreds of bark and husks.

I spend the time in quietness, arranging my belongings into smaller bundles and tying them from the rafters, searching for my handkerchief which I can find nowhere, washing the sleeping mat in the pond and placing it on the roof where the sun will dry it.

I stop in astonishment to hear sounds coming from my chest, the unfamiliar sounds of humming that join with the drone of insects into strange resonance in the small interior of my hut.

Realizations halt me in my actions. My God, how far have I come? — how far have I drifted from the man who would probably be preparing his classes at school about now? — anxious for Fridays to get here so he could spend them with his family. What day is this? What month? Is there ever again to be a week end, a Sunday? There need to be Sundays in a man's life, and indeed Mondays and all the other days which have their own special colorings and tonalities.

What would today be? — just from the feel of it? Perhaps Saturday with the housecleaning and with the general aura of relaxation throughout the compound. Saturday at home, sitting on the veranda and listening to the baseball games, drinking a cup of coffee.

How far have I come? How far have I drifted from all of that? And yet this is real. What is coffee? A name, a word with but faint overtones in me now. What is a veranda, or baseball? But even when these words will have ceased entirely being image-makers, the days will continue to evoke their own peculiarities, and today is most certainly Saturday.

Smoothing out a square in the back corner, I print SAT. in the mud with my forefinger, deciding that I will keep my own calendar, that each day I will erase the spot and print SUN. or MON. or TUES., for there must be retained some connection with the other John Harper, even though I am no longer he. That is the change and the vague shock to me — and also the relief. For such a long time I have been that other man, playing a part, trying to fit it in, calculating every move and every reaction from his background; but imperceptibly I am becoming Jon, a rauka, a naked and bearded man, begining to live again, beginning to love again, beginning to live and love on another level as my thoughts center around the soft nucleus of the present instead of the past, around the sparkling clarity of morning outside, around my responsibilities to the child, who fills the center of my being during these moments when I putter around in our home and attempt to bring some cleanliness and some order to it.

"Kulangu?"

It is Veedlie's voice, sounding hesitant and somewhat constrained. I step to the door and peer out. He stands some feet away.

"Kulangu," I answer, smiling at him, and he relaxes to become that Veedlie of other times, the Veedlie of the tiny head and the wise eyes and the sardonic smile. The village simmers in a health of sunlit activities behind him. Truly this must be Saturday.

Across the way men are gathering in the alley beside Tombani's hut, seating themselves with their backs to the walls of the two buildings.

"You come take betel?" Veedlie asks, absently grasping my hand and staring up into my face. It is the first time since Tombani's suspicions about my manhood that I have been asked to join with the men in the betel ceremony.

"I come take betel," I say, stepping over the frame and bracing myself against the onslaught of sunlight.

Little Veedlie struts with his belly pushed far out, holding my hand and walking so close against me that his
shoulder repeatedly bumps my thigh.

Tombani, seated beside fat Oai, raises his scraggly eyebrows to look into my face. The small clay pipe is clutched
in the center of his mouth so that his wrinkled lips are
pursed in a kissing attitude around the stem. He elbows
fat Oai away to make room for me to sit between them.

When I am settled, the patriarch removes his pipe and
leans toward me, with his mouth almost against my ear, and
tells me that in Zinai there is much of Veedlie's eye sick-
ness, that I must go there and cure the villagers.

"Who tells you this?" I ask suspiciously.

He nods toward a squat, fat-faced young man sitting
against the opposite wall. "He tells me."

"How do I go?"

"He takes you."

"Does Ririkinger go?"

"No. . ." he snorts derisively, pulling back and frowning
at me for even suggesting such a thing.

"This is not Rauka's plan?"

"No, no, no, no, no," he says with such certainty that I
believe him.

"I do not like to leave Ririkinger."

Again the old man gives me a sidelong glance of
contempt.

"You cure them like you cure Veedlie," he commands
coldly.

"Who guards Ririkinger from Rauka Tataolagi?" I
counter with the same coldness.

"I guard her."

"You guard her well?"

"I guard her well and very well. You take the thing you use on Veedlie and cure the people of Zinai."

"Do you see the thing I use to cure Veedlie? It is gone from my hut."

I have not spoken loudly, but a hush falls over the group. Veedlie, talking with the villager from Zinai, stops and raises his head to look at me. An elder, lifting the poki stick to his mouth holds it poised in mid-air. I listen to wind shuffling leaves overhead as the black bodies sit motionless. Tombani pokes his pipe back into his mouth and stares at me through a puff of smoke so vile I must wave it away with my hand.

"What is it?" I ask. "Do you know where the thing is?"

In the same chanting, crooning voice he uses to explain the obvious, the old man tells me what I should seemingly already know, that I am going to die. He tells me as casually as though he were still speaking of the sore eyes of Zinai. Wondering what my handkerchief's disappearance can have to do with my death, and wondering too how all these people appear to know about it, I feel my view drawn away from this narrow alleyway toward the other side of the compound to find Ririkinger.

"What do you mean? How do I die?" I ask, locating the group of children, who are playing at the edge of the forest.

The keura branch is passed again. Low talk and laughter resume about me.

I order Tombani to explain. Fat Oai leans his head across my chest, dropping sweat on my upper thighs, as though he alone among the group were intent on hearing Tombani's explanation.

The old man turns to face full toward me. Something softens in his eyes and a hinted smile shows me a fragment of stained tush. Warmth emanates from him, primitive indications of affection as he explains in a gentle voice that Rauka kills me with snakes which she keeps in woven bamboo baskets.

"I know about the snakes," I say.

"She starves them and tortures them by tossing hot coals on them. When they are mad with pain and hunger, she puts the thing belonging to you in with them. They think your smell is the cause of their torture."

As he talks, I can feel the muscles in my face relax.

"When she turns them loose, they go to the smell, and they bite you and you die," he concludes pleasantly.

I realize that I am smiling broadly, certain that such sense-association and such a degree of memory are impossible in Rauka's snakes; and even if they were possible, the handkerchief would smell as strongly of Rauka herself as it would of me. But when could she have stolen it? It was missing yesterday when I cured Tombani's headache. Perhaps while I was bathing in the pond with Ririkinger yesterday forenoon.

Tombani answers my smile with an expression of bewilderment that softens his eyes to great benevolence, and even fat Oai draws back and beams, apparently impressed that I should be so gallant in the face of death from a serpent's fangs.

"You have betel and then go to Zinai," the old man says gently.

"If I have betel, I cannot walk to Zinai," I answer, filled with relief at this ridiculous threat to my life, for it means that Rauka's plan is to regain the child by my death and that she will probably not attempt to harm her during my absence, that she will wait for the fruition of her plan. I grasp the hut wall behind me and hoist myself to my feet, telling Tombani that I will be in my hut, that the young man from Zinai can come for me whenever he wishes to leave.

"And tell Rauka Tataolagi," I say loudly down to him, "that if she touches Ririkinger, I kill her."

It is almost noon when the swimmers return from the ocean and one of the boys appears at my door with a handful of sea slugs. Grinning, he drops the gelatinous mass into my palm. There is no time to wash my hair and beard now, but I decide to launder my undershirt which I can use to cleanse the sore eyes of Zinai.

Commanding the youth to build a fire near my door, I dig into the bundle for my undershirt.

With my feet drawn back into the narrow margin of shadow remaining before my hut, I sit on my window frame and watch the tiny fire and the water wherein my undershirt boils amid tough-fibered bubbles that catch rainbows from the sun. There is a strange ruffling of irony that my youthful ambitions to be a doctor, that my midnight readings of Chase and Paré, of Vesalius and Galen return to find caricatures of fulfillment here in these elemental practices of curing.

Shading my eyes from the smoke with my forearm, I stoop and fish the white cloth from the water on a branch.

My guide approaches through wavery lines of heat, and I call Ririkinger for a farewell talk.

31

There is something in the depths of a terrified woman's eyes that is almost unbearable to witness, something noble and infinitely secret to womanhood, something of the plea for mercy, something of the helpless need, drawing man forever out of himself and clubbing his heart with love and pity and longing, for he sees woman's mysterious essence stripped of its veilings, sees it pure and therefore sees its most profoundly touching characteristics.

The male holds her, his fingers tight around her biceps, and gently pushes her toward me, smiling in an expression full of pain and uneasiness.

They are lined up in front of my hut, the men silent beside their women who fill the afternoon air with wails and shriekings.

The young woman's face is within arm's reach now. I hold the soaked and folded undershirt in my right hand ready to apply it to the sore on her eyelid, but her expression holds me back. She cringes, her eyes opened wide in anguish, dancing about in her skull, and all the muscles in her face sweep outward to her rounded lips in the strange symmetry of terror.

I smile, my heart strangling with pity, and tell her to try again, that it cannot hurt her as she has already discovered during these three days.

How damning is this to Rauka, for it is a terror born of their youth, born of the pain that accompanies every moment of change in their lives from the first horror of tattooing, through the brutal matings, through childbirth in the most sordid and uncomfortable of huts, through every condition of their lives in which Rauka Tataolagi participates. Seeing this, the obscenity of ignorance, even of the benevolent ignorance of Rauka, appears as a contaminating thing.

I place my left hand behind the young woman's head and hold it still while I apply the cloth. The moment it touches her eye, the indrawn, bleating screech of agony rises to silence the birds above us, the screech of a woman touched by a snake rather than a comforting cloth.

When it is over, and her eye is clean, her man walks her stumblingly away and the next in line is pushed forward. Again the eyes dilating in fear, again the preliminary whimperings as I dip the cloth into the boiling water again and smile again and speak gently again.

Then men, no less frightened, maintain a stoic, petrified calm, bracing themselves before me. During these two hours each morning and afternoon, Zinai is a place of wailings and moanings; but in between times, there is no indication of fright or even of dread. Indeed, they treat me with the most complete kindness and gentleness, producing an atmosphere far different from that of Vanua, as though this were another land and another race of people. Even though there is here much of the same impersonality as in Vanua, the tone is gentler, quieter, and my affections have gone out unforced to these people. I cannot imagine a woman like Rauka Tataolagi being spawned of this stock; and now that I have been away from her presence for these three days, all of Vanua seems to bear the imprint of her domination as some hidden violence, some diseased violence to hearts and souls under her influence. And yet Zinai is only a few miles through the jungle, and all of the children here are tattooed as they are in Vanua, so she must come here occasionally, or else they send their young to her.

After the treatments are finished, I boil the cloth again and hang it from the eaves of my hut to dry; and then I walk around to the rear of my hut where I can sit on a grass hillock and look through massive tree trunks to a view below of valley and river and beyond to a patch of small mountains, perpetually blue. I judge that somewhere in them, perhaps eight or ten miles away, live the bushmen; and although I can see no habitation, smoke funnels rise from the distant hilltops.

These are the finest moments I have had since the crash, for all is tranquillity here, and it is good to rest after my work. Zinai is tiny compared to Vanua, and all is emerald shadings as though the sources of light were filtered through colored glass.

Whereas in Vanua the huts were built in a circle around

the large open compound, in Zinai two rows of huts face each other across a narrow span of ankle-deep grasses, not more than ten feet wide. It is an alleyway of only twenty-four huts on a ridge above the river, with forest at each end and each side of the rectangle, a forest so tall that treetops overlap above in a solid mass of foliage. Vanua appears gaudy and metropolitan compared to this glade where only the vaguest sunlight ever penetrates, where the drainage is so perfect that hut floors are never muddy, and where the grasses underfoot are so luxurious no earth shows through even in the paths.

How tempted would I be to move Ririkinger and live here in preference to Vanua, except for the eternal gloom of the place which turns noon into dusk and makes the harsh sunlight of Vanua irresistibly appealing.

I sit here, dreading only the night, for the nights are filled with loneliness for the child, and I wish I had insisted on bringing her with me. I recall when Cindy was only a few months old and we let her spend the night with her grandmother; and we lay there feeling the tremendous void in our house. Lying inside on my mat each night there is the same void, the same incalculable loneliness for the child, as I imagine during the moments before dropping off to sleep where she is and what she is doing. Perhaps I could send the young guide to —

"Kulangu?"

I turn as widely separated first drops of rain begin spattering against leaves overhead. Looking back along the side of my hut, I see Veedlie standing at the corner.

"Kulangu," I answer, getting to my feet and going to him. "Why are you here? Is everything all right?"

His smile reassures me, and he reaches for my hand.

"Everything is all right. Tombani tells me to come."

"Good," I say, patting his head, truly glad to see him.
"We go in out of the rain. Are you hungry?"

"Yes," he says as I stoop down and grasp him under the
armpits to lift him through the opening.

"What does Tombani want?"

"He sends me to bring you back for the feast," he says,
his face beaming into mine and his feet feeling for the door
jamb.

"What feast?"

"The death feast for the little one you call Ririkinger."

I am aware of dense sweat mingling with raindrops on
my cheeks and the gurgling of blood in the large vein at
my temple, flooding it until I am waiting in profound calmness for it to burst.

"You are hurting me."

Veedlie's squirmings and whimperings break into my
vast concentration on the throbbing vein at my temple,
and I realize that I am holding him suspended in the air,
my fingers bruising into the flesh at his armpits. Relaxing
my grasp, I lower him gently back outside.

"Ririkinger is dead?" I hear words, calm words, coming from my lips, but they are words spoken by some other
force than myself. "How?"

"No, but she dies," he assures me in exactly the same
voice he would use to inform me it is raining.

"She is not dead?"

"No," he says, rubbing himself beneath the armpits with
his arms crossed over his chest. "But she dies soon."

Grasping his shoulder, I shove him in front of me and we
are off walking beneath a dome of thunder.

"Kulangu," he protests, wrenching to get away.

"Take me to her."

He drags back, clutching my hand and arguing that it is soon night, that we might meet bushmen, that we cannot go until the sun's rise.

Anger rises fresh in me, and the violence of the emotion is a benediction, freeing me from the suffocation of a moment before.

"We go now. Take me to her," I command so harshly the child releases my hand and slinks on ahead of me past the last shadowy huts of Zinai.

"Where is she?"

"In Rauka's hut. You cannot go there. It is taboo."

"I tell Tombani to guard her," I roar, as we brush under trees into a world of greater somberness.

"Tombani guards her," he insists, glancing over his shoulder. "She gets sick."

"How?" I demand, catching up to him and stopping him with my hand on his head. "Tell me how?" I ask more gently, kneeling before him with my face close to his.

"She drinks the stuff you leave in the coconut shell," he confides embarrassedly, his teeth gleaming in a grin. "It is evil. It makes her sick — oh, sick."

"Why do you laugh?" I ask, wondering what sea-slug water could possibly do to the child.

"It is evil to drink," he whispers deliciously, hunching his shoulders forward like a little boy telling a nasty joke.

"What does it do?" I demand furiously.

"It makes men crazy," he whispers against my ear. "It makes them want to do things. It is bad and very bad, kulangu."

"What things?"

"Bad things."

"Tell me what it does," I command loudly.

Reluctantly, he makes an erotic gesture, showing me that it is a stimulant, an aphrodisiac.

"What does it do to the child?"

Bending forward, he grasps his stomach and makes signs of violent retchings.

"Is that all?"

"It makes her burn with fevers."

"Then it does not make her die," I say, rising to my feet. "It only makes her sick."

"She dies," he reassures me casually.

"Why does she die? Why is she with Rauka?"

"She dies from the cutting," he answers simply, turning to feel his way down the path.

"Rauka cuts her?"

"With the sun's rise. But Ririkinger dies. She is too weak now. Tombani says for you to come for the feast. The boys leave for the hunt today. I come for you."

"Why does Tombani let Rauka cut her? I tell him to guard the child."

"The little one gets sick. Tombani sends her to Rauka to cure," he explains, his voice angling off into the monotonous chant, imitating his grandfather. "Rauka says it is evil not to cut the little one. Tombani cannot go to Rauka's hut. It is taboo for man to look at it. But Ririkinger hangs too long, gets too weak. Rauka says she dies with the cutting."

"Take me there the shortest way."

"If you go there, kulangu, Rauka kills you," he argues,

walking now at a faster gait. "It is taboo. You are male."

"Hurry. I am a rauka too. It is not taboo for me."

"She kills you if you go there. She kills you with her snakes."

"Take me there. Hurry."

He slithers forward, his weaving body little more than a rain-slaked shadow before me, dim in the night. I flounder at his heels, lashed by soaked leaves, the two of us alone in a universe of underbrush and rain. An image returns again and again to my mind, the image of that terrified woman's eyes this afternoon, dancing in her skull, pleading for mercy, in helpless need; and all of that is transferred to the guileless eyes of the child, hanging there at the stake in Rauka's hovel, full of the mystery of livingness that will soon be murdered, tied up in the filth of that place throughout these drizzling nights with no other companionship than the mummified head and the sorceress with her snakes. And the idiot logic, the idiot logic of these people, sending Veedlie for me not so I might save Ririkinger, but only so I might be there to help celebrate her death by participating in the feast.

The eyes dancing in the skull are stippled deep in my consciousness, in some core of infinite tenderness and fear, casting the future before me, the future nights and days alone, the future returning to the past when I had no human to hang my life to. Now that I have been granted Ririkinger, the thought of living again that solitary existence, of breathing alone the airs of my hut, drives out the immediate pains of roots cutting into my bare feet, of scratches and slaps against my naked body, and I plod on at Veedlie's back, goaded by the terrified eyes.

Slavery to laws older than they. Slavery to laws that allow them to murder a child, for if Rauka knows that Ririkinger cannot live through the cutting, and she insists on
doing the cutting regardless, it can be nothing but murder,
or slavery to a tradition over which they feel they have no
control, driven along paths not of their own choosing . . .

Veedlie halts so abruptly I stumble into him and both of
us fall into the mud. The child is sobbing when I haul him
to his feet and lift him up against my chest, and we shout
above the pouring rain that turns the world into a sheath of
crystalline obscurity, grey-black. He says that we are at the
edge of the wide river, that without being able to see we
risk running into one of the gators near the opposite
shore. He pleads with me to go back to Zinai for the
night.

Carrying him cradled in my arms, I plunge out into the
silent current, through reeds that cling to my hips. My
feet proceed from soft mud to the gravel bottom near the
center of the river. Again its silence is eerie, and here,
without the protection of overfoliage, rain streams against
us in gusts. Walking with my legs widely separated to
brace myself against the currents, I ease forward in water
up to my armpits, as silently as possible so as not to attract
the gators.

Veedlie, his voice strained to an agony of fear, manages
to tell me that I must flounder, stir up the water, create as
much disturbance as possible in order to frighten the gators
away. I lower him into the water enough to splash his
feet, and hurtle forward in leaps, struggling against the
downsweep of the rapids.

Looking up, the sky is soft grey and the masses of jungle

on the opposite bank are indistinguishable in the splintering downpour.

My calm surprises me. Nerves cringe in anticipation of teeth tearing into the flesh of my legs, but the eyes, the anguished eyes and the static image of the child hanging from the stake, drive me on, not frantically, but coldly, almost as though I were standing off somewhere and directing the movements rather than participating in them.

Veedlie wriggles from my arms when we enter the shallows, and grabbing my hand, wades and runs, splashing to the spot where the branch materializes over our heads. I toss him through the darkness up on the bank and reach for the branch. Swinging myself out of the water, my feet strike his body and I feel him grasp them to his chest and hold them steady while I pull myself in hand over hand along the branch. We crawl forward on hands and knees with my arms at each side of his hips and my chin near the small of his back, for some distance until the path allows us to rise to our feet and begin the slippery climb upward, dragging ourselves from tree to tree up the hill.

At the top, although the storm has not abated, a greater dimension of lightness settles about us, the diffused light of the moon penetrating layers of clouds. Veedlie sits down and slides to the bottom of the hill. I call into the boiling greyness below, asking if he is all right, and hear his faint answer that he is.

I follow him, sliding feet first down the embankment.

We are not far from the pond. Catching up with Veedlie, I grasp his shoulder and bend to shout in his ear that I want to take the path leading to Rauka's hovel.

"It is taboo, taboo," he argues. "I cannot look on her hut."

I tell him he will not need to look, but simply to lead me to the edge of the banana grove, and then he can return to his dwelling.

My respiration becomes short as we grope our way forward. Now that we are here, calmness rustles into uncontrollable tremblings, requiring me to breathe deeply.

Veedlie stops before me in a dim seepage of moonlit rain and I can make out the giant folds of a banana leaf beside him.

"It is there," he whispers mournfully, keeping his face averted from the clearing.

"Tell no one you bring me here," I command. "Go and sleep." The moment I release his arm he is gone.

I push back the banana leaves and gaze into the miniature compound. The scene is like an ancient and faded photograph, with no dimensions of light and shadow. Pale through sheets of rain, Rauka's solitary hut is etched in faint outline, standing silent and infinitely peaceful.

I rake dribblings from my eyes and slosh across the open space to her door, deadening all thoughts, deadening all feelings, blanking my mind to all possible consequences. Above the flurried freshness of the rain, above the ozone freshness of the air, the hovel's stench filters out to surround me.

I take a deep breath which sucks water into my nose, and, stooping, shove my head through the door where the immediate clatter of rain is muffled through thatch above me.

The interior is a black hole, full of chill dampness and rot.

Dropping to my knees, I inch forward with hands outstretched, wishing for a momentary flare of lightning to orient myself, but the downpour drones steadily without thunder.

My knee touches flesh and flesh is quickly withdrawn. I kneel motionless in the mud, waiting for an outcry, but hear only a vague settling of movements as Rauka probably changes positions and drifts into renewed sleep. I hear no whimper, no sound except water from the eaves bubbling into puddles at the open door behind me.

Rauka is to my right then, and beyond her there would be room enough only for her clutter of baskets and the head. Ririkinger, if she is still alive, if she still hangs from the stake, must be back to my left. Reversing myself, I waddle through the mire on my knees, with my hands outstretched and following the soaked weave of the wall opposite the door. My fingers guide me to the corner seam where the wall turns, and between the seam and me, flesh touches my wrist, flesh that is on fire.

Muscles melt in my legs, obliging me to sit back on my heels as I bring my other hand to the fore and trace the body of Ririkinger hanging motionless, not responding to my touches but blazing with fever and therefore still, thank God, alive.

My hands follow her arms up to the knotted bark above her head, tied not to a stake, but to one of the low ceiling beams. My fingers tear at the knots, manipulating them loose. She sinks forward and I bring her fevered body full length against my rain-chilled flesh, holding her tightly and trying to cool her. Kissing her cheek, it is as though I could see clearly her face, see clearly her eyes closed, see clearly her head wobbling to one side on her neck, see even the expression of utter peace on her unconscious features. How similar to the look of death is the look of sleep.

A loud rattling, as though a stick were raked across a corrugated surface, causes me to jerk my head up. A blow cracks against the back of my neck. I am jolted forward, squishing Ririkinger into the mud beneath me. Hugging her tightly with one arm, I roll to the side and see the door full of dribbling greys. The pole rattles again across beams, accompanied by Rauka's screech, and thumps into my ribs as I lurch for the opening.

Rain from the eaves sloshes cold across my neck and my free hand sinks into water up to my wrist. I rise to my knees, struggling to my feet as the pole drives hard against my kidneys, sprawling me forward again. I twist in mid-air and land splashing on my back with Ririkinger on my chest. Rain streams mud from her head into my mouth.

Rauka appears in the doorway. Her screams are faint above me, faint through the sizzle of rain, faint through the sizzle of pain in my kidney.

She bounds toward me, a grey form emerging from the slanting backdrop of rain. Covering Ririkinger's head with my hand and pressing it into my beard to protect it from the blow, I kick out with my right foot, kick out so violently my entire body slides forward. I feel my foot contact her belly and her wailings are abruptly silenced. The pole streaks inside of my thigh and falls on my stomach. She is skittering backward, flinging out her arms.

I struggle to my feet and hobble toward the wall of banana trees, unable to straighten up for the pain in my kidney.

As the first broad leaf slashes across my face, I reach up and break off a handful of bananas, and without glancing back, plunge into the jungle.

The deserted compound huddles rainswept, a shallow lake when I wade across it to my hut.

Inside, I bolt my door with the heavy spear and rip down my bundles of clothes until I find my shirt and coat. I dry Ririkinger as well as possible with the shirt and hold her high up against me, listening to the faint regularity of her heartbeat with my ear pressed against her chest, and hearing the counterpointing pounding of my own.

I shake her gently and talk to her, my voice hoarse and lost above the thuddings of storm, until, of her own accord, she lifts her head and groans.

Wrapping her in my coat, I lie down and place her on my stomach to keep her from the mud. I wait, expecting to hear Rauka come battering at my door at any moment. I wait, sleeplessly, with my arms around her as pains within my own body filter one by one into consciousness; the incessant grinding of my kidneys, bringing exaltation that I have saved the child; the pain across my ribs, bringing further exaltation, and then the pain at the base of my skull, changing exaltation into a vast and spreading fatigue. I wait, feeling the rise and fall of the child's good sleep against my chest.

I close my eyes and hug her to me, listening for Rauka, remembering another life in another world where children are protected, where I slept in a night of dry sheets and the comfort of another body that was equally mine. For a moment the sheer discomfort of lying in slime, the sheer exhaustion of pain, the sheer starkness of this land where

Rauka prowls always in search of death, unhinges my exaltation and brings me to a view of desolation. But the
mummified head of the other afternoon is highlighted in
the sinkings, dangling above me again, telling me that at the
door of many years from now whether I have slept in a
bed of slush or one of down, whether in pain or comfort,
will be seen as having little importance, and that it is folly
to mourn over the momentary wetness or dryness, fruitful-
ness or fruitlessness of a night when there is a lifetime of
nights to be lived. The recollection persuades me of the
goodness of all that seemed torment a moment ago; and I
lie here subjected to the invasion of peace, beginning to
understand a phrase I once memorized because it bewildered me, the haunting phrase of ancient Lamachus, blind
and paralyzed, answering Phrynicus the Poet who con-
soled himself in captivity by saying that at least he still
had a view of the sky through his dungeon window:
"What is your patch of sky to me, Phrynicus? — I who am
without eyes or legs? I think for an instant and the answers swarm back, a thousand things to astonish and en-
chant me this very night of storm when creatures huddle
deep within the woods against the elements; when I can
feel and sense and become a part of every huddling thing
out there, and see, yes, see — see fish suspended in brooks,
see owls facing into the rain with their eyes tight shut.
How much richer are your fortunate guards and my
fortunate landlord, pacing about their rooms this night,
seeing everything and therefore nothing, hearing everything and therefore nothing, waiting for an end to their
boredom, their eternal boredom?"
Above the drizzle, above the stench, an aura of health

pervades my being, and for the first time since childhood I do not need to voice words in order to be praying: my emotion is prayer, the night is prayer, the relenting storm outside is prayer and the protection within is prayer, quietening the afterflush of emotion, quietening all thought and all rebellion as I wrap the splattered coat more closely about Ririkinger.

32

The need to urinate awakens me to the chill of beginning dawn, without struggle, without fatigue but strangely refreshed.

I reach under the coat and feel the joy of Ririkinger's flesh, cooler than last night, telling me that the fevers are breaking. Retrieving the little pile of bananas I brought last night, I peel one of them and offer it to her lips. Her head droops forward against my chest but she takes the nourishment, instinctively chewing and swallowing without ever opening her eyes until two of the small bananas have been consumed and her mouth has fallen slack in slumber.

The frame is cold to my hands when I crawl through the door and gaze about me at a compound reposing placidly in a world of washed greys. A faded full moon hangs above massed foliage behind Tombani's hut, and stars are slowly disappearing from a pale and cloudless sky.

Massaging warmth into my arms, I pick my way stiffly around the side of my hut and stand facing the bushes, not bothering to hide my act in this soaked world of dawn where nothing else stirs, where I alone am awake and about.

When I have finished I check on the child who sleeps profoundly, and then, unable to bear the muddiness of my body any longer, I start for the pond.

Pains from last night's beating arouse themselves with my walking, until the walking becomes hobbling before I have crossed the compound toward Oai's hut.

The coolness, the calm of jungles coming awake in occasional isolated squawkings and chirpings as I pass down the path, the promise of clear skies and torrid heat later in the day, make me wonder if last night could have been real, make me breathe deeply in relief that I forced Veedlie to bring me back.

Unwilling to destroy the silence, I ease myself breathcatchingly into the pond and bathe completely submerged in gestures made violent by the cold.

Fear that Rauka might be up and waiting for her chance to steal the child back makes me hurry until I am once again alongside Oai's hut where I have a clear view of my own. I am halted and my glance is drawn from the monochrome world of greys to an infinitely fragile cloud, tinted by the invisible sun. It floats high above opposite spires of forest like a twirl of pink gauze, and beyond it, far in other spheres, a solitary star flecks the clear pool of heaven.

From the stillness, from the profound tranquillity, a

muffled cough wafts to me. Someone coughs. Someone else is awake for an instant in the swamp of his bed. In which of these huts, behind which of these walls does the cougher sleep? Would I know him in the light of day? Have I ever seen him? Gazing about the sleeping compound, it occurs to me that I know very few of these people and very little of their lives, and I realize in some surprise that I could live here forever and not know more, that they are as much insulated from those with whom they share bloods and intimacies as they are from me; each passing his own hours and days in that aimless and static detachment one associates with a herd of animals driven along paths not of their own choosing — or with slaves deadened to animal status by being driven along paths not of their own choosing.

This morning, as birds begin to enliven the brush around me, shuffling leaves and splattering raindrops which fall into puddles at my feet, the dawning sights of this land make the other land of my past fade to distances beyond recall, and the heart which has known sorrow begins to perceive that core of intense joy buried in the substance of sorrow. Standing alone at the edge of the compound, looking on these sodden huts, a phrase haunts my brain in repeated chantings:

> *driven along paths not of their own choosing*

What are they? — these beings that surround me with their sleeping. How is it they seem so dead and yet so move my affections, bound up as they are in the paraphernalia of snorings and flesh and hungers and salivas and hairs?

> *driven along paths not of their own choosing*

Affection excites my heart with answers that cannot be formulated by the brain, truths from some far memory of the soul, intimate truths forever strangers to the intellect, truths stemming from:

driven along paths not of their own choosing

as though that were the key, the fugal theme to the soul's infinite variations — a clumsy theme, a sturdy theme, an uncadenced theme, rendered majestic and gracious as all men within the breast of man: the lover, the scholar, the hater, the dilettante, the historian, the philosopher, the curser, the saint and the poet intermingle their own harmonies into the crude beginnings of truth.

For here in this primal world of dawn there is a truth that men and women and children sleep next to each other in their huts, but each is forever separated from the rest, each is tied up within himself by outside forces away from the dualism which constitutes man as part spirit as well as part matter, part angel as well as part animal; and each personality lies bound up in the sack of its singularness by a slavery to laws etched into its being by Elemental Nature — the merciless and blind laws of air and water and earth and fire that creep from stagnant jungles or bolt down from thunders. Each soul is deadened until there is no living from within, but only from without:

driven along paths not of their own choosing

An intelligence is born within me, floating around the uncadenced theme, for what man has not felt himself grow dead within himself when another's demands rather than his own threatened the freedom of his destiny, and felt himself tied up within himself by the outside thing?

driven along paths not of his own choosing

The intelligence is transferred to the emotion, evoking an ox's flared nose and an ox's blared eye, and the creaking wheels of a jungle cart, and the *hola* shouted with the crack of a whip, driving the young beast along the path of another's choosing, until plodding the path becomes the ox's necessity, forever ambling before squeaking wheels in uncadenced turnings:

driven along paths not of its own choosing

The emotion modulates to affection, evoking Rauka's flared nose and Rauka's blared eye, and those of her people, and the *hola* shouted with the crack of Nature's whip, driving the human along the path of Nature's choosing, until plodding the path becomes the human's necessity.

The affection fades the chanted theme to understanding, to the infinite implications riding on silence when I consider that in their total immersion into Elemental Nature, they see themselves as one of its revolving parts instead of the free beings they were created, they see themselves as akin to the leaves and the ashes and the winds and the raindrops, tossed about in their lives as helplessly as lightning is tossed about in the skies, their every act commanded by subservience to the outside thing. They move through life in a semblance of living; they move like the raindrops or like thunderheads tumbling across heavens, which seem to live but have no inner living:

driven along paths not of their own choosing

The theme returns in brass trumpetings, and the understanding modulates to contemplation when I think of Tombani who moves unresisting before the same laws that move the thunderheads or swish the rains, so preoccupied with the whiplash and the *hola* and the creaking wheels of Elemental Nature, so preoccupied with that outside thing which tells him to mutilate his children, and when to mate and when even to destroy himself that it has reduced to dim and distant proportions the spiritual content, the angel portions of him and his people, until it no longer dwells in them as an integral part, as the source of man's intensest living, but only as a vague and nostalgic memory of something older and better than now — the ox's vague memory of the pasture or the slave's vague memory of freedom, the original freedom of the spirit born in the soul to be the mother of all other freedoms, a freedom having its essence in duality which allows man to choose his actions in conformity with his soul's hungerings for good. But viewing Elemental Nature as the guide and controlling force of all life, all fate, their movements have become movements of submission to it, until their living is the living of leaves curled in the sun or of coconuts pulled by gravity to the earth. Their souls, deadened because there is no living from within, cease to animate their hearts and bodies without ever ceasing to hunger for the inflooding dynamism which alone comes when the spirit is free to move men along paths of its own choosing.

And the variations of the fugal theme combine from harshness into a vague and minor harmony as contemplation modulates to intense sympathy for them, as the gross and cumbersome head of Oai fills my heart with clear knowledge of the things that changed his eyes from those alive one day to those dead the next:

> There at that point where you forgot, as the others have forgotten, that your will could make your body walk even when Elemental Nature desired it to remain still, and that your will could make your body remain still even when your passions desired it to walk;

> *driven along paths not of your own choosing*

> and there at that point where you traded a concept of destiny dependent on freedom for one of destiny dependent on slavery to Elemental Nature;

> *driven along paths not of your own choosing*

> and there at that point where your acts became those of the tides and the seasons and the cycles of nature;

> *driven along paths not of your own choosing*

> there at that point, no act could any longer satisfy your spiritual appetite, no act could any longer bring you happiness.

They lie sprawled in attitudes of sleep in their huts and sympathy modulates to sorrow for them, for they are hopelessly ensnared now as their slavery has become as much a part of them as the path a part of the ox and no act, no matter how perfect, can have any significance in their poor souls, because the soul rejects and must forever reject the goodness of an act that is unfree, any perfection that is commanded by an outside force rather than the own free will of the actor:

driven along paths not of his own choosing

And no love can have any significance in their poor hearts, because the heart rejects and must forever reject the goodness of a love that is unfree, any love that is commanded by an outside force rather than the own free will of the lover:

driven along paths not of his own choosing

Man's greatest gift, freely given love, has no opportunity of being born when the soul has no opportunity of freely choosing. That which splashes color into humanity's shadowed conditions is here forever veiled, for the soul insulates itself from light and expansion when forced to love a stranger.

Intelligence and perception, which raise man above the ox, become here nothing more than instruments making him aware of his ox helplessness before the whiplash and the *hola* of grinding fate. Stoicism becomes merely the deadened face of abandoned struggle in the conviction of defeat, giving despair the respectable countenance of stones instead of tears:

driven along paths not of their own choosing

And as the leaf curls up in sunlight, not only because of the outside heat but because of the inner tendons and fibers of its make-up, so their wills curl up in slavery, not only because of the outside thing which captivates them, but because it allows the inner tendons and fibers of their passions to rise up and captivate their wills without struggle, until slavery to Elemental Nature becomes equally slavery to their animal nature while passion counters passion in hopeless bludgeonings of the personality, passion canceling out passion until only the passion of despair remains:

driven along paths not of their own choosing

The theme resounds in a startlingly different key, sounding the chords of affection, understanding, contemplation, sympathy and sorrow into a dissonant statement that overwhelms me with its unsuspected truth — that the clumsy theme, the sturdy theme, the uncadenced theme, so chanted and so primordial in its tonality, is equally the theme of me and the people of my world, different only in its counterpoint, in its treatment and its preoccupations . . .

driven along paths not of our own choosing.

It was muffled for a time in the beginning, when we were taught to remember once more, through mysterious redemption from Elemental Nature by a God-Man, our spirituality, the memory of which revived our freedom in us. We were redeemed from the controls of this primal nature and allowed to throw off the whiplash and the *hola* and to move along paths of our own free choosing, to move in living-from-within, where alone good that is the product of a free spirit has any significance, any reality.

And the theme is almost unrecognizable now, tempered as it is with harmonies of celestial release, wherein the new man was allowed to rise above fate, was exalted above Elemental Nature, and could view it not as the terrifying Creator of all life, but as the inspiring creation of a greater Creator, fixed here for man's uses; not as a vast and living organism controlling man's fate, but as a wonderful complex of energies to be harnessed and controlled by man. Freedom from the first slavery showed the new man his equal freedom from the second, wherein he came to look on the passions not as a vast and living organism controlling and driving him, but as a wonderful complex of energies to be harnessed and controlled by his will in the freeing of his personality from their bondage.

But the transition passage, wherein my heart has been filled with the muted harmonies of celestial participation, gives way to the theme's slow return in an orchestration of vigor and dynamism, clanging with cymbals and brasses, thumped out of cadence with tympani, no longer the creaking wheels of the oxcart, but the roar of geared smoothness and the clankings of steeled smoothness, as man attacked the ancient slavemaster with all the exultation born of his new perspective, mechanizing Elemental Nature, harnessing it into subservience to him; becoming more and more absorbed in its mechanization until the pagan theme blasts again to the fore in all of its primal accents, until the new man ends up as the old one:

driven along paths not of his own choosing

And the two themes whisper together, in exactly the same uncadenced rhythms in slow denouement, telling me that here in this compound, I am at home more than I would ever have dreamed possible, for the essential slavery is the same, with only vague differences of accent. Here, the primitive is so completely absorbed in Elemental Nature that it has contrived to make him forget the forever hungering goals of his spiritual being.

In civilization, the new man became so completely absorbed in Mechanized Nature that it has equally contrived to make him forget the forever hungering goals of his spiritual being. Here, where their enslavement to Elemental Nature destroys the delicate balance of dualism in man's nature by decreasing his living-from-within through compulsions from without; there, in civilization, man's enslavement to Mechanized Nature equally destroys this delicate balance by decreasing the intensity of his living-from-within through compulsions from without.

Oai, Tombani, Rauka — they live in the heaviness of their slavery, their lives anchored in Elemental Nature; loveless and unloving lives wherein those perfecting forces in their natures, that complex of energies: the passions of love, hate, desire, aversion, sorrow, joy, hope, despair, daring, fear and anger are no longer guided by their captivated wills, but drive their wills to the destruction of their personalities.

But the intellectual, the engineer, the salesman and the buyer, the housewife and the professor — we live in the same heaviness to the same essential slavery, our lives anchored in Mechanized Nature; desperate and anxious lives wherein those same perfecting forces in our natures, that complex of energies, the passions are no longer guided by our captivated wills, but drive our wills to the destruction of our personalities.

For the essential slavery is neither in Elemental Nature nor Mechanized Nature, which are only vast preoccupations to divert man and make him forget his angel part for the length of time it takes to change his freedom into necessity and compulsion, the length of time it takes to turn him into a surprised slave to an outside thing:

driven along paths not of his own choosing

The theme returns to its primitive purity, telling me in a unison swelling, that man's eternal drives to his goals, his restlessness and impatience to find happiness in the goodness of both his angel-demands and his animal-demands, have in no way altered in the centuries separating Tombani from me, separating his people from my people. Man falls, with what terrifying ease, back into his primordial condition of slavery, subject only to different exterior forces, different whiplashes and different *holas*, with us scarcely more aware of the details of our slavery than these people:

driven along paths not of our own choosing

In these calm and silent moments, in these moments when all of life's currents flow through me, I realize clearly for an instant that the great ascetic saints, through freeing their own perfecting passions from those forms of elemental compulsion and necessity inherent in all slaveries, and subjecting them to the dominion of their wills in freely given

love, became the only free personalities in history by remembering that their wills could make their bodies walk
even though their passions desired them to remain still, that
their wills could make their bodies remain still even though
their passions desired them to walk. And the small gap separating civilized man from primal man is that remnants of
sanctity continue to offer us moments of consonance in
our lives, where they can never have any place in theirs;
for our happiness remains in the saint's dream, a dream unknown to them: the saint's dream of bread, of health, of
tenderness and robustness and heroism, all involved in love;
blazing the word *love* in a final majestic coda to the theme,
changing it from minor tonality into that mysterious modality which is neither major nor minor, but multi-hued in
strengths and tones and softnesses;

love — not in the modality of a wrathful moral which
　　　　puts all humanity into hell;
love — not in the modality of a niggardly preoccupation
　　　　with sin and evil;
love — not in the modality of presumptuous logic that
　　　　demands that God's intelligence inhabit the
　　　　brain of man;
love — not in the modality of finical refinements lead-
　　　　ing man to be shocked by things not shocking
　　　　to God;
love — not in modality of dullard clichés and stereo-
　　　　typed formulae for happiness; but love in the
　　　　modality of the heart, of sanctity and jubila-
　　　　tion, filling the air with its pipings, repeating
　　　　the theme in rich-toned pumpings; and all of

the images of this love are comfortable ones, fine ones, sweet ones telling man that sanctity exists wherever harmony is produced between angel-hungers and animal-hungers in a true climate of freedom:

moving along paths of his own choosing

The final consonance, the final chord echoes in my soul with infinite overtones of tranquillity. I focus my eyes on the twirl of cloud, blanched now in a lighter heaven, and begin trudging around the perimeter to my own door. And the vast complexity of the fugal structure is resolved to warmest simplicity in my belly, as I see sanctity in all things sustaining man in grace: in each second of his living, whether cooking, creating children, working to support life, brushing his teeth, sleeping; as long as they have significance from his free choice of them and his free gift of them as acts of love.

Such a degree of harmony between man's physical and spiritual appetites is nullified here in this land of unisonal acts, and it is nullified under all compulsions. For a moment I think of the quagmires of both animalism, which denies the angel-hungers of man, and certain types of angelism in our own gracelessly selfish morality which deny even the basic animal-hungers of man: those two guarantees of despair to humanity; each sundering the life-drive through the invisible murder of the will, which, though created free in order to give itself in freely chosen acts of love, dies under those forms of outside compulsion which are subtle beyond understanding, but which, whether they be the controls of a social system, of a wrathful morality, of another human, of habits, of Mechanized Nature, or — as here — of Elemental Nature, succeed equally in destroying man's responsibility for his acts and therefore in destroying their significance within him.

Crawling through the opening into my hut, I turn to see the shadowy movement of Tombani as he ambles out of his door on footsteps that seem to yawn and drifts around the side of his dwelling toward the brush, and I wonder that all things remain forever the same with men's souls and if there will ever be an end to humanity's cry of *Exsurge:* "Arise . . . our bellies cleave to the earth . . . help us and deliver us . . ."

Now, in the peculiar stillness of morning, I hear others stirring about in the brush, breaking sticks, splashing sleep from their eyes in the brook. How united do we become in these early morning hours when all struggle from sleep and stumble about, swallowing the salivas of night and seeking a return to feelings. In these moments, we here are the same as the Harvard Intellectuals, the ancient cenobites, the kings of all times and the beggars of all times. All hang on to a remnant of the innocence of sleep and are made infinitely lovable in their unmasked humanity. There is something in the early morning yawnings and stretchings and water dabbings and eye rubbings that reduces all to the same unbuffeted level of new birth. Even the perverse, the devil-dedicated, become momentarily children for the time it takes to awaken.

Only the day, the gradual tentacle radiations of the day with all of its multiple diffusions and crystallizations, brings to the fore those traits that distinguish the king from the beggar, the professor from the student, the salesman from the buyer, until finally, with wakefulness, all of the various pulls and tugs of compulsions and necessities converge into the slaveries that set each being off from the rest in the sack of his personality. But all start out exactly alike every morning; all are the same for these few moments when dawn becomes the climate of wakefulness and smoke begins to rise from breakfast fires.

33

The air is rich with the crusting odors of pork. They are going ahead with the feast then, and this time the fatty smell unhinges ravenous hunger in my belly as I stand before my hut, cradling Ririkinger, and watch the festivities in preparation, watch for some sight of Rauka among the women.

The sun reflects from a small sheet of water caught in the center of the compound, casting ripples of gold on the face of Tombani's hut and on the trunks and underfoliage of the towering trees beyond.

It touches me with some regret that Rauka Tataolagi is not here, and the vision of her huddling alone and crushed in defeat pushes into the soft corners of my being. If I should go to her and placate her she would only begin again. We will never be safe from her. No, it is better to leave her in her misery, to let her accept in her own way what has happened to her. But all the while I find myself preparing words and phrases in the dialect, words and phrases that might explain to her and help her to salvage her self-respect. It is better to have a lively enemy than a crushed victim. I am conceding points. I am degrading the quality of her opposition, but to bring her from shame is more important than the ethic of our enmity.

I putter about my hut, attempting to forget her, attempting to read. Giving that up, I go and kneel in the corner and wipe out the faded letters where I printed the word SAT. for Saturday. That was the day I left for Zinai. Today must be Thursday. I print THURS. with some excitement, waiting for Sunday, waiting to know Sunday again.

In the brilliance of morning, villagers go about their occupations preparing for the feast, carrying in firewood, spreading banana leaves on the ground and gathering in knots to chatter. Tombani sits in full sunlight, his back against his hut and his clay pipe between his teeth, ignoring the world.

Surely in all of this day, in all of these lullings and hummings of joyous calm there could be some way of bringing Rauka to an understanding that would allow us to live peaceably here in the same village.

Shoving the mat to the highest ground in the room, over the word THURS., I place Ririkinger on it and arrange her into a comfortable position before heading for the door.

The path is fulled with undercurrents of tranquillity and

quietness made light by the unrestrained chirpings of birds. The buttercup meadow sparkles deserted and full of color when I pass the pond, drawing me to it.

And again there is a strange detachment when I limp stiffly through the shadowed grove toward the green speckles of sunlit navundi leaves with its surroundings of birdsongs and leaf rustlings, detachment as I see myself from another perspective: a bearded and naked old man hobbling toward the miniature compound, a man who will attempt to explain his love for his child to a shrunken black crone with tufts of white hair who stares desolatingly at her feet, defeated in her benevolent designs to kill his child and murder him.

Pushing aside the large flat leaves of the navundi, I squint, adjusting my eyes to the new blaze of sunlight, and gaze toward the door of her shanty.

The sights and sounds of a doorway filled with the thrumming iridescence of flies quieten my heart and make me wish I might drop the navundi branches back in place and leave this area to the secret and sacred reclamation of nature which is being carried out before me. But she cannot be left there to join in her own proper time with the earth and the skies. She must be buried.

I walk slowly across mud crusts that blister into my feet. She lies on her face at the entrance of her hut in the mirrored pool which has been gutted from the earth by constantly dripping rain water from the eaves. Kneeling beside her, I see a line of silt and dust tracing across her face where the water has receded in evaporation as the pool has become shallower. She drowned apparently without ever regaining consciousness after I kicked her and sent her reeling back to knock her head against the door jamb, for there is no indication of writhing or struggle.

I retrieve her pole from the congealment of drying mud and start back to the village to tell them they may have the death feast for Rauka Tataolagi. But at the navundi wall I turn, drawn back to her, remembering the laughter and clowning that accompanied Maigna's burial. I could not bear for her to suffer that indignity. The urge to bury her myself surprises me and grows in me, the urge to bury her secretly and decently, to bury her gently and kindly, to bury her reverently, as a friend, and then never to tell anyone about it, to let her death and resting place become a private affection I shall carry through my days.

But first I must return to the village.

At the cooking hut, I pick up a coconut husk and light the edges of it from the fire, gasping for breath in the smoke-filled, pork-filled interior where others are nothing but shadows. Quickly I wrap the fire inside the husk and escape before anyone can question me.

In the center of Rauka's little compound I kneel and break through the thin crusts with my fingers and begin scooping out a shallow grave.

I reach water about two feet deep, water to which my own pouring sweats are added. I line the bottom of the grave with navundi leaves, sober in my task and filled with a peculiar gratification that nullifies all somberness, all macabreness.

Her emaciated body is as light as though it were made of paper. I carry it to the grave and lower it to its bed of green leaves, arranging her mud-caked staff beside her. With the sun full on my back, I straddle the mound and begin covering her when I remember the mummified head. Bringing it from the hut, I place it with her and kneel in the blazing heat to cover them both, repeating again and again the words of the Requiem: "Rest eternal grant them, O Lord, and may the perpetual light shine upon them . . ." I work in automaton, drunk and dizzy from the heat and the effort, mumbling the prayer above the cicada's distant raspings.

When the churned mud of the grave is level with the surrounding earth, I stumble back and pick up the smoldering coconut husk. Holding it against the ragged eaves of the hovel, I blow on it, seeing the black ash turn pink with each respiration. My throat aches from the effort and I am almost ready to give up when an upshoot of orange flame crackles into being and spreads, shooting off sparks and enveloping the rotted roof of thatch until its roar silences the cicada, silences the birds and drives me out of the clearing.

Needing desperately to get some food into my belly and to get into the pool, I rip off a handful of bananas and limp away from the holocaust of flame and smoke, fighting against the vertigo that sweeps over me.

At the pond, I drop my bananas on the grassy mound and with my last strength fall face forward into the chilling waters.

The scent of flowers floats to me from the meadow when I climb out on the bank. I sit down and stare at my flesh, blue and stippled from the refreshing coldness. Peace drifts to me on the lively twitterings of birds overhead, on the return of heats to my body as I begin to eat my bananas.

Sunshine makes the surface of the pond sparkle through leaf shadows. Smoke from the fire in Rauka's compound mingles with smoke from the cooking fires of the village and casts a faint bluish haze over the meadow. The jungle will reclaim the ashes of the pest hole, the compound of the raukas. Already it seems no more insidious than the field of yellow buttercups stretched out beneath the sunlight before me.

From Vanua I hear the bawling of a baby and the lazy chattering of a mother. And the atmosphere is new, freed of the taint of evil, freed of constraint and fear.

Rising stiffly, I head back toward the path, back to my village and my hut and my child, back to erase the word THURSDAY and print the word SUNDAY in the corner beneath Ririkinger's mat.